FLIGHT *of* SORCERY *and* SHADOW

MEG COWLEY

Published in 2020 by
Eldarkin Publishing Limited
United Kingdom

Second Edition

ISBN: 9798668714889

For my parents
This all began at the making table...

AUTHOR'S NOTE

Welcome to a new adventure in the Altarea World!

I'm so thrilled to invite you to adventure with Aedon and Lief into the living forest of Tir-na-Alathea, to delve into the deepest, darkest vaults of the legendary Athenaeum with Venya and Nyx, and to soar with Vasili and Icarus on dragon-back! This was a hugely fun tale for me to write, and I hope you have just as much enjoyment reading it.

If you've read the *Chronicles of Pelenor*, a sister series to the *Tales of Tir-na-Alathea*, you'll recognise some familiar faces, and I hope you will be glad to see them.

If you haven't, then I welcome you to the realm! Feel free to jump into the story here; it's a great introduction to the world of Altarea. All of my series can be read together, or as standalones.

Without further ado… happy reading, my friends.

Warm wishes,

Meg

Meg Cowley

Books by Meg Cowley

World of Altarea novels:

Books of Caledan

A fast-paced fantasy filled with magic, dragons, and intrigue, that epic fantasy fans will love.

The Tainted Crown
The Brooding Crown
The Shattered Crown

Pelenor Chronicles: Rise of Saradon

A sprawling epic fantasy quartet of intrigue, betrayal, peril and romance.

Heart of Dragons
Court of Shadows
Order of Valxiron
Mark of Fate

Tales of Tir na Alathea: Darkness of the Living Forest

A fast-paced epic adventure of unlikely allies facing darkness together, coming in 2020.

Flight of Sorcery and Shadow
Ascent of Darkness and Ruin
Purge of Flame and Song

Lore of Aurauria: The Treacherous Courts

A darkly romantic epic saga of revenge, betrayal, and redemption, coming in 2021.

A Prince so Heartless
A King so Wicked
A Queen so Ruined

Other fantasy books:

Morgana Chronicles

Discover Arthurian legend as you've never heard it before in this original and gripping high fantasy tale of a young Morgana Le Fay.

Magic Awakened

Relic Guardians

Tomb Raider meets Indiana Jones plus magic in this fast-paced magical urban adventure fantasy, co-written with Victoria DeLuis.

Ancient Magic
Hidden Magic
Cursed Magic
Gathered Magic

ONE

Finarvon had not woken that day intending to murder his entire garrison. Yet when the black mist descended, nothing else mattered.

More. More. More, it called to him.

His twin blades sang as he swirled in a deadly dance, his long, auburn hair flying around him with the force of his movements. The element of surprise was his best weapon, for who would attack an elven stronghold in the midst of a secure realm that had not seen war in an age?

It was their shock, the moment of hesitation from his dearest friends, that sealed their fate.

They were no longer the elves he had grown up with, trained with, feasted with, his closest companions in life. They were only targets. Their slender throats begged to be opened. The pure, light fabric of their clothes was too unsullied, calling for him to blacken it with death.

So he did.

Those slim throats yawned with crimson smiles, rivers of

blood cascading onto the pale garments. A canvas of scarlet soaked into the ground. Around him, the twisted bodies fell still, moans and screams silenced by the black smoke surging from his fingers and forcing its way down their throats to choke them where they stood, fumbling for their weapons, failing to call forth their own magic, which would have been enough to end his rampage.

He laughed maniacally with every strike. Their bodies stilled and their rich, warm skin paled in death as black tendrils snaked under their flesh in a ghastly, dark spider web, the darkness clouding their unseeing, amber eyes.

More. More. More.

Was it Finarvon's blade that sang to him? His own blood? Or a voice beyond his being? He could not discern, for it seemed to come from everywhere, within and without, filling him, charging him, until he was blinded by the compulsion, unable to even string together a tendril of free will, let alone rationalise or refute the urge.

At last, he stood alone. No more came for him. No more could he find. And only with the death of the last of his comrades, the thump of the last body upon the stone, did Finarvon halt.

Slowly, his hand fell to his side. The laughter ringing in his ears, tearing from his own throat, faltered.

Gradually, the black mist receded enough for him to see the devastation all around him. The twisted forms of those he had called friends, their blood splattered up the whorled, wooden walls, the iron tang of their life permeating the room. The only sound to be heard was his own panting, for even the wildlife outside, usually so squalling, had stilled in the face of his ferociousness.

Finarvon had woken from a dream into a living nightmare, and his gaping mouth formed around a wordless howl of agony as he understood what he saw…and now remembered every painful moment.

He had done this.

Killed all of them.

He was still screaming as the black mist descended upon him once more, choking the life from his body and leaving him to join his comrades in death.

If anyone had been left alive, they would have seen tendrils of black rising from the mouths, noses, eyes of all those present, coalescing into a brooding cloud that filled the room before it seeped up through the levels of the tree fortress and evanesced into the night beyond.

They would have also seen Finarvon rise to his feet once more with unearthly grace, his slack face spidered with black veins testament to the will that held his still-warm corpse upright.

Around him, the dead rose anew.

TWO

Lief passed through the forest as silent as any woodland creature, her soft-soled, supple, leather boots making not a sound with each light step she took across the verdant cushion of moss. She turned her head as she walked, her sharp senses attuned to any hint of something untoward.

Squirrels with glossy, red coats bounded past her in a cacophony of shrieks as they chased each other from tree to tree and through the bushes. The corner of Lief's lips tugged up into a smile as she slowed to watch them for a moment, resting a hand upon the full quiver of arrows belted to her hip, the other tightening around the bow strapped across her chest. As the stray breeze brushed a tendril of auburn hair free from her braid, she hooked it behind her ear once more.

The creatures passed from her vision and the rustle of their chase faded, making way for the chorus of birdsong in the canopy above her once more. The giant oaks here soared high above their counterparts outside the magic of the forest's borders, their trunks thick and strong, their branches stretching wide – silent guardians of the forest. Now they slumbered, but if the need arose, they could walk the earth, for the realm of Tir-na-Alathea held the *dhiran*, the living forest.

Like almost every other patrol she had made, this one was unremarkable. The summer sun cast dappled warmth upon her in a pattern of shadow and light through the canopy high above, warming her uncovered head pleasantly. It was cool near the edge of the forest, for it was the depths of winter outside Tir-na-Alathea's borders, and even though Queen Solanaceae's magic was powerful, She could not prevent a trickle from bleeding through, blurring the edges of the protections upon the endless summer of the living forest.

Lief welcomed it. A novel and fresh change from the usual humidity that clung to her skin. As she picked her way down into the gully that marked the edge of her patrol, the chill deepened. She shivered, pausing at the unnaturally steep change in temperature.

The loud bickering of birds now far behind her, she realised not a thing rustled in the foliage around her. And she knew where there was silence in the forest, there was danger. It was the first instinct any creature learned, and wood elves were no different. The lifeblood of the forest beat through her, as innate as magic. All wood elves felt it. Now, the oaks seemed to watch, too, the air still, like the forest held its breath with her.

Lief stilled upon the game trail and strained her hearing for any trace of life, her long, pointed ears quivering with the effort.

Moving with liquid grace, she readied her bow, the supple, smooth wood warm under her hand, and slid an arrow from her quiver, nocking it and holding the bow down, ready to draw. She was the quickest, most accurate archer in the patrol, but target practice was different than being out in the field. Her chest swelled with a deep, steadying breath as her eyes scanned back and forth.

Nothing. Just the unnerving silence. Anxiety coiled within Lief as she crept forwards, avoiding every crunching leaf or cracking twig that might give her away. Was it her imagination, or had the sunlight darkened? It seemed like the winter beyond the forest, the dark clouds she could see at the edge of the horizon, had somehow tainted the brightness of the living forest. It should have been impossible for the outside to bleed in so much.

Lief frowned. *Is there a trespasser?*

It was not uncommon for folks to venture into the living forest of Tir-na-Alathea. In search of riches, stories, sanctuary, or war, it did not matter. They all failed. The Queen guarded Her realm without quarter. Yet something felt…*off*, in a way Lief could not describe. As she edged up the gully, a sense of unease stirred, a sickly swoop in her stomach. With each step, the light faded, the sounds of the forest behind her receding. Her own breathing was loud. Too loud. Every step felt like the beat of a drum announcing her presence.

Focus, you fool, she admonished herself, sending out her magic before her – sensing, testing, seeking…and protecting, for it cloaked her in silence. She felt a tendril of regret that she had not waited for Finarvon to patrol with her, but she slapped the thought away. His tardiness had nothing to do with her, and she could patrol without him just as well. Besides, she could not bear to see his smug, philandering face, let alone work with him. It was a violation, the way he had the nerve to *smile* at her. A reminder of all the hurt he had already caused her… and that he seemed to bear no regret for the matter at all.

The gulley wound its way to the edge of the forest and beyond, into the land of Pelenor. It was the closest she had ever come to setting foot outside the living forest, save for a time on her first patrol long ago when she had lingered on the border between the summer and the fading autumn, wondering at her Queen and Her forest's power.

Now, the winter beyond did not capture her attention, for with quickening dread, Lief saw the tell-tale signs that something was indeed amiss. The taint washed over her, physically and magically – and she sensed the forest felt it, too.

It feels…sick, she realised, as though some slow, dark poison spread through the air, earth, and forest itself.

A slight breeze brought the scent of decay to her nose, and Lief fought back the urge to gag on the stench of death. Still, nothing moved. Yet she could feel something pulsing through the forest around her, slow and inexorable.

At her feet, summer leaves that ought to have been fresh and green in the canopy above were blackened and rotting to mush, and each trunk she passed had darkened bark and oozed viscous, sanguine sap, leaving trails of tears down the oaks. Lief was sure she could feel them groaning, creaking in agony as whatever this malevolence was choked the life from them.

This part of the forest had been destroyed. There was no other word for it. Every part of it was tainted. It could no longer sustain life, and what there had been had withered away.

She reached out to the tree next to her, stopping just shy of resting her hand upon the bark. Her natural sympathy for the forest was tempered by caution for her own safety. Lief knew the forest as well as she knew herself, but she had never seen the likes of this. Whatever it was, even if she could not fix it, it was her duty to return to Lune at once and report what she had seen.

Lief glanced towards the border of Tir-na-Alathea and Pelenor, her very body filled with nervous energy and brimming with the urge to leave. But something stopped her. Looking closer, she sucked in a breath. Normally, the very air of the border was filled with a flicker of magic that blurred the land beyond. The only visible thing to suggest the edge of the forest. But as the gulley crossed over into Pelenor, she perceived a jagged hole in the shimmering veil, the land beyond as clear as day.

A swear hissed through Lief's lips as she crouched low and ran through the squelching mulch and over rotting logs, hurrying to the barrier. She shouldered her bow and returned the arrow to her quiver, then drew her hunting knife, holding it ready as she backed to the edge of the forest realm.

The magic of the border hummed against Lief's back, a faint buzzing the only indication of the unimaginable power it contained. She reached back, her palm brushing against it. Although she moved through the air, her hand stopped as it connected with the invisible wall, as though it were solid. It was reassuringly hard, with no give as she pushed against it. Yet as she slid her hand closer to where the tear frayed the magic, her fingers, then her arm slipped through, into the biting air of the land beyond.

Lief snatched her arm back with a gasp as the cold bit into her exposed skin. Her sleeveless tunic was well suited for the eternal summer forest, but no protection beyond. The chilly breeze seeped in from the tear.

As Lief looked back along the gulley, the trail became clear. The darkness and smell of death bore straight into the forest, bleeding out of the edge of the gulley and into the trees beyond it, where all around, the summer greens of Tir-na-Alathea lay as though nothing had been disturbed.

Lief suppressed the urge to vomit as the cloying stench clogged her throat. After one last scan of the silent, deserted forest around her, she turned back to the barrier.

I must repair this. No matter that it was beyond her skill or power. Even a temporary fix would be better than nought. *Then I have to track what has entered Tir-na-Alathea through it.* Lief had no doubt something dark had ventured into the living forest. She would have to find it and remove it by any means necessary.

You should return to Lune, make your report, and leave this to someone far better qualified, her subconsciously obedient nature reminded her.

I can do this myself, her stubborn defiance answered.

With that, Lief turned back to the barrier and pulled forth her magic, what little remained from the earth beneath her and the plants around her. She began to hum – she did not dare sing, not wanting to shatter the silence – as she wove a song of building, healing, and mending, knitting the barrier together one delicate strand at a time, hoping it might be enough to keep anything else out of the woodland realm, the living forest of Tir-na-Alathea.

THREE

Aedon yawned and stretched, his fists bumping the smooth, wooden wall of his cell, as they did every morning. He blinked up at the light filtering through the small crack in the tree roots – what passed for a window, yet too narrow to escape through, for he had tried that long ago – and ran a hand through his shaggy hair.

The Epic of Mireanor slipped from where it had rested all night, lying open across his chest, where he had fallen asleep reading it, to the floor, crumpling the worn pages. Aedon cursed under his breath and retrieved the cracked tome, smoothing the pages and shutting it neatly, before placing it on the foot of his cot.

"As good as new," he muttered. "What they don't know can't hurt them."

Though not as fastidious as some, the wood elves would not be happy if he started damaging their books. It had taken him twelve years of captivity to persuade them to even let him borrow them in the first place, and he had no inclination to return to the mind-numbing infuriation of long days spent staring at the walls of his cell, tangled tree roots of giant proportion wrapping around him, or staring through the crack to his paltry source of daylight.

At least I find some escape in the stories. Not that I deserve one.

Twenty-five long years… He had tried every trick in his repertoire to escape, to no avail, until the wood elves had lost patience, stripped him of his magic, and locked him in the dusty hole he now called home, where the only company he had were scurrying mice and one objectionable door. A cruel joke of the wood elves, he was certain.

"Ahem." Aedon cleared his throat. "May I have breakfast, please?"

The door creaked. "I shall ask, thief," it answered, its rough, whispery growl as snooty as ever.

"Call me Aedon," he replied, as he did every day.

"I will call you what you are."

Aedon sighed and smoothed the front of his green, woollen tunic. "Maybe by the time I've been here fifty years, this blasted thing will be more friendly," he muttered to himself.

"I doubt it."

Aedon shot it a venomous glare. "You know, for a door, you have a lot of attitude. You're a *door*, for goodness sake. Are you sure you can't let me out?" He had tried, and failed, to trick, wheedle, and flatter his way out for a quarter of a century.

"No."

"Not even to stretch my legs? They're getting rather stiff,

cramped in here day after day."

"Not my problem."

"Curse you, you rotten old piece of wood."

The door did not deign to answer.

Whilst he waited, he carved another line in the cot with his nail – he had learned early not to disturb the tree that comprised his cell, for those roots were powerful and quick to crush – to mark the passing of another day. There was precious little room left now, almost twenty-five years of marks upon it, the lines getting smaller and smaller the less space he had.

A quarter of a century in a dark hole, he thought glumly.

It was not *unpleasant*, per se. Dark, earthy, a comfortable temperature, and at least they had been generous enough to give him clothes and a blanket, as well as a bucket to use as a privy, which they emptied daily. They fed and watered him, too. He was permitted outside for exercise every day, short though the reprieves were. He had seen worse. *Been* in worse.

Yet it had been a quarter of a century with no contact from the outside world, no freedom to roam the forest above. His life was this cell. Alone. Always alone. The ghosts of all those he had left behind in the world outside sat beside him. He felt their accusing stares boring into him.

He dropped his head into his palms, trying to banish the imaginary phantoms that haunted him, and waited, each long moment yawning into the next, for night to fall once more so he could at least eliminate his demons for a few hours of sleep.

Breakfast did not come.

Nor did lunch.

Nor did dinner.

The faint hubbub of life outside turned to screams, then silence, as Aedon waited in the dim cell with nothing but a surly door and his rumbling stomach for company – as well as a growing fear at what he had heard.

The early evening sun cast the roots in warm shadows, and still, no food arrived, no change of guard. All Aedon could hear was unearthly silence. He realised even the birds, usually so raucous, had been absent all day.

He could not expel the curl of unease that writhed through his belly, the sense that something was amiss. Instinctively, he felt for his magic, though he knew it was far beyond his reach…and froze as he touched it.

The sensation shivered through him like a lover's caress, lighting his senses on fire and banishing the stiffness from his limbs. It was as though he took a deep, rich breath after being saved from drowning. Aedon drank it in. It had been so long since he had had access to his power, and like a starving soul before a feast, he revelled in it.

The barrier the wood elves had smothered him in to cut him off from the innate magic within had driven in as deeply and painfully as a knife. Aedon still remembered the curl of Queen

Solanaceae's lip, her glee at causing him so much suffering. For an elf to be without magic was akin to death. Aedon had felt empty inside ever since.

But now, it filled him to the brim and spilled out, warming him, lighting up the cell with a warm faelight as he let out a breathy, surprised chuckle.

After a long moment, his joy and relief subsided, the wariness returning. Aedon knew the wards they placed upon him were sustained by the magic of the forest and the elves there. They would never release his magic by choice. The fire magic within him, the remnants of his dragon rider days, was feared and reviled among the folk of the forest. He was fairly certain the wards had not been willingly broken. If they had failed…

Aedon could draw few conclusions, and none of them were pleasant. Within him, the wary thief and the former warrior vied for control, curiosity melding with caution. Above all, Aedon's spark of self-preservation ignited once more.

"What's happening out there?" he asked the door.

But the door did not answer, shuddering. That unnerved him more than the eerie silence that seemed to smother the entire place, for it had never been without a rebuke or retort.

"Let me out."

The door shivered again.

Aedon called forth his magic, and hot flames burst into life in his cupped palms. He edged closer to the door, until the fire warmed the wood. The door creaked and shook on its hinges, as if to get away from him.

"Let me out, or I will be forced to use this upon you."

Despite the many ways the door had infuriated, offended, and contained him over the years, he bore it no malicious will. After all, it was just a door. After a last, creaking shudder and a whine, failing to get away from the flames, the door flew open with a bang. It echoed down the silent halls like a beacon.

"Thanks."

Aedon slipped into the darkening halls, which were empty of all life and the light that normally lined them. The hovering sconces where the heatless faelights normally sat, flickering and fluttering, were devoid of magic.

Aedon's apprehension grew.

Through the gaps in the gnarled roots that made up the walls, he could see the canopy outside darkening with the coming gloaming. Still, the wood elves ought to be busy with their daily business, for they did not cease until sunset proper, then made merry long and loud into the night. However, all Aedon heard was silence.

The faint breeze carried the usual fragrant flowers upon it, but tonight, it held something else. He ceased padding down the hallway to take a long, full breath of it and gagged, scrunching up his face. Putrid. Rotting. Tangy. Like blood and death.

What is that stench?

On half a thought, he backtracked to the guards' room and peered in. Empty. Aedon crossed swiftly to the weapon rack and donned a dagger, sword, and belt. He reached for a bow and quiver, too, then dropped his hand.

Twenty-five years.

He probably would not be able to even hit the biggest target now. *Better I use blade and magic.* Where his aim did not strike true, Aedon hoped his magic would.

He returned to the corridor, skulking silently from pooling shadow to pooling shadow as the sun passed below the horizon and darkness fell. Coming to a winding staircase of roots smoothed with centuries of wear, he climbed, until he cautiously emerged into the grassy yard that was the sole part of the outside world he had seen for over two decades.

It was deserted. Yet the feeling of something there, watching, lurking, brooding, did not fade. Blending into the shadows as best he could, Aedon skulked around the edge of the yard. On the walkways above, bridges connecting the branches of the behemoth trees, shadowy figures prowled. Somehow, he knew that he ought not draw their attention.

Aedon's senses were fully open to the night, searching for any trace of life, as well as threats, as his heart thundered and limbs quivered with the urge to bolt. He had been in far worse situations than a seemingly deserted courtyard, no matter how long ago, and no matter how safe his former cell now felt against the yawning vastness of the forest around him.

Aedon flitted between the giant trees, cloaking himself with magic to cross the open spaces in order to silence his steps and scatter his shadow. There were no walls in the city here, for within the borders of Tir-na-Alathea, none were needed.

An unearthly shriek, wild and feral, rang out into the night. Aedon jumped as the sound scraped down his spine, sending chills through him and fraying his already worn nerves. He eased the dagger from its sheath. Another screech rang out across the clearing, as if in answer. He had never heard anything quite like it, save for the inhuman caws of the goblin scourge that had been banished from the Kingdom of Pelenor, with his help, a quarter of a century before.

Aedon darted into the shadow of a tree, his thundering pulse masking any other sound…until he heard the sharp crack of a nearby twig. A shadow crossed in front of him, bulging and contorting strangely. Aedon shrank back into the small hollow of the trunk as he watched it, transfixed.

A figure came into view, faintly illuminated by the waning crescent moon.

Now the shadow's movement made sense, for this creature shuffled and lurched awkwardly. It looked vaguely like an elf, but it moved like no elf Aedon had ever seen. Holding his breath, he watched as it lumbered across the clearing, before stopping between the trees and raising its nose to the sky. One long, deep, rattling breath, followed by another, the sound travelling through the still air.

Slowly, the figure turned, and Aedon stifled a cry.

It was a wood elf – or had been.

Its tanned skin was as pale as the moon, and black veins crawled across its face like branches. What once had been warm, amber eyes had darkened to voids too terrible to behold. And across its throat yawned a gaping slash. Crusted blood trailed down alabaster skin and marred its pale green doublet, the blood so dark it looked black.

Aedon knew without a doubt that it was dead. Yet it stood in front of him.

He looked up to the walkways above him, seeing the figures there had the same stumbling gait. Aedon wondered how many more were around that he didn't see.

How can this be?

He had no answers. The only thing he knew was he must flee immediately. He did not want to be seen, or caught, by them.

He chanced a glance around the trunk. Pure terror gripped him as the dead elf's head whipped around unnaturally fast on its mangled neck at his movement, those black voids seeking him out.

Like a predator, it skulked forwards with silent, eerie grace, belying the lurching movements Aedon had just seen. Panic rose. He was outnumbered, outmatched, surrounded, and had no idea where he was. He could flee, he could hide, but how far would he get?

He renewed his wards, checking that they were strong enough to conceal any sound of his passage, then summoned an errant breeze. It rustled bushes across the clearing, as though something thrashed through them.

Aedon barely dared watch as the creature quickly spun around, regarded the bushes for a moment, and bounded towards them.

Then Aedon ran.

Strides long, and with as few glances back as he dared, he ran through the forest until his legs could not carry him anymore, burning for respite. Shrinking into the shadow of a tree to catch his breath and slow his thundering heart, he looked around, frowning. He was entirely lost, having no idea where the wood elves' garrison was, or the rest of the world.

All he heard was silence.

Aedon did not dare believe he was safe yet. After as long a reprieve as he dared, he ran again, hoping against hope that he headed towards some kind of safety, but the forest looked the same in every direction. Not to mention in ducking around giant trees, he had no idea of the trueness of his course any longer.

Aedon glanced up and swore softly, seeing the moon ahead. He had come full circle. For all he knew, he could be heading right back into the arms of…

He shivered, energy running through him. That thought was

enough to bring fresh strength to his step. He turned away from the moon and–

Smack.

Aedon stumbled away from the shadowy figure, who tumbled to the ground with him.

FOUR

Lief followed the trail of devastation into the heart of the forest for hours, until darkness threatened from the approaching night. The forest around her did not thrum with life as it ordinarily would. Instead, the usual cacophony seemed to shrink away from making a racket, as though it, too, feared what she tracked. The rustles were muted, the birdsong a staccato that quickly silenced as she passed, as though fearing her passing.

She had seen no trace of anything other than the fetid, rotting trail of death that led her through the forest, tainting everything it had touched with black poison that rotted, puffing a putrid stench into her nose with every step she took. Lief checked the rising moon again, hoping it had somehow changed bearing, but it hung just as it had before, silent in the sky. And with its inexorable hushed progress through the heavens, her heart grew heavier, for the trail led her back to Lune.

Lief hoped she would not return to find conflict in her home. That the fair oaks that cradled Lune amongst their boughs and roots had not sickened like the bleeding trees she walked through, which burst with pustules of bloody sap and shed blackening leaves. She could hear their creaking groans, a constant dirge to their excruciating demise, as she flitted through the yawning shadows.

She held her bow ready, an arrow nocked. Lief slowed, thinking, then returned the arrow to her quiver and re-strapped the bow across her chest. Magic would serve her best in the dark.

She paused to survey her surroundings. Over the next rise and at the end of the valley, she would find Lune. Her heart quivered at that. The darkness bored straight through the forest towards it, but she could hear nothing upon the breeze.

All is well, that's why, Lief told herself sternly.

There was no reason for fear in the living forest, for it was as much a weapon as the wood elves who inhabited it. Even this, whatever it was, as destructive a force as it had shown to be, was no match for the elves of Lune.

Her fingers slid across the handle of the leaf-shaped dagger belted to her hip, but she forced herself not to draw it.

There is no threat, Lief na Arboreali. Stop letting shadows scare you. You are a ranger of Tir-na-Alathea.

Straightening, she continued, her steps quickening until she ran, fleet of foot and silent as the night through her forest, skipping over the ruined moss. A figure appeared before her out of nowhere – utterly silent and half a shadow. Lief could not stop in time.

Smack.

Lief stumbled and skidded on the ground with a sickly squelch. A moment later, black slime smearing her bare arm and the back of her tunic, she jumped to her feet, dagger drawn, looking down at the figure she had run into. He was tall – too tall for any of the wood elves she knew. What was he doing out here in the dark of night?

"Who are you?" Lief asked sharply, her magic pooling under her skin, ready to erupt at the slightest provocation. "What are you doing here?" There should be no stranger in the living forest, but a stranger in the midst of unimaginable destruction to her beloved Tir-na-Alathea? Lief did not believe in coincidences.

The figure groaned, but after a moment of groggy hesitation, he rose too, his own magic blooming at his fingertips, a faint light of...

Lief hissed. *Fire*! The mortal enemy of the forest. No element was greater feared than it, nor more forbidden.

"Did you do this?" she snarled, sweeping her dagger out at the destruction around them.

"What?" he retorted, straightening a little. "Wait... You're... You're not like them. You're...*alive?*" He looked at her, brows furrowed.

That halted her brimming assault. "Pardon?" Confusion stayed Lief's hand. In the faint light of his magic, she could not help but examine him.

He was an elf, she could see the point of his ears, but unlike the long, tapered point of hers, his were short. *He is a Pelenori elf.* Tousled, brown hair tumbled down to his shoulders, and his forest green eyes, which she could not help but be drawn to, twinkled in the light. Seeing he wore a simple woollen tunic, she gasped.

"You are the prisoner – the thief. How did you–"

An unearthly shriek rang out in the distance. The thief swore and grasped her arm, tugging her with him. Lief cried out at his unwelcome and unexpected touch, trying to wrench herself away, but he held firm.

"We have to go – *now*!"

She had not expected the urgency in his voice, but that did not erase who he was.

"I won't help you escape, thief."

"I'm not trying to escape," he growled. "At least not the way that you think. Did you hear that? We need to get to safety."

"I'm not an imbecile. You're coming with me. I don't know how you escaped, but I'm taking you right back to Lune."

Lief shrugged off his grip and reversed their roles, gripping him firmly by the upper arm, digging in a little more harshly than was necessary. But she did not mind seeing him flinch. He deserved it. After all, he was a thief, a liar, and a crook. Her Queen had decreed he rot in a cell, and she would see it done.

The thief's eyes flashed with anger. "Listen, wood elf. If you go back there, you will *die*, like the rest of them. Do you hear me?"

Lief recoiled, frowning. "What are you talking about?"

"Everyone in Lune is dead, and if we stay here–" He faltered as another shriek rang out, closer this time, "we will meet the same fate. I don't intend to die today, so step aside."

Lief bared her teeth and brought her face into his, even as a jolt of uncertainty rushed through her at his wild claim. "I'm taking you back, no matter what you say."

He just raised an eyebrow. Not the reaction she had expected. Why was he not scared of her? Yet he bounced upon the balls of his feet, as though keen to be away.

When something crashed through the brush behind them, Lief spun around, but she could see nothing, for the moon had disappeared behind the clouds, casting the forest floor into deep shadows.

"What is that?" Lief's voice wavered with uncertainty.

He blew out a breath and his shoulders slumped. "Ugh. Damn my noble disposition. If you're going to be so foolhardy as to return, I cannot let you go alone. I know what awaits you, and I would not wish that fate upon anyone."

"You're coming with me?" She eyed him suspiciously, a coil of unease swirling in her belly.

"You leave me no choice," he said through gritted teeth, and despite her determined resistance to any of his thieving, lying ways, she had to admit, his acting was convincingly fervent. "But be warned, you're making a damn stupid mistake."

She bristled at that. "Get moving, thief." She tugged him more harshly than she needed to, but he came meekly enough.

After a few steps, he shrugged off her grip. "I won't run. You have my word."

Lief glared at him, but he seemed sincere enough. She still did not trust him, though, and stayed close as they passed through the dark forest, barely breathing for the anticipation of what they would find. A dappled light returned as the moon shook its cover and returned to bathe them in a pale glow. Whilst the warmth of the summer forest surrounded them once more, far from the tear in the border of the living forest, chills still crawled across Lief's exposed skin.

"Wait." He halted. "I'm warded, so they cannot hear me and will struggle to perceive me. I'll extend my wards to you." His voice was even, but she thought she sensed a slight tremor.

"I don't need any wards. I'm returning home."

"I'm *not* asking. You'll thank me later."

She felt his magic bloom over her with a warm caress that somehow soothed her rising hackles, no matter how much she wished it did not.

Lief raised her chin, gestured for him to get moving, then stormed after him in the direction of Lune.

The rotting trees and soil soon ended, fizzling out after a copse of birches that looked stark and bare, their leaves blackening on the ground, sanguine sap trailing like claw marks down their trunks. Lief slowed for a moment to note where it ended – just before the borders of Lune.

To her surprise, the thief drew close, until she could feel the wool of his tunic brush her shoulder. "Whatever you do, please promise me… Do not speak. Do not approach them. They are no longer the elves you probably knew."

As if in answer, a shadow ahead bulged, stumbling between the trees. The thief gripped her wrist in warning, but Lief shook it off and drew closer, her confidence tempering only slightly. What reason did she have to fear her own home? Just because of the mad ramblings of a prisoner who had probably gone strange in the head after so many years captive? Who was no doubt trying to execute a hare-brained scheme to escape?

As the creature drew close and turned towards them, Lief's jaw gaped, but no sound emerged. With wordless horror, she beheld the monstrosity before her.

Its black eyes captured her gaze, sucking her into the dark void within. Black veins stretched across its ghastly pale face. Yet it bore the attire of her kin, had the long, mahogany hair, the slim, pointed ears…but it was like no wood elf she had ever seen. Everything about it felt *wrong.*

Lief shook with confusion and fear as the creature stalked closer, hissing and gobbling wordlessly. Dark magic roiled off it in waves, the moss and grass around it curling to blackened, shrivelled ash.

"Run."

The thief's command in her ear, as well as the yank upon her arm, was enough to break her free.

They bolted. The thief sent a blast of magic back at the creature, lighting up the forest around them with an orange glow for a moment. The creature emitted a head-splitting screech that cut right through her. Lief did not stop to look, did not turn back, and ran faster, now tugging the thief along in her haste to flee, every instinct within her telling her to get as far away from it as she could.

She heard crashing through the forest behind them, and the thief's long strides outstripped her own. More creatures dove through undergrowth, over roots, and dodged between trees with uncanny agility. Lief glanced to her sides as she fled and cried out as the shadows matched her pace, drawing closer, reaching for her.

Lief dodged one. The other snatched at her, its fingers clawing through her hair, ripping part of her braid free. She screamed, leaping away, her lungs burning as she tried to run faster, to outpace them somehow.

A cold hand grasped her bare arm and dragged her back.

FIVE

"You know, if you really wanted to show me how clever you were, you could just *tell me*," said Venya airily, placing books one by one along the dark and dusty shelves. Each time, she stood back, raised her hands, and watched with satisfaction as a fine, golden net of binding magic erupted from her fingertips and wrapped around the grimoires, binding them to their shelves and slumber.

One rustled its pages, the chain tethering it to the shelf gently clinking. "Where's the fun in that?" it teased, its papery voice holding a mischievous edge.

"Oh, you're *impossible*, Sylvio." Venya shoved the book in her hand onto the shelf, to its muffled protest, and glared at the grimoire, folding her arms.

"Junior librarians aren't meant to know such interesting things." Now it was the grimoire's turn to be airy.

Sylvestri di Niano Verdiatris, The Book of Gateways groaned as he adjusted on the shelf, his aged, thick, leather binding creaking as he shifted. The chain tethering him, which glittered with magic and metal, also shifted. He looked like nothing more than an innocuous old tome, but Venya knew better.

Those pages held powerful magic, the kind that could devastate cities, and Sylvio was not the restraining type. The library had only just recovered after his last rampage. Some of the new plaster on the vaulted ceiling was still damp. Sylvio now had a padlock to hold his covers together, too, just to make sure.

Venya narrowed her eyes at him. "You know, I don't have to talk to you. I could leave you in this dark hole…" She clenched her fist, and all the faelights illuminating the windowless space with soft, warm light blinked out of existence, plunging the room into darkness, "where no one else ever bothers to come and visit. All alone for the rest of time."

"Oh, dear elfling, you and I both know you could not resist me."

Venya scoffed, but with a flick of her wrist, lit the faelights hovering around them once more. She was not afraid of the dark, per se, but there was something very unnerving about being trapped in a pitch-black room with a bunch of malevolent – or, at the very least, darkly mischievous – sentient magical tomes.

"Would you like to try me?" she said sweetly, turning away and making to leave.

"You know, I'm trying to rest here," an indignant, wheezy, trembling voice piped up.

Venya gritted her teeth and turned towards it. "Sorry,

Marcus," she apologised to the ancient grimoire behind her, which coughed on his own dust. "We were just talki–"

But her words were lost as Marcus spoke over her forcefully in the unrelenting drone that she so hated. Venya sighed. She knew she was about to endure at least a ten-minute lecture about courtesy and consideration from the pompous historical tome before she could make her escape – not to mention now she would not discover Sylvio's interesting morsel of knowledge.

Mouldy pages! she cursed to herself, sending her eyes skywards – through there was no sky to be seen in the deep vaults under the mountain – and edged towards the door.

"Maybe I'll tell you how I escaped next time!" Sylvio shouted over Marcus's droning, then cackled.

Venya gritted her teeth and slammed the vault door behind her. She pulled out her junior librarian's token and pressed it to the intricate seal of the matching depression on the door, securing it. Warm magic breathed over her hand in a small gust of air, a momentary flare of golden light. Then she was alone once more, Marcus's voice and Sylvio's cackling silenced behind the impenetrable door.

Well, almost impenetrable. Venya had no doubt the crafty old grimoire would try to escape again. She vowed to be the one to catch him when that happened.

For a moment, she paused in the hallway, eyeing the token, the brass metal bright with the newness of it. Her parents had sent her a letter of congratulations for completing her probation as a trainee librarian and graduating to a junior position, but still, she felt no pride in it. Only the continuing niggle that it was not good enough.

Two years, Venya. You've only been here two years, she reminded herself, though it never eased her frustration. She was used to being at the top of all her classes, the best in her cohort, and it did not come easily to pursue ventures that were beyond her skills and knowledge… Ventures that measured her level in time more than prowess. It would take her another three years to make a full librarian position in the Royal Athenaeum, the archives that held all the wisdom in the Kingdom of Pelenor.

That meant it would take another three years before she could access the more interesting, and dangerous, grimoires on the lower levels, never mind that she had already surpassed the rest of the fully fledged librarians in terms of magical skills and power, thanks to the potency of her elven blood. If she chose to do so, she could have broken the padlocks and chains of most of the grimoires under the wardenship of the junior librarians, but it was not the ability to do so that attracted her.

One day, I'll be first librarian, she promised herself resolutely. Then her parents would be so proud, and no amount of bad blood, thanks to the ancestors who had cursed her with their name, would be able to hold her back, shame her, any longer.

Venya made short order of filing the remaining grimoires in

the next vault, dodging past the fog cast by a mischievous weather grimoire, and ignoring the agonised moaning of a healer's journal that she knew, once unchained, liked to pick apart its victims sinew by interesting sinew.

Venya grumbled and stomped up the stairs just as the finishing bell pealed down the endless hallways of the grimoire-filled vaults.

SIX

Venya yawned and stretched, the woollen blanket slipping down as she did so. For a moment, she lay still, staring up at the pitched roof of her bedroom, where light streamed in through the small dormer window. It was a tiny space under the eaves that barely fit her small bed, washstand, wardrobe, and teetering piles of books. Such was the luxurious life of a junior librarian. It was a far cry from the space and extravagance she had grown up with, but Venya had never cared for typical finery. Books were her treasure.

The morning bell rang again, and Venya slid out of bed with another yawn. Slipping off her nightgown, she dressed in the simple, practical garb of the librarians – warm leggings, a long-sleeved top that hugged her slim figure, and a tunic bearing the crest of the Royal Athenaeum, the archives of Pelenor.

Venya belted the yellow-hemmed tunic around her, the colour signifying her rank as a junior librarian, checking each of the pouches upon her belt were intact and that her spelled dagger was secure in its leather sheath. For most of her peers, the belts were the only line of defence they had against rogue grimoires. Not all of them were as lucky as her to have magic in their blood.

Venya quickly brushed through her long, raven hair, then braided it. She had learned early on that loose hair was never a good idea in the vaults.

"Come on, ladies and gents!"

Beatrix's jovial voice rang out down the corridor. As a fully qualified librarian, she had been assigned to their wing to oversee the half-dozen junior librarians in Venya's cohort, despite only being a few years older than Venya herself.

She grabbed a small book from the top of one of her piles – a tiny volume of exquisite poetry she was slowly translating from the elven script of Tir-na-Alathea about the living forest itself – and hurried out of her door, almost crashing into Beatrix, who was just passing. Venya stumbled backwards, bumping into the doorframe.

She blushed as Beatrix tucked a stray piece of her short, flyaway, chestnut hair behind her ear and turned a warm grin her way. "Morning, Vee."

"M-morning," Venya stuttered as her face heated, barely able to meet Beatrix's emerald eyes. She dashed past, cursing herself for her utter inability to act normal, and fled down the stairs to the canteen, where all the librarians dined.

With a bowl of porridge and her book in hand, she found a quiet corner and tucked away with her poetry, ignoring the chatter of others around her, whilst they ignored her, too.

It was not uncommon for librarians to read at mealtimes, but the others had learned to give Venya a wide berth.

"She thinks she's so much better than us with her fancy blood."

"That girl's going to turn into a book."

Venya gritted her teeth at the jibes and giggles from the table behind her, knowing they had meant for her to hear, and focused on her book. It was not the first time she had wished to turn into a grimoire and get revenge for the two years of merciless teasing by some of her fellow juniors.

She raced through the rest of her porridge, eager to get away from them.

A great shadow loomed over her. Venya smiled without looking up, already knowing who it was.

"Good morning, Beorn."

"Morning, Venya," Beorn replied, his voice a low rumble. According to Beatrix, the hulking librarian had been a fixture in the library for decades, and his kindly nature earned him respect and affection from everyone. "Still translating, eh?"

At her nod, he leaned over. "Ah, Miss Venya. I know I tell you every time I see it, but your handwriting is most beautiful. Befitting of translating that book." He smiled kindly.

Venya's cheeks warmed, but she could hardly accept praise like that, awkwardly bobbing her head at the book instead. "Did you know this word has *sixteen* meanings, depending on the context?" she blurted.

Beorn raised an eyebrow and slid onto the bench next to her. "No, I did not. Go on. I shall bite. Tell me more."

Ignoring the tittering, whispering junior librarians behind her, she did so.

Venya hurried to the main archives to be assigned her day's tasks, her footsteps echoing with the other librarians' as they all headed down the high-ceilinged, marble-floored halls, peeling off one by one or in pairs for their various duties.

Beatrix fell into step with her. "I'd heard what they said. It was me who told Beorn to put them in their place, but I guess he preferred your company instead. Ignore them, okay, Vee?" She smiled sympathetically.

Venya forced herself to smile, though she could only glance at Beatrix for the barest second. "Thank you."

Beatrix was everything she was not, yet wanted to be. Cool, calm, confident, pretty – inside and out – *qualified.* The red of the librarian rank suited her warm skin and chestnut hair.

"You're with me today." Beatrix nudged her, catching Venya off guard. She stumbled, and Beatrix's warm hands steadied her shoulders as she laughed – though not unkindly. Venya's cheeks fired hot and red all the same.

Beatrix explained at Venya's stunned silence. "Cleo is ill this week, so I need you with me."

"But, um..." Venya gaped for a moment. Cleo was a librarian, not a junior.

"I know, I know." She waved a hand through the air. "Don't worry about it. I've cleared it with Nieve. There's no other librarian available to take Cleo's place, and between you and me..." Beatrix leaned closer to whisper, her warm breath tickling Venya's pointed ears, "there's no one I trust more than you. Nieve agreed." Beatrix leaned away again and flashed her a smile.

Venya's mouth gaped. Nieve was in charge of the entire Athenaeum...and a stickler for the rules.

"But... But I'm not qualified," she protested numbly.

"I know. I was surprised, too. But she obviously thinks highly of you, else she wouldn't have agreed. Sorry I can't promise you any of the really juicy stuff." She sighed. "Neither of us are experienced enough for that."

Venya caught the disappointment and yearning in Beatrix's voice. Venya knew how she loved to work with the more feisty grimoires, longed for the rank of a senior librarian in order to access the restricted volumes.

Beatrix's voice brightened again. "But today I need someone who is quick, efficient, with an eye for detail. That's you."

"Oh, well... I mean... A-anyone can–"

"Oh, Vee." Beatrix rolled her eyes. "Just take the compliment!"

They turned down another hall, and Beatrix led her to a room she had never been allowed in before – the librarians' lounge. At their entrance, a few eyes flicked up to them, hovering on Venya. At the colour of her uniform that so clearly marked her out of place there. She lingered in the doorway awkwardly until Beatrix beckoned her in through the tall, ornate, carved wooden doors. She slunk in, feeling entirely out of place in her yellow-trimmed robes amidst the flurry of red, yet with Beatrix by her side, no one questioned her.

Beatrix led her past nooks where plush, faded armchairs were tucked away amidst the bookshelves, set next to fireplaces that crackled merrily, and arranged neatly around coffee tables stacked with books. Plush rugs lay on the polished parquet floors, and despite the high ceilings, the space was warm, the lead-paned windows well-sealed against the winter climes outside. It smelled of books, with a hint of freshly baked bread and cinnamon from the baskets of rolls and pastries that stood invitingly upon the low tables.

Venya could not help but dawdle, gaping at it all. It was a far cry from the small common room the juniors shared, crammed with too few mismatched chairs and one small fireplace that never seemed to warm the stone-flagged room with its cracked window that would never shut tightly.

Beatrix snagged two pastries and pressed one into Venya's hand with a wink. *No one will know*, she mouthed.

Venya tucked the still warm pastry into a pocket, glancing around, as though she expected a librarian to jump out from between the shelves to throw her out. Beatrix ate hers, small flakes of pastry flying away with each crunching bite, then grabbed a pile of papers from a sideboard, flicking through until she found their assignments for the day.

"Here you go, Vee." She handed her a sheet. "You've got these to shelve and these to retrieve." She pointed to each list respectively, then singled out a few. "Watch out for this one and that one. They're not the nicest. Oh, and that one bites. Wear gloves."

Venya winced, looking up at Beatrix with an apologetic smile that was more of a grimace. "I forgot mine…" They were somewhere in her tiny bedroom, between the piles of books. She admonished herself for the mistake. Every librarian needed gloves. Not all grimoires were toothless, and their bite was *nasty*.

Beatrix chuckled. "For someone who's so smart, you can be awfully forgetful, Vee. Don't worry. I have a spare set you can borrow. Come on. We'd better get started. Oh! I almost forgot."

Beatrix rummaged in her pocket and pulled out a silver seal – that of a librarian. "Nieve says you can borrow this for the week. I know it goes without saying, but take care of it, don't misuse it, and if you lose it, Nieve will have both our heads."

Venya could have laughed at the idea she would ever do anything she was forbidden to. She had always been one for following the rules. When it came to grimoires, rule breaking was literal life and death, not to mention her career would be ruined. Only a fool would risk it.

Her hand closed around the warm metal, their hands brushing. She was both hungry to use it and annoyed that at the end of the week, it would be taken from her. She would not earn it for years to come yet.

As if summoned by her name, Nieve appeared around the bookcases. "Hurry yourselves, ladies. You're late." Nieve's stern gaze turned upon her. "Venya, don't let me down." She felt a rush of fear at her words. Venya was top of her cohort, but grades meant nothing when faced with an unbound grimoire that could maim or kill. Or Nieve.

Somehow, even though the first librarian was firm but fair, Venya feared her, though she had never given Nieve cause for reprimand. Perhaps it was the way her mouth was always set in a thin, clamped line, or the way true warmth and mirth hardly ever seemed to reach her eyes. Perhaps it was the severity of her cropped, silver hair, or the depths of her obsidian robes, trimmed with the purple of her rank.

"Y-yes, Nieve."

In short order, they entered the archives at the back of the Athenaeum. Soon, the windows vanished, for the Athenaeum was built into the mountainside, tunnelling deep into the ancient stone, so sconces had been set at regular intervals along the halls, faelights illuminating their way. Beatrix soon peeled off with a wave to file the pile of grimoires that bobbed along behind her, enchanted by the magic of the place, and Venya continued to the stairs ahead, and the vaults waiting below.

The third level… She had not been permitted to go there before. Venya hesitated for a moment as she looked at the imprint in the door where the librarian seal was to fit. With a nervous smile, hand slightly shaking, she put the seal to it, bracing herself, expecting it to reject her, blast her away with the fierce protective magics with which the Athenaeum was renowned for warding its vaults. Instead, a warm ruffle of magic flared and the door clicked open.

Venya left the other grimoires floating in the hallway as she directed the one to be filed through the low door. The vaulted ceilings were lower than the first two levels, seeming to close in on Venya with every step. The air was thick with muttered rustlings and papery whispers that ceased the moment she entered, layering the air with silence, before starting once more. She glanced around for the source, but it came from all the grimoires around her – some bound in chains, others concealed within heavy, iron caskets, still others behind physical bars that bore signs of escape attempts.

Venya swallowed, excited, yet growing more apprehensive by the moment. These were not the slumbering, mild grimoires she had first trained with as an apprentice, nor the more chatty and malevolent, though hardly potent, grimoires on the second level.

She turned to check her reference for filing the first grimoire and hurried down the long aisles of books until she found the correct space for it. She wrinkled her nose at the stench of rotten eggs wafting through the air, trying not to think what might be the source of such sorcery.

Using her magic, Venya directed the grimoire onto the shelf, being careful not to touch it, and chained it in place as quickly as she could, fingers slipping for a second on the cold, smooth metal that flared with warmth as she activated the spells with a touch of the silver token.

The grimoire snarled as it momentarily awoke from its ensorcelled slumber, and Venya's fingers fumbled with the padlock. The book was as large as her torso, and the edges of the gnarled, worn leather held vicious teeth dripping with venom, which had already singed and burned the edges of its own pages. As she watched, a drop fell upon the bookshelf and hissed, scoring a dark mark upon the varnished wood.

Gritting her teeth, Venya finally snapped the padlock shut, and warm magic rippled over the grimoire. When it shuddered and growled, Venya jumped backwards, nearly knocking into another grimoire on the shelf behind her, before it fell into an ensorcelled slumber again. Venya watched and waited, heart thundering, making sure she had contained it before daring to move closer again.

This was the first grimoire with teeth – and *venom* – that she had been able to approach so closely. It both fascinated and unsettled her. Torn between curiosity and apprehension, she drifted closer to the quivering teeth, trying to read the words etched into the worn, cracked, acid-damaged surface.

How are grimoires made? She had not learned that yet. At least not the true art of it, though she longed to make her own one day. *How do they come to be so malevolent? Are they caged because they are evil, or is it being caged that makes them so?*

She resolved to ask Beatrix…or Nieve, if she could. An aspiring first librarian ought to know everything one could about grimoires, she reasoned.

As she leaned in to decipher the title, the book stilled and quieted. Venya realised its intentions. She jerked back just as the grimoire launched itself at her, jaws as wide as the padlock would allow. She stumbled to the floor as it crashed back onto the shelf once more, snarling and growling, acid spraying from its gnashing teeth

Venya took the hint and fled.

SEVEN

Aedon used the faint moon as his guide through the otherwise dark, unfamiliar forest, hoping the wood elf kept pace, as obstinate and insufferable as she already seemed to be. Hearing a cry, he looked back and swore as the shadowy figures converged on them. He cursed her foolishness, even though he knew she had no reason to take him at his word. After all, he *was* a thief.

She screamed, and he glanced back again, seeing her fall between the creatures, tugged this way and that as the dead grappled for a hold on her. Aedon snarled in frustration. Every part of him screamed to run, to save himself, yet a shred of who he had been at one time still remained.

Aedon skidded to a stop, looking forwards, then back at the scuffle. Now was his chance to escape. After a quarter century of captivity, freedom beckoned him, in any direction he chose… An empty taunt, for the forest stretched unbroken in hundreds or thousands of miles in each direction. It would be easy for him to get lost. What would freedom matter if he wandered the rest of his days lost in Tir-na-Alathea? He owed the wood elf nothing, less than nothing, yet he could not leave her knowing what her likely fate would be. Could he?

Attracted by the commotion, more of the shambling dead crashed through the trees.

Aedon swore again, then dove into the fray, the putrid scent of death gagging him. With a savage thrust of his clawed hand, his magic obliterated one of the dead, even as the wood elf despatched another.

"Believe me now?" he cried out, blasting, yet still they came, shambling through the night, their pale faces deathly white against the dark forest.

"Yes," she snarled, slashing her dagger at any that came within reach. She dodged away from another, before knocking it down and stabbing it through the heart.

Yet as she turned away, it rose anew, black blood oozing from the wound upon its breast.

Aedon cried out, but it was too late. Feet away, he could not reach her, not whilst engaged in his own fight.

The dead creature latched her in its grasp, its arms snaking around her torso as it pulled her close. With a gurgling shriek, the wood elf thrashing, it sank its pointed, blackened teeth into the soft flesh where her shoulder met her slender neck.

Her scream was pure pain as she struggled fiercely to free herself, to no avail. The creature's arms only tightened around her until she silenced, the very breath slowly squeezed out of her body.

Aedon exploded.

The welcome return of his magic had led to the reappearance of his most treasured gift – dragon fire. Even though it was forbidden to use in the forest, Aedon had no intention of dying there, and so he let it fill him up, engulf him, burst outward and spill into the clearing, sending everything whirling into an inferno. His wards protected the wood elf, but the creature that held her vanished into flame and obliteration with the rest of them.

Outward the fire swept, engulfing everything around them. Aedon had to throw up an arm to shield his eyes from the brightness of the blaze.

Once it died down, he turned, a vicious smile upon his face. It felt so good to be powerful once more. His wild euphoria vanished when he beheld her.

In a moment that seemed to slow, the wood elf's eyes rolled upward, then she collapsed.

Aedon cut off his magic, rushed to her, and scooped her up into his arms.

"I've got you. Don't worry," he said, as much to reassure himself as the silent form in his arms. "Come on."

Once he had stemmed the flow of his power, the inferno receded, which meant they did not have long before more of the creatures returned.

We must be long gone by then.

Though his own body ached with the lagging response of so much power used, the rush of battle euphoria ebbing, Aedon pushed on through the forest, holding the wood elf close. Her limp legs swayed against him, and her head nuzzled into his shoulder, a tangled cascade of hair draping over them both. She was lighter than he expected, but with fatigue setting in, along with no meals and little water that day, Aedon's arms burned from the strain.

"Put me down," she moaned through a grimace, stirring against him.

"You're in no fit state."

"I can walk myself." She pushed away from his chest, recoiling with sudden vehemence, repugnance dripping from her.

Aedon sighed and gently lowered her feet to the ground, keeping his arm under hers to support her. Unexpectedly, she did not try to shake him off, and he could tell why. Her legs tremored violently. If he let go, she would fall. He had a feeling the strange wood elf's pride would not suffer it.

Yet he saw her grit her teeth and lock her legs to stop them shaking. She pushed him away. He stepped back.

"Fire is forbidden!" she gasped out.

"If you want me to take you back, I'll be more than happy to oblige," Aedon forced out through gritted teeth, snaking a hand around her waist and lifting, dragging her forwards faster than her own legs could manage.

"What are they?" She stumbled along beside him.

"I'm not sure," he admitted. "For now, we have a more pressing concern. We need shelter…and water and food if we can muster it."

She nodded with a grimace and pointed. "This way. There are some tors. A few places we can hide…"

Aedon shivered – at what they hid from.

They stumbled on in silence, occasionally punctuated by the she-elf's grunts to adjust course, until they came to the stone monoliths soaring high above them. He helped her pick her way through them, the she-elf leading him to a cave burrowed into the depths of one, hidden entirely from the world outside and raised far up from the forest floor, with a cleft allowing them a slender view of the forest.

It was silent and earthy, peaceful and safe. Aedon was grateful that it was warm enough in the summer lands to not need a fire, for he did not want to risk one. He did not fear the forest denizens that night, but they did not need any unwelcome company. Even so, he lit a small faelight to illuminate the small space, which would not be seen from outside.

They ducked to enter the cave, which was half the height of an elf and sloped downwards a way before ending. It was bare of anything, but Aedon did not mind that. He had slept in far worse places before, though the stone would be uncomfortable.

It's better than being dead, he reminded himself, shuddering at the thought of those terrible, dark eyes fixed upon him.

With a groan, Aedon helped the she-elf sit, setting her gently against the rough wall at the end. Her eyes slipped shut with a sigh as she tipped her head back against the stone, her breathing shallow and rapid.

She looked tired, with shadows under her eyes, her curtain of red-brown hair tangled and littered with debris. Her skin, which he knew ought to have been a warm, tanned hue, was pale, her face drawn in pain. Even the smattering of freckles across her cheeks seemed paler than usual. Her slender body trembled as the rush of adrenaline faded.

Her eyes fluttered open, looking at him in absolute horror. "They were… They were…" She shook more fiercely now, her teeth clacking together with the force of it, and her eyes once more scrunched shut, as if she could block out the nightmare.

Instinctively, Aedon squatted in front of her, his hands upon her shoulders. "I know it's hard. You're in shock, but you must try to push it away. You cannot afford to fall apart now, or it will be the death of us both."

Her wild, fearful eyes met his, her face slack with unspoken horror. It had been terrifying for him, but for her? Aedon imagined that she probably knew each and every elf who lived there.

Aedon sucked in a sharp breath. "Your neck…"

In the faint light, with her head tipped back, his eyes were drawn to the crook of her neck where a hideous wound marred her skin. Crimson blood oozed lazily from it, and the skin around the bite bloomed dark purple, but what he could not tear his gaze from were the thin, black veins creeping away from the wound.

Her dirty hand covered it, feeling the wound and wincing. "It's not that bad, is it? I mean, it hurts, but it's only a bite."

Aedon gave her a dubious glance.

"What?"

He quietly described what her wound looked like. She stilled, her fingers clenching around the wound. "What… What does that mean?" she breathed. "Am I… Am I going to become a monster like them? Is it poisoned?"

Aedon bit his lip. "I don't know, but it cannot be good." He reached towards her, pausing as she recoiled. "I'm sorry. May I?"

After a pause, she nodded.

He placed his slim fingers upon the skin at the edge of the bruise. "Tell me what you feel," he murmured as he pressed, working his way inward.

She hissed and winced as he drew closer to the bite mark. "Burning. Stinging. Throbbing."

Aedon nodded solemnly. He sent a small pulse of magic into it. "Better?"

"No," she ground out, her face pale, and shrugged away from him.

It didn't work? It should have been impossible for it to fail. Such magic was basic. "I don't understand…" Yet, deep down, he did, for there were dark magics that repelled such things.

He put aside thoughts of his own safety and freedom for a moment, easily slipping back into the duty that called him to protect others – though he was not certain what it would mean to be free at this point, having not experienced it for so many years.

"You need to see a proper healer – immediately. This is beyond me. Where does the nearest one reside?"

"Far away," she replied with deliberate vagueness.

Aedon pursed his lips. "Look, elf. I'm not after your secrets. I've been minding my own business here for twenty-five years, and I'm not about to change now, thank you very much. To be quite honest, I don't want any part in what you people do here, but I'm not about to let you die."

"I don't need your help, thief," she insisted, the fire lighting within her once more, her amber eyes glaring at him with defiance.

He raised a brow. "Really? Didn't seem that way back there," said Aedon, voice oozing with sarcasm, as he glanced down at her wound. She bared her teeth at him.

"I wasn't about to let you go," she fired back. "You're the Queen's prisoner. It's my duty to see you returned to serve at Her pleasure. I have no inclination to be your minder. I have far better things to do, elf, thank *you* very much!"

She is feisty, I'll give her that, he thought, smirking. It only seemed to infuriate her, which gave him more wicked pleasure. If there was anything left he enjoyed in life, it was aggravating haughty wood elves.

"Well, for now, it seems we're stuck together," Aedon said, pursing his lips as he sat across from her, their legs almost bumping in the small space. She looked as unhappy about that as he. "It's late. We'd better rest. Tomorrow, we can make the trip to a healer. I'll keep guard."

"Nothing will find us here."

"Hmm," replied Aedon noncommittally. He had learned to never be complacent, though he hoped she was right. He was not sure either of them could survive another attack so soon. "Just get some rest."

He needed it, as well. He blinked furiously, trying to force his stinging eyes to stay open. His empty stomach rumbled again, more rebelliously than before, echoing in the silent space. The worst thing, though, was his thirst. He licked his parched lips.

"Here." She passed him a half-full waterskin from her belt.

He widened his eyes as he took it, surprised at her generosity.

"Can't have you dying on me," she said snidely.

Any sympathy he had for her vanished, and he took a deep swig of the cool water within before handing it back to her. "What do they call you?"

She glared at him and clamped her mouth shut.

He rolled his eyes. "Oh, come on. I may not have the slightest clue where I am, but if this place is like the rest of Tir-na-Alathea, we're a good week away from any trace of civilisation, maybe more. Since I'm stuck with you…" At her narrowed eyes, he said more sweetly, "and you with me, I cannot exactly call you 'wood elf' the whole time, can I? That wouldn't be polite." When she just blinked at him, he smiled. "I'll start. I am Aedon Lindhir Riel of House Felrian of Pelenor." He inclined his head in a small bow, which was limited by the confines of the stone right above his head.

She watched him, suspicious, deliberating, before she finally inclined her own head ever so slightly. "Lief na Arboreali."

"A pleasure to make your acquaintance, Lief," Aedon said, as was customary, though it was a bald lie.

She snorted.

He rolled his eyes. *She is going to be insufferable.*

EIGHT

Lief burned as she tossed fitfully on the cold, hard stone, shaken from nightmare to nightmare as the wound upon her neck shot pain into her, as though she had been speared and still writhed upon the weapon.

For a moment, she could feel something cold and wet upon her forehead. Then it was gone, and she returned once more to the dark void, tortured by feverish nightmares.

As her eyes opened, it took her a long moment to recognise the strange, pale face before her. The previous day's events flooded back. Lief struggled to sit up, but his firm, warm hand pressed against her shoulder.

She had never meant to fall asleep, had stared at him until her eyes had burned with exhaustion long into the night, determined to not let him out of her sight. Lief groaned.

"Steady, Lief. You have a fever."

She blinked up at him, clearing the grit from her eyes. He

looked exhausted – dark shadows under his eyes, slumped posture. "You did not sleep."

He shook his head. "I…tended to you through the night. You slept peacefully for a while, then started murmuring, tossing and turning. I had to hold you down at times so you wouldn't injure yourself." With a frown, he glanced at the hard stone beneath her. "Not an ideal bed, I'm afraid."

Lief cringed at the thought of being so vulnerable before a stranger, her cheeks burning with shame. "Thank you," she ground out.

Despite his exhaustion, his lips twitched and eyes crinkled with faint amusement before he offered her the waterskin. "If you're able, we should move on today, get as far away as possible. We'll need water and food, too."

Lief nodded, savouring the relief of the cool liquid trickling down her dry throat. Her head felt fuzzy, as though she were not fully in control, the sharpness of her senses and the full force of her magic hidden behind a veil. The pain had faded to a dull, stinging ache, uncomfortable and unpleasant.

Lief set down the waterskin and tugged aside the collar of her tunic, trying to catch a glimpse of the bite, but could not. Aedon's sharp intake of breath did not reassure her. "What?"

"It's…spread…"

Lief quickly looked down, bending her neck as far as possible. At the periphery of her vision, she could just make out the snaking, black veins spreading faintly across her shoulder. Her fingers tremored as she let her collar fall back into place.

"We should leave," she said abruptly, her tone brooking no argument, not willing to admit how scared she was, for she could already feel its ill effects lagging through her body.

She groaned as she forced her stiff limbs to crawl out of the cave. After a night sleeping on stone, her entire body felt like it had petrified. Once she made it outside, she stood and stretched her arms up to the azure, cloudless sky above, looking as though the previous day's events had been nothing more than whispers of a nightmare – if not for the wince when her shoulder throbbed in angry reminder.

"Where are we going? Emuir? Solanaceae ought to know."

She shot a look of annoyance at the elf. That he knew anything of her forest, let alone the capital, and that he spoke of her Queen with such informality… "Do not speak so disrespectfully of my Queen. If you knew Her power, you would n–"

Aedon let out a bark of laughter. "Oh, believe me, your Queen and I are rather more well acquainted than you might imagine. I dare say She shan't be glad to see me, especially with such tidings, but perhaps if She is feeling generous, She will give me a swift end. At the very least, my misery will be done with."

Lief frowned. "You want Her…to kill you?" She did not understand this strange elf in the slightest. He spoke of it so lightly, as though he did not seek his own demise, and yet inside him, she was certain she could sense a kernel of bitter grief, tainted with denial.

Who would desire their own death? What is he running from? She doubted he would answer truthfully even if she asked.

Aedon shrugged. "It'd be better than being stuck in a hole in the ground for another quarter century – or more. Come on." He did not wait for her as he scrambled down the tors to the forest floor below.

Lief sighed and followed the strange Pelenori elf.

Her strength seemed to return with each step, especially when they found a stream to fill their waterskins and a crop of berries to feast upon.

They had stopped at a scout cache in the forest, taking cloaks, packs, some dried food – though there was precious little there – but she had not permitted Aedon to take a dagger. She did not like the way his face clouded at that.

Tough. He's a criminal, a prisoner. Even though he saved me, I cannot arm him.

The pale, dead faces, cold hands, and black, spidery veins of the previous day seemed nothing more than a hallucination. The forest now around them burst with life, deafeningly vibrant. No hint of anything other than the greatness of the living forest.

Only the presence of the elf at her side convinced Lief that she had not dreamed the entire thing. Well, him and the wound on her neck, which still burned and ached. She had learned not to rub it. It offered no relief, instead lancing white-hot pain through her at the slightest touch. Already, she tired, and the sun had not yet peaked. Such fatigue was unheard of for her. Lief knew it was the bite. Her worst fear was that she would become like *them.*

But what were they? They had been her comrades, her kindred, her people, though she had few she would call friends, and no family to speak of. Lief could not help but wonder about all who resided in Lune. Had they met the same fate?

Aedon noticed her shiver. "Are you all right?"

"Fine."

He shrugged and stood, having drunk his fill from the stream and refilled the waterskin.

As they continued, the forest's normalcy lulling them into a leisurely stroll, she broke the silence that had lasted all morning. "What did you do?"

"Hmm?"

"What did you do to be punished by the Queen?"

He raised an eyebrow. "I stole from Her."

Lief huffed. "Yes, I know that. Everyone does. But what did you take? You must have angered Her severely, taken something of great value, for Her to punish you so."

"Does it matter?" Aedon shrugged. "It happened. It's in the

past. Nothing can change it now. I'm here to serve my punishment, for as long as Solanaceae sees fit."

Lief frowned. "And you're all right with that?"

He shrugged again. "I accepted my fate a long time ago. It's no less than I deserve." A bitter note crept into his voice.

"I don't think you believe that," she said boldly.

"Where are we going?"

She cast a sidelong glare at him. "All right. Keep your secrets, Aedon Lindhir Riel of House Felrian. We're going to the nearest city, and no, I'm not telling you where that is."

Aedon laughed and cast his arms wide, spinning. "You overestimate my abilities, Lief. Where would I run to by simply knowing where we are headed? I have no wish to spend the rest of my days lost in this infernal place. That would be an even worse punishment."

Lief scowled at his insult to her beloved home. She took advantage of the pause to mark their direction by glancing at the way the moss grew on the silver-barked trees surrounding them.

"Are we to walk there?"

She glanced at him, curious at the note of inquisitiveness in his voice. "How else would we get there? You may have noticed neither of us has wings."

"Every other wood elf I've met could evanesce. Travel a day's distance in a moment. Can we not do that? Surely it would be faster."

Lief gritted her teeth, furious that he should force her into the position of admitting a weakness. "I have not yet mastered the art," she ground out and stormed off, not looking to check if he followed.

Soon, they would begin to climb into the foothills. The fastest way to Emuir, which she would not admit to Aedon as being their destination, was over the mountains via a pass she had not taken in many years, preferring the leisurely route along the river around the mountain's base. Now, she did not have time to dawdle. If the Queen did not already know of the dark creatures that plagued Lune, she had to give her report as soon as she could. Not to mention return the thief, who appeared willing, to the Queen's custody.

A wave of dizziness washed over her, then the world tilted. With a cry, her legs wobbled. Aedon grasped her, his warm hands tightening as he gently lowered her to the ground.

NINE

Vasili clung to the saddle, his thighs holding firm, his head flung back and arms wide, whooping as Icarus roared with the joy of flight. The emerald dragon's wings snapped closed as he plunged from the sky.

Laughing, Vasili grabbed the pommel and bent low over Icarus's back, narrowing his eyes as the wind sliced past. It was ice cold, but the winter chill was kept at bay by the warmth of the dragon between his legs, the crimson cloak of the Winged Kingsguard around his shoulders, and the protective shield of his own magic.

He ought to have been terrified. Anyone would have been at the thought of hurtling to the ground far below. The first test of a rider and dragon was always to see that both had a head for heights. It had never been a problem for Vasili. He still remembered his first flight vividly. On his sixteenth summer. The summer Icarus had chosen him for a rider, and together, they had joined the Winged Kingsguard, the legendary ranks of elven dragon riders who had defended Pelenor for an age.

Vasili still had the same jolt of excitement every time they launched into the sky. No matter how high they flew, he had never been scared. Icarus's wings would never fail them. What was there to fear?

As closely bonded as they were, he felt everything Icarus sensed, and the dragon's senses layered over his own with such depth and vividness, it was almost dizzying. The air smelled fresh, and the cold seared inside Vasili's nose, but for Icarus, it was a kaleidoscope of scents, from the pollen of the grasslands below, merging with the stone-tainted air of the mountains, to the pure sweetness of the higher atmosphere. Even the colours were richer, the grey mountains behind them almost blue, the sky violet, and the grassy plains below a golden green.

Blue skies disappeared when Icarus shot through a cloud. A moment later, light bathed them once more as he broke through the other side. The elf lapped up the sun, weak as it was, as Icarus flared his wings and pulled them out of the dive. Vasili's head always swam for a moment with the force of it, but nonetheless, he grinned and clapped his hand on Icarus's thick, scaled neck.

"I've missed this, my friend."

"As have I." The dragon's reply came directly into his mind.

The winter storms had kept the entire outpost holed up for weeks. At the first sign of the storm abating, the outpost emptied, riders and dragons taking to the alpine skies for a taste of freedom.

Vasili let Icarus have his head. Not that he ever tried to really control the dragon. They were one, acted in all things together, and for all intents and purposes, Icarus was bound to him, but Vasili had never taken that for granted, for the reverse was also true. He was bound to Icarus just as strongly. Icarus was the one being he felt an equal to. Besides which, the young dragon had an *excellent* nose for adventure.

Icarus took them both high over the edge of the mountains, rising on the thermals that circled above the borders of the grasslands of the Indis tribes, outside Pelenor's lands that ended beyond the eastern mountains. Vasili was rarely permitted to patrol this far, but Captain Tristan had allowed them all to fly where they would for the day, since they had been cooped inside for weeks. Vasili and Icarus simply planned to bend that instruction slightly more generously than their peers. He stifled a grin.

At the screech above them, Vasili and Icarus looked up. A roc – a legendary giant eagle – soared above them. Twice the span of Vasili's arms, yet half the width of Icarus's wings. Its wings outstretched, Vasili could see every inch of the intricate, golden feathers on the underside. Dragons and rocs held a wary respect for each other. A dragon could snap a roc's neck, but a roc could render a dragon sightless with vicious ease. So, the two predators lived and let live in the mountains.

Vasili rarely got to see one of the enormous eagles so closely, and as they rose to the same height, both spiralling up on the thermal, he met its steely grey gaze. Had he encountered it alone, it would have killed him instantly. Those eyes were as big as his palm. The beak as large as his head. They were so close, he could even see the serrations on the edge, the sharp, pointed tip perfectly honed for killing. Unflinching, the roc evaluated them, before banking out of the thermal and dropping away.

Icarus roared joyfully. "Shall we?"

"As if you even have to ask," Vasili laughed.

Icarus followed the eagle, streamlining himself as he dived, picking up speed. Vasili flattened himself to Icarus's back, the smooth scales warm against his cheek. He loved the rush of wind through his already tousled hair, the tug of the cloak flapping behind him, the feeling of simultaneously floating and falling.

Icarus drew level with the roc, adjusting his wings so they plummeted together. The bird screeched again and wheeled away, ceding the prey it had targeted to them. Vasili shared Icarus's joy, their moods mingling just as much as their senses.

Icarus soared over the plains, much lower than before, whilst the eagle's annoyance echoed overhead. The herd of wild horses thundered over the grasslands below, spooked by their presence. No doubt the roc was angry at the loss of its prey – one of the previous spring's foals would have been an easy meal – and would sabotage their own hunt out of spite.

Icarus slowed, yet still far outstripped the horses cantering below, sticking tightly in their herd. He had no need to eat. He had taken a mountain goat a day before and would not need to break his fast for another three days. Though he was partial to horses.

Once upon a time, Vasili would have turned up his nose at the meat, but the life of a ranger scout of the Winged Kingsguard was not glamorous, and he had none of the privileges of his former life, the son of Lord Dimitrius Vaeri Mortris of House Ellarian and Lady Harper Ilrune Caledan of House Ravakian.

In the mountains, Vasili was a nobody, and the only currency that meant anything to the riders was respect – won by hard work, not coin. He had a long way to go before he earned that from anyone in the Winged Kingsguard. Even then, he still would have a long way more to go than his fellow riders, given the black mark against his name, thanks to his blood.

Soon, they were alone again, soaring low over the seemingly endless grass sea of the plains. And there, between the heavens and the earth, Vasili and Icarus were momentarily free.

TEN

Warm lights welcomed Vasili and Icarus back to the outpost as dusk came early in the mountains with the winter climes and the threat of another storm to the north. The only way to access the complex was from the air. It was fondly nicknamed the Dragon's Nest for precisely that reason. Icarus landed running, as he preferred, on the giant outcrop that served as the landing strip and loped through the open gate and into the training square.

The dragon slowed, ambled over to the troughs of fresh, flowing glacial water, and took long, slow, deep drafts as Vasili unstrapped his legs and dismounted. He deftly unfastened the buckles and catches that secured the scarred leather saddle around the dragon's belly, front legs, shoulders, and neck.

Another dragon alighted behind them, and Vasili raised a hand in greeting.

"Fair winds?" Captain Tristan called from astride his dragon, Ycini, which rumbled in greeting at Icarus. He laughed at Vasili's wide grin. "Excellent. I'll see you in the mess hall."

"See you there." Vasili's stomach already rumbled from a full day in the air.

He hefted the weighty saddle from Icarus with a grunt, then lugged it to the tack store. "I'll see you after dinner." He stroked Icarus's muzzle.

The dragon huffed in reply and turned away with Ycini. They launched into the sky, battering Vasili – Tristan had already gone ahead – with a great gust of wind. Vasili watched them go, a small smile tugging the corner of his lips.

Watching dragons in flight never became mundane. The way their scales scattered the dying light – Icarus's emerald, Ycini's violet. Their membranous wings warming red as the dwindling sunlight passed through them. Their joyful roars splitting the sky. And, through his bond with Icarus, feeling the dragon's innermost peace at being one with the sky.

The sound of their wings faded as the dragons passed out of sight around the peak. His sense of Icarus faded, too, until it was gone with the distance between them. As Vasili turned to leave, the sound of approaching wings – an unmistakable, muffled thud – stayed him. He frowned at the dragon approaching. Far larger than any others stationed at the outpost, and its colour…dark silver. He knew only one dragon with such a hue.

Britte… With General Elyvia, leader of the Winged Kingsguard, atop her. *Why is she here?* They were typically stationed in Pelenor's capital, Tournai, far from the Dragon's Nest, and the outpost was so dull, a rider of her importance had no business there, in a place so far below her notice.

His mind whirred with questions as he watched the giant dragon land with a soft crunch that belied its size.

The general would not come unless something is afoot.

A tingle of excitement curled within Vasili. He had joined the ranks of the Wings for adventure, not to be stationed at the edge of the realm running patrols on a border with allied lands that never saw anything interesting happen at all.

Vasili hurried to the mess hall, slipping through the ranks of his fellow riders and catching Tristan by the elbow just as his mentor sat to eat.

Tristan looked at him and frowned. "Is everything all right?"

"The general is here, sir."

Tristan's frown only deepened. "Elyvia? You are certain?"

At Vasili's nod, Tristan straightened, his food abandoned on the trestle table. "Thank you. Have my supper," he said with a wry smile and a sigh. "I had not yet taken a bite, and it will save you having to queue."

Vasili sank onto the bench and watched Tristan dash away. As hungry as he was, he would far rather know why the General of the Winged Kingsguard had appeared at their quiet, lonely outpost. Still, at the lowest rank, there was no way he could discover why the general had arrived, unless…

There might be a way.

He knew it was wrong to eavesdrop, but he could not help the urge. Not after three months of the most interesting news being the changing weather.

"Oi! That's not fair." Nikolai, a fellow recruit similar to him in age and experience, sat on the bench beside Vasili. "I had to queue an age for mine after Harys took the last of the pot, the greedy pig. Must be nice to be captain's favourite."

Vasili elbowed him good-naturedly.

And earned a wet finger in his ear for his retaliation.

Vasili growled and squirmed, cursing Nikolai, but the young man only laughed and turned to devour his meal. Such teasing was all in the spirit of the Winged Kingsguard. Living and working in close proximity forced friendship upon them all.

He hurriedly ate his supper, bid farewell to Nikolai, and made for the store cupboard on the ground floor. It was his week for cleaning duties. The floors needed sweeping, washing down, and fresh rushes laid. But nothing said he could not start outside Tristan's quarters.

He grabbed a pail, a cloth, and a sweeping brush, rushed outside to fill the bucket with icy water from the pipe system that fed the dragons' water troughs, then shot back inside – almost slipping on a patch of ice in the courtyard.

As quietly as he could, Vasili dashed up the twisting stairs to the upper halls where everyone had their sleeping quarters and Tristan, as captain of the outpost, had his study. Quietly setting down the pail, he took the brush and began to sweep haphazardly down the deserted corridor towards Tristan's rooms.

At the end of the corridor, having abandoned all pretence of cleaning, he hovered, ears straining to hear the muffled words inside. A flurry of his magic, and their voices jumped into focus. Vasili suppressed a twinge of guilt. He had crossed a line from curiosity to deliberate nosiness beyond his rank.

"I have heard nothing," Tristan said, and Vasili could hear the confusion in his voice. "Shae's last correspondence was…last full moon, I think. Four weeks ago."

Vasili knew Shae was Tristan's younger sister, who was stationed at a neighbouring outpost several hundred leagues south of them.

"News reached me late last week, so no wonder she did not make mention of it to you then. I came as quickly as I could. I visited them first, of course, but they still had no news. Since then, I have visited two other outposts. No one has heard a thing."

Silence fell. Vasili leaned closer to the door, barely breathing, his cheek an inch away from the whorled wood.

"It's impossible," Tristan murmured.

"I know." Elyvia's voice sounded grim.

"Three dragons and three riders don't just…*vanish.*"

Vasili held his breath. *Did I hear that correctly?* He gripped the broom so tightly it hurt, and the shiver crawling up his spine had nothing to do with the chill of the air.

"Indeed."

"You don't think…"

"In all honesty, I don't quite know *what* to think, Tristan. It was a routine patrol. Three days. They simply never returned. I have considered all possibilities, yet none seem likely. I know the riders, as do you. They would not have deserted their duties, nor could an accident befall them so big as to incapacitate them all. Our lands are safe…" Elyvia hesitated. "Well…*were* safe anyway."

"Have there been any other reports of anything unusual?"

"Six months ago, an accident befell a rider and dragon just north of here. They had strayed as far south as their patrol dictated. Their injuries were consistent with that of a wild dragon attack. I might believe one rider to fall foul of a territorial wild dragon, or perhaps suffer a calamitous accident, but not three."

"What are the other options?"

"None that I care to consider."

"Could we have found them at last?"

Tristan's voice was so quiet, Vasili had to press his ear to the door to hear – and froze when the wood creaked under him.

Elyvia's reply was even quieter. "To vanish with no trace… I can only think it is the work of the Order of Valxiron, and I do not wish to even give such thought a voice."

The broom nearly dropped from Vasili's hand. He clutched it with both hands before it clattered to the stone flags.

The Order of Valxiron…

Devout followers of Valxiron, the Dark One, who sought to place the entire world of Altarea under his dark domain. An ancient evil, millennia old, that seemed to endure without end. The old enemy of his parents' generation, vanquished a quarter of a century ago, yet it seemed the remnants of his disciples had fled into the shadows, licking their wounds and regrouping in secret.

"It's been almost a decade since we found them last."

"Aye."

Tristan chuckled. "I was wet behind the ears then."

"And still one of the best scouts we had, worthy of joining the Noble Order." The Noble Order of Dawn was Elyvia's legacy, formed after the fall of Valxiron and his Order to hunt down and crush any remnants of that twisted legion. To mark the dawn of a new era, unscarred by Valxiron's malice. It was Vasili's dream to join them. What better glory could he wish for than to see the cause of his blackened family name exterminated?

Yet he was too young, too inexperienced, Tristan had chided. Vasili secretly wondered whether Tristan also feared his interest. After all, Vasili's father, Dimitrius, had been led astray by the Order of Valxiron in his younger days. Perhaps Tristan, like everyone else, still feared the Ellarian and Ravakian names that his parents, and thus he, bore. It only made Vasili more determined to prove himself worthy.

"They were always smoke in the wind. One step ahead of me," Tristan muttered angrily.

"Yet you and Dimitrius were always adept at staying hot on their heels. They never had a moment's peace to settle, to strengthen, and that is thanks to the two of you."

Pride swelled in Vasili's chest that his father was held in such high regard by the general. There were few his parents could call true friends, but Vasili remembered Elyvia's presence in his life from his early childhood.

"We may need to call upon him again."

"And you."

"We are at your disposal, Elyvia."

"As always, I remain grateful for your unwavering support, Tristan. Send word to your sister's outpost. We must get to the bottom of this. For better or worse, we must know the truth."

"Do you fear them?" Tristan's question was soft, almost apologetic.

Elyvia sighed. "I think I would be a fool to dismiss them. I cannot say I fear them, but I fear whom they serve. We defeated him. We watched him fall. Yet a power like that, so old, so dark, so clever, does not simply disappear. I have always feared his return, much as I so desperately wish to believe that it will not – *cannot* – come to pass." A bleak darkness passed through her voice.

Vasili guessed she remembered the battle a quarter of a century before, when she and his parents, along with the whole realm of Pelenor, had made a last stand against Valxiron's forces.

"What would you have us do?"

Vasili could hear the waver in his voice. Tristan was still young, looking to his leader for reassurance.

"We hunt," Elyvia replied grimly. "I want every single dragon and rider out there. We will either find that patrol or discover what befell them."

"And if we find…the Order of Valxiron?" Tristan's voice hushed on the last word, as though he did not dare speak it for fear of invoking the Dark One.

"Then we will do as we have always done, Tristan. We will face them."

ELEVEN

Darkness clouded her vision again, but Lief tried to blink it away, struggling to see the blurring forest before her. Her skin prickled uncomfortably, the sensation seeming to sap her strength and the ability to move, her senses appearing to be far away.

"Lief? *Lief?*" Aedon shouted, but it sounded as though he stood across a valley, muffled and distant.

She tried to respond, but only a mumbled moan emerged. Aedon swore. She felt the warm caress of his magic rippling over her and through her, but it did not banish the pain of the wound, which seemed to throb all the more in angry defiance.

When she slowly opened her eyes, it was inching towards sunset. Around her, the forest was dim, the light golden upon the leaves high above. Smoke wafted into her face. She had a brief moment of panic, thinking the forest was on fire, then the mouth-watering aroma of cooking meat reached her. She lay upon her cloak on a nest of moss, Aedon's cloak over her. She groaned and propped herself up on an arm.

"Welcome back," said Aedon gravely, looking up and sitting back from the spit he tended over a small fire.

Lief did not answer for a moment. "This saps my strength," she croaked. "I do not understand it."

"There is dark magic at play here, Lief. I know its taint. I have given you what strength and protection I am able, but I do not think I can stay it or rid you of it. The few things I know of that can cure all ills, we do not possess."

Lief stilled. She did not need to look to know that the dark veins had spread, tingling down her shoulder blade and stinging at her collarbone. She felt nauseous, and the exhaustion had not abated.

It was a long journey to Emuir. She had never doubted her abilities before, but it now crept at the edges of her resolve like a hungry wolf on the prowl.

I cannot fail.

She sat up, and only sheer force of will kept her from toppling over. Aedon watched her closely, but he made no move towards her, as if he understood the mental war she waged with herself.

"It seemed safe enough here," he said, his tone carefully light. "I've warded us. We ought to be all right."

"I'll take first watch," Lief insisted, though she was not sure how she would remain awake. The exhaustion crushed her, the heaviness of her head almost forcing it to droop down, as though it bore a physical weight. Yet she refused to leave herself unguarded against him.

"Eat. Drink. It'll help." Aedon offered her a haunch of the rabbit and a skewer of tender meat upon a bare stick.

"Thank you." She bit into the hot, dark meat, savouring the rich taste, juices trickling down her chin. With the other morsels he had managed to forage – mushrooms, some herbs, berries – he had made an even richer sauce to baste it in that had seeped into the meat as it cooked, adding an earthy, light, sweet aftertaste to the smoky meat.

As they ate in silence – which was less frosty than it had been, though hardly companionable as they covertly examined each other – Lief scrutinized the clearing Aedon had chosen.

An uneven ring of sycamore trees nestled around the slight hollow they sat in, and as darkness fell, the canopy above them blocked out the clear sky, the smallest opening in the very middle allowing Lief to see the gentle twinkling of stars. The silvery bark seemed to glow in the dark, and the leaves whispered in the faint breeze.

Lief could feel the trees' looming disapproval of the fire in their midst, the groaning, creaking anger that was missed by the ears of outsiders as the forest awoke around them.

"Aedon, we must put out the fire."

"Hmm?" Aedon glanced up, blinking owlishly, before he followed her gaze to the trees that surrounded them. "It's cold," he complained.

She scoffed at him. To her, it was a balmy summer's night, perfect for sleeping under the stars with only the canopy for shelter. "You Pelenori elves are soft."

"We're *practical.* I'm not about to eat my supper half-cooked. Who knows what grotty, woodland parasites this meat has in it."

Lief drew herself up indignantly. "It's no wonder they never let you out, if this is how rude you are."

Aedon snorted. "Believe me, you don't endear yourself to me, either. No woodland elf I've ever met could be accused of good hospitality."

"Not to *thieves*," she ground out, glaring at him from across the fire.

"I'm not putting out the fire."

"You don't have to," she said with a vicious grin, rising to her feet, even though it made her head spin – but she did not allow her exhaustion to show. With a few sharp stomps, she crushed the fire, then kicked dirt over the glowing embers to smother them, too. "As far as I'm concerned, you're still a prisoner of my Queen, and it's my sworn duty to see you returned to Her custody."

"What of the dead? The dark magic?"

"Not your concern, *thief.*"

"Oh, we're back to that, are we?" he growled. "Fine, *wood elf.*

Have it your way."

"I will. Go to sleep. We have a long trek tomorrow."

He crossed his arms over his chest. "I don't want to."

Skies above, he is mulishly stubborn.

Lief ground her teeth and called upon the forest in the silent language only wood elves spoke. It rustled in answer. A moment later, vines slithered across the ground, pushed up through the earth, uncoiled from the trees, all converging upon the unsuspecting thief.

Before he could move, they were upon him, twining around his limbs and binding him to the earth, splayed before her.

"Let me go!" Aedon exclaimed, writhing, but he could barely move as the vines tightened, leaves hissing as they slid across each other.

Lief only smiled at him with venomous delight, swaying slightly against the dizziness that threatened to topple her after the effort of what ought to have been nothing more than a thought in invoking the forest to her aid. "Sweet dreams, thief."

Darkness clouded her vision, and the wound upon her collar throbbed. With deliberate carefulness, she settled between the roots of the tree opposite Aedon, trying to betray none of her weakness to him.

His curses broke the peace of the evening. Lief's head throbbed. She had quite enough of all of it – her own vulnerability, his damned insufferable presence. It took all her will to dig deep to beg for the forest's help once more. Moments later, a vine threw itself across the elf's mouth, silencing Aedon's protests.

Lief trembled, no matter how much she tried to still herself. The wound seemed to burn hotter, and sweat beaded upon her forehead as she alternated between feeling afire and ice cold.

When it came, the nausea was sudden and violent. Lief turned her head weakly to one side and vomited over the moss beside her, her supper still as fresh as it had been when she ate it, albeit tainted by the acrid stench of bile. She could barely hear Aedon's muffled attempts to reach her as she slipped into unconsciousness, still shuddering with pain.

TWELVE

The taste of earth was bitter upon his tongue, but no matter how much he bit and gagged, Aedon could not shift the vine across his mouth. Nor could he move any part of his body, so tightly were they wound about him. It seemed impervious to his magic, and he did not dare release fire upon the forest around him, for fear of what it would do to him in revenge.

Damned wood elf!

They had always been an unpleasant race to deal with, even before his captivity, and if Lief was anything to go by, he liked them no more now.

Yet when he looked at her, the spike of dislike surging through him was tempered by pity. She was pale, her tanned skin sallow in the moonlight, and with her head tipped to one side, he could see the black veins trailing up her neck, farther than they had been that morning. Aedon cursed silently.

A shriek rang out in the night. Aedon stilled, listening. The woods had fallen silent. A chill crept down his spine that had nothing to do with the cold earth pressed into his back.

A moan followed the shriek, and with it, Aedon's pulse raced. The living forest held many a dark and dangerous denizen, but that had been something else entirely. Something that ought to have been dead…and was now rustling through the foliage, drawing closer.

"Lief!" Aedon tried to say around the vine, but it emerged as a strangled, wordless noise. The wood elf did not move. When the shriek came again, an unearthly, shrill cacophony that drilled into Aedon's head, Lief moaned and tossed in her sleep.

He reached into her mind. Walls of obsidian met him, strong, high, and thick. Impregnable. The rustling drew closer.

"*Lief, you must wake up! Free me! A beast comes. We must protect ourselves!*" He pounded against the defences of her mind, to no avail.

The rustling had stopped. But now Aedon could hear snuffling. A twig snapped somewhere behind him, sending a chill of fear through him. Aedon realised how vulnerable he was, and it did not reassure him.

A deep sniff, like a hound taking in the scent of its prey, rattled through the clearing.

A rustle of leaves.

The heavy step of a foot upon the dry bark of a root that cracked under the weight.

Aedon shrank into the earth, and the vines seemed to shrink with him, away from this fell beast.

Its shadow fell upon him, blotting out the moonlight. Upon

two legs, it hunched forwards, its head swinging this way and that, tangled, dark locks of hair trailing with its movement.

Somehow, it had not seen or scented him, though that did not give Aedon any comfort. It would only be a matter of time before the scent of earth and the forest covering him did not provide a shroud.

It stepped over Aedon's vine-covered legs, as though they were natural forms of the earth, and stalked closer to Lief, drawing in great, snuffling breaths with each step.

Aedon could do nothing but watch as it drew closer and bent to sniff her, hissing as it did so.

"*Lief!*" Aedon screamed into her mind.

Her eyes flickered open.

He saw the moment disorientation turned to pure terror, eyes wide as she beheld the monstrosity before her. Lank, dark hair framing a white face covered in black veins. Black, lifeless eyes. Sharp, pointed teeth in a dead mouth.

Lief screamed, and the silence of the night was broken.

THIRTEEN

Venya hurried down the stairs to the next vault, the line of bound grimoires trailing after her, to catalogue the next one. It floated before her, directing her back to its shelf in the narrow, tall vault that felt altogether too much like a dark alley. She was glad to leave it and head to the next, which was cavernously huge and held a collection of books in languages she could not read, arranged in diverging rows around a circular, central space, like the rays of a bookish sun.

Soon enough, she had just one grimoire left. Beatrix had not warned her of it, yet she had felt its incessant crooning, persuasive voice following her all day with the persistence of an irritating fly. She could not wait to be rid of it.

"Just one little second, my sweet," it said to her in a voice husky with allure. "That's all it will take, and I shall make your wildest dreams come true… Just free me for a moment, and I can show you a taste of the magic you deserve to wield."

"I don't need sorcery. Still your tongue!" Venya snapped as

the grimoire led her down several more levels to its vault.

"O-ho," it chuckled. "Already bestowed with powers? Come, let me taste them. Then we can join and wield magic in sweet, powerful harmony. Think of the great things we could do together…"

Venya glared at it. The tome was pristine, glittering leather, as though imbued with gold dust. It was meant to allure, with its decorative corner caps, embossed designs upon it inlaid in gold, and precious gems embedded into the leather itself. Her hands twitched of their own accord, and she fought back the urge to caress the glimmering, supple leather, to do exactly as the grimoire asked.

How can it do that? she wondered.

She knew magic could be used for ill as well as good, knew it could be used to manipulate and master others, but to feel it in herself was disconcerting to say the least – and from a *book*, no less. She resolved to pluck up the courage to ask Nieve of it when next she saw the first librarian. She always welcomed questions of those seeking knowledge, and it was the only time Venya did not fear approaching her stern boss, for Nieve had never turned her away when it came to learning.

"Enough of that," she growled. "I am a librarian, and you will not seek to enchant me."

The book chuckled, throaty and low. "If you say so, Mistress *Junior* Librarian."

Venya gritted her teeth and inserted the silver seal into the door of its chamber – another restricted section she had not been permitted to enter before. This one was wide and long, holding a central aisle that led to a blank, smooth rock face, with rows of books to either side. She followed the grimoire as it led her back to its place, bound by the magic of the library to do so, no matter how much it wished not to.

"Come on. On the shelf," she told it sternly, gesturing to the large, empty space set aside for it. Venya glanced at the grimoire again, noticing how the cover seemed to shimmer in the glow of the golden faelights. She longed to trace a finger across it. Before she knew it, her arm stretched out, fingers splaying as she reached for the beautiful book.

However could I have been afraid of it? she wondered, her thoughts hazy and slow. Just to stroke it would be to honour the knowledge and wisdom it contained, and those gems embedded upon the cover were so pretty that she longed to feel how smooth and perfectly cut they were…

"I wouldn't do that if I were you, Venya," called a mildly amused voice behind her.

Venya whirled around to find the first librarian standing a stone's throw away, smirking, with a stack of bound grimoires from the *Dark Magic* section following her. Venya froze, petrified.

"Jaakobah, to your place," Nieve said sternly, her level gaze fixed upon the tome.

Without another word, it floated to its place, dropped to the shelf with a muffled thump, and stilled while chains and padlocks slithered around it, clinking and clicking as they bound it in place.

"I… I'm sorry…," blurted Venya.

To her surprise, Nieve chuckled. "You aren't the first, nor will you be the last, to succumb to that deceitful tome's whisperings."

Venya's relieved breath escaped in a gush as she realised she had not landed herself in trouble.

"I'm sorry," she said again, her attention flicking from Nieve to Jaakobah and back again.

"It's no trouble. Are you finished in here? Let me escort you out."

"Y-yes, thank you." Venya hurried to Nieve's side.

Now's my chance.

"Nieve?"

"Hmm?"

"How did it, well, slip inside my mind like that?"

Keeping up her mental walls came as easily as breathing after a lifetime of tutelage at the hands of her parents and professors. Nieve knew of her magical prowess, and Venya sometimes wondered if Nieve and Beatrix were the only ones who truly did not seem to judge her for her blood, for the sins of those who had borne her family name before.

"Grimoires are interesting creations," Nieve mused as they

strode down the long aisle, Venya hurrying to keep up with the woman's longer stride. "Part sorcery, part life, each one is unique, and their sentience is uncommon. The magic within them sometimes combines in unexpected ways, and the magic we possess–" Nieve was an elf, like her, "–cannot quite grasp it. Thus, they have the ability to slip inside our defences. Sometimes it can be easier to be non-magical, to not have that sense; other times, it is harder, of course, because a mortal mind cannot shield itself so well."

"You mention they are part sorcery and part life. How are they made? I've heard that blood ma–"

"Blood magic is forbidden," Nieve said sharply. Then her tone softened. "But yes, some grimoires are…were made with blood sorcery, such as those in our most restricted vaults. Others were made with dark magics. Still others were made with light magic. Not all grimoires are evil."

Venya nodded, not daring to ask the thousand questions peppering her mind.

"Curiosity is a fine trait to possess, but it must be tempered with caution. I know you understand that, for you tread cautiously above all else, which is most sensible when dealing with unknown magics. Keep to your studies, Venya. Such powerful magics are not your business yet. You have not earned the right to know, nor proven yourself enough to practice. That will come with time, as well as your ascendance through the ranks of our library."

Nieve swept through the exit, waited for Venya to pass, then flashed her seal – the iridescent seal of the first librarian made of a metal Venya had never seen elsewhere – to close and bar the heavy, metal door behind them. With a gracious incline of her head, Nieve swept up the stairs and out of sight. Venya listened to her footsteps fade, mulling over her words.

That evening, when night had come to the wintery land of Pelenor – not that she could tell, being in the bowels of the mountain – Venya ascended the stairs for the final time, a stack of grimoires that had been checked out from the archives in tow.

As she hit the last stair, she tripped and went sprawling, biting back a curse as the corner of stone bit into her shins, and her elbow cracked on the floor. The grimoires behind her jolted at her sudden movement, tumbling out of their pile. Giggles reverberated down the stairs as a cohort of other junior librarians passed her.

She glared up at them, her face burning with shame as they tittered and smirked, nudging each other and whispering. Some did not bother to whisper. None stopped to help.

"What else would you expect from a daughter of Houses Ravakian and Ellarian?"

"I know. She must be a charitable cause…"

"Well, no one else would have her, not with family like hers. No wonder they buried her down in the archives."

"Where she belongs!"

"They all ought to be exiled, dreadful folk that they are. Leave them to rot in sin."

"Oh, no. They're so strange, they might *like* that."

The whispers and mutterings were drowned out by a cascade of laughter as they disappeared from sight.

Venya scrambled to her feet, nursing smarting shins, an aching elbow, and bruised pride, as she gestured for the grimoires to stack neatly once more, leasing a trickle of magic to guide them.

Venya stood for a long moment in the gloom of the spiral stairwell, her eyes scrunched shut against the burning tears that threatened to fall, biting her quivering lip. She did not know how they managed to drive a knife into her heart with such ease when she tried so hard to remain below their scrutiny, not worthy of their notice, and no harm to anyone.

Yet no matter what she did – whether she was top of their cohort with flying grades, tutored them when they demanded, followed them around in the hopes it would make them like her – Venya had never fit in.

True to her family heritage, she was truly the black sheep of them all. The daughter of Dimitrius Vaeri Mortris of House Ellarian and Harper Ilrune Caledan of House Ravakian. The shame of her father's House name was only bested by the disgraced stigma of her mother's. Though it was not their fault, neither was it hers. She did not know how her twin brother, Vasili, seemed to bear it so much better than she. He took it as a challenge – much like their father, she supposed. The complete opposite to her preferring to blend into the background.

The tears started falling unbidden, slipping through her closed eyes, and she clasped a hand over her mouth to stifle a sob. She hurried through the almost deserted corridors, taking back ways and shortcuts to ensure she did not meet a soul, until she reached the librarians' lounge.

At the timid presentation of her borrowed seal, the door creaked open. Venya swiftly dumped the pile of grimoires into the ornate, varnished, glass-fronted cabinet next to the door that Beatrix had told her of. As she turned to leave, she stopped, groaning.

There was one stray grimoire that had yet to be returned. A small, tiny, tatty thing… No wonder it had been left behind. She bent to look at it, discarded at the bottom of the basket next to the cabinet. It was not even padlocked, so she could only presume it was not dangerous. *The Book of Beasts* was stamped into the cover. A cover that, Venya realised as she leaned closer, was not made of leather at all, but a dusty brown, short, coarse fur. The letters had been branded onto the skin underneath.

Venya closed her puffy eyes, weighing her options. She did not feel like working anymore. Did not feel like chancing meeting anyone when she felt so despondent and longed to flee to the quiet sanctuary of her room. Not to mention, the rest of them had finished half a bell ago. She had been delayed finding unfamiliar vaults and shelves.

Yet, as a librarian, her first order of service was to the Athenaeum, no matter her lowly rank. Venya sighed, hung her head, and summoned the grimoire into her hand with a flick of her wrist.

FOURTEEN

Down into the depths of the vaults, the grimoire tugged her, pulling her hand, as though an invisible being held it. The fur was warm, the coarse hair rough, though not unpleasantly so. Almost like the pelt of a deer. It was smaller than any other grimoire she had seen, slightly larger than her splayed hand, though she knew size was no indicator of potency. Underestimating a grimoire sometimes meant death. That had been one of Nieve's first lessons to them all upon joining the Athenaeum's ranks.

It cannot be this deep.

Venya frowned, glancing at the small book in her hand as it led her past yet another vault. They were well past the junior librarian vaults now and into the librarian vault levels below. She wondered if it would lead her farther still, where she was not permitted. She both hoped so and dreaded it. She did not want to spend forever walking to a faraway vault, but neither did she want to descend all those stairs if she could not enter the vault the grimoire belonged in.

At last, the incessant tugging ceased and nudged her sideways, towards a slim door of rich, red wood inlaid with iron, carved with animals and unusual beasts feasting on berries and…

Venya swallowed. She looked closer. *Feasting on…people.*

She stepped back and ran her gaze over the door. The iron was a ward against the magic within. And a warning to her to not underestimate what the vault contained.

The floor, the handle, even the surface of the door was covered in a thick layer of dust.

No one has been in here for years. She fleetingly wondered if the grimoire had been checked out for that long.

She glanced at the grimoire again, her earlier unhappiness forgotten. Now she felt only trepidation, wondering if she had overstepped her bounds as a junior librarian to come this deep into the Athenaeum, even with the best of intentions.

Just because I have the seal of a librarian does not make me one.

The Book of Beasts tugged her towards it more insistently. Venya bit her lip. *Just a quick in and out.* She was the top of her cohort for a reason. Nieve trusted her. Beatrix trusted her. Venya tried to use that as a reason to trust herself.

Before she could second-guess herself, she placed the silver librarian's seal into the door, watched as it faded into nothingness, then strode in, her heart beating quickly.

The grimoire guided her through the dark vault, dimly lit by the customary faelights. Venya did not dare to brighten them. It would do her no favours to attract the attention of any grimoires in this vault, which she might be woefully unequipped to face.

Shelves loomed in the darkness. Tall, wide, deep, narrow, with grimoires bound in the shadows upon them. And between the shelves…

Venya paused. *Cages…*

She dared not breathe as she passed the first, which puffed out clouds of smoke, flickering embers within. She had never seen a grimoire like that, and she did not want to awaken it. Venya edged past, stifling a cough at the acrid tang that hit the back of her throat.

In a nook, a tiny gap awaited the book in her hand, but it looked too small. Venya set *The Book of Beasts* down upon the shelf to clear some more room for it between the grimoires resting there. She moved them gingerly, one small inch at a time, her gloved hands tremoring with fear that they would waken, that she would be within striking distance of whatever magic lay within.

A prickle on the back of her neck. The sense that she was being watched. Venya frowned and turned.

Beatrix leaned casually against the edge of a shelf at the end of the aisle – which they both knew was against regulations, for it was all too easy to accidentally unleash a grimoire – a cocksure grin gracing her usually carefree face.

Venya frowned. She knew Beatrix would have finished her own filing ages ago. "What are you doing here? Did Nieve send you?"

"I came for you, Vee," she crooned in a sultry tone, pushing off the bookcase and sauntering towards her.

"W-what?" Venya stammered.

"Oh come. You think I don't see the way you look at me? It's written all over your face. You want me, don't you?" Beatrix ran a hand through her wavy, cropped hair.

"I-I-I–" Venya could not speak around the lump in her throat. It was her fantasy and nightmare come true. How had Beatrix known? She had never said anything, been so careful to not give any impression of anything other than professional courtesy. Did she return her feelings, or was this a trick? Yet she knew Beatrix's nature. Knew she would not be so cruel.

"I feel the same, you know…," Beatrix whispered, biting her lip, slowly, deliberately, and smirking when Venya's attention snapped to it. She closed the gap between them, until she towered before Venya.

The faelights cast light and shadow against her warm skin. Her moist lips glimmered, and under the shadow of her hair swept across her face, her eyes were dark.

"Just this once, I want to kiss you, Venya." Beatrix's hand slipped around her waist and pulled her close, as her other hand twined up Venya's neck, caressing the nape, fingering the sensitive point of her ears.

A quiet moan escaped Venya. Her heart thundered, breathing quick, body tremoring with anticipation and fear of the moment she had imagined so many times, never expecting it would happen. Yet it was coming to pass, and in such an unexpected manner that she could have never dreamed it.

However, intuition prickled at Venya. A deep, instinctive fear, not just the fluttering nerves of a heart scared for its attentions to be unrequited. It screamed at her to wake up, to run.

Something was wrong.

Venya dragged her eyes away from Beatrix's lips as they descended towards hers, open and inviting, and looked up into her eyes.

At once, she knew.

They were black and cold, without irises or pupils.

Venya shoved the woman away, stumbling backwards as she fumbled for the pouch of powdered mint and asphodel root at her belt.

Beatrix's face contorted in a too-wide smile that stretched from ear to ear, her glistening teeth elongating to cruel, serrated fangs.

Venya bumped into the shelving behind her, the grimoires hissing at the intrusion, and dived to the side. *The Book of Beasts* flopped onto the floor. Venya did not even spare it a glance.

Over a few moments, Beatrix morphed into a long-limbed beast with brutal claws, her head a sleek, hairless monstrosity with stubs for ears, a slit-like nose, and that cruel, too-wide mouth filled with razor-sharp teeth. She grew taller, until she had to crouch in the vaulted space, with her arms spread wide across the whole of the aisle.

Venya's fingers finally grasped the pouch, the round, palm-sized ball wrapped in rough gauze easy to tug from her belt. As the link broke, the neck of the pouch opened. Venya hurled it, still not sure whether she dealt with a creature or an apparition, but knowing that the pouch would give her the moment she needed to act.

It smashed onto the floor, erupting into a cloud of powder that engulfed the beast. Its snarl told her the magic-infused powder had worked to constrain it for a moment.

Think, Venya!

With a sinking heart, she realised that the door, her only means of escape, lay behind the creature. She could try and charge it…

No. She dismissed the suicidal notion at once. If she put herself within reach of those long, vicious claws and teeth… She shuddered.

Her magic flared, longing to be used, but Venya knew she could not risk it. Not in a room full of grimoires. She did not know which would be worse – damaging them or accidentally freeing them.

Her foot nudged the small grimoire on the floor, just as the beast emerged, angrier than ever, from the cloud of minty, musky mist. Taking a step back, her heel caught on a raised, jagged edge of a paving slab that had come loose. She tumbled to the floor, landing hard on the stone with a jarring crash that winded her.

Gasping for breath, Venya could hardly move as the mist dissipated, with the creature none the worse for wear, yet twice as aggravated. Venya's reprieve was over.

The beast lunged.

FIFTEEN

The earth shuddered around them as roots and vines broke through the surface. So desperate were they to answer their mistress, to seek out this new threat, they slithered over Aedon, gagging and smothering him. Dirt stung his eyes, trickled into his mouth.

The beast before them was trapped, lashed upon its knees by the forest's power, as Lief scrambled backwards, falling over roots in her haste to escape. More vines assailed it, trailing up its body, constricting, until the beast's shrieking became a keening wail, and then a gurgled cry as they wrapped around its throat.

Aedon watched in horror, trying to blink the grit from his eyes, as with a sickly squeezing, ripping, and the ear-splitting pop of limbs being pulled from their sockets, the roots and vines tore the creature apart.

Its dismembered torso thudded to the ground. Silence fell.

Slowly, the roots and vines uncurled with a hiss of leaves, arms, legs, and a head – frozen in a deathly snarl – thumping to the ground, too. Obsidian blood soaked into the ground, sizzling as it burned through the moss and leaf litter, shrivelling anything it touched to a black, rotted pulp.

Silence fell across the clearing once more. Aedon could hear nothing but the thudding of his own heart in his ears as he watched Lief's heaving chest, her wide eyes frozen upon the monstrosity before her. As they both watched, its bodiless hand curled and uncurled in a grotesque imitation of life.

Lief whimpered, slowly inching back, until she bumped against the trunk of a giant tree that creaked as it leaned towards her. Aedon's eyes widened as he watched the branches lower around her, almost protectively.

"Lief!" he tried to say around the vine.

At his strangled cry, she finally looked at him. He could see how dazed she still was. He struggled against the vines and growled in frustration when they did not give.

Her hand rose to caress the giant root of the tree around her. A sigh shuddered through the clearing. Slowly, as though distrustful of his intentions, the vines and roots retreated, slithering back into the disturbed ground, around the trees, and as immobile upon the forest floor as they had been when Lief and Aedon had arrived.

Aedon did not move, glaring suspiciously at the innocuous roots he had so promptly dismissed. It had been foolish of him to forget the immense and fatal power of the forest, even after all these years. He suppressed a shiver. A part of him longed for freedom, yet he could never leave until the Queen and the forest willed it. This had reminded him of that.

Lief did not speak as he slowly sat up, just in case the forest attacked, and edged around the dismembered corpse. He wrinkled his nose at the sour, acrid stench rising from it combined with the cloying, sickly sweetness of decay. Her eyes were fixed upon it – black eyes, he realised with a sharp strike of fear.

He conjured a faelight before he moved any closer, and breathed a sigh of relief as the warm light brightened her amber eyes anew.

Suddenly, their earlier argument seemed so petty in light of this far more serious threat facing them.

"Are you all right?" he asked.

Gazing at him, Lief did not answer, her expression bleak and filled with horror, before her attention went back to the beast before them. The mossy carpet continued to gently hiss as it bubbled into black, putrid mulch around the severed limbs.

"We need to burn it," Aedon said. He glanced at the trees around them. "It's the only way to ensure it…won't come back."

The trees around them creaked audibly, the leaves shivering, but no vines or roots came to assault him anew. Aedon took it as the forest's approval. They could not sleep that night with the remains of such a beast betwixt them. He conjured an ember, then a small flame, listening, watching, waiting for the forest's response. Though it continued to creak and rustle around him, it made no move to attack.

"I will be quick," he promised. Though whether he said it for Lief's or the forest's benefit, he wasn't certain.

Lief's eyes warmed as they reflected the fire. It burned hot and quickly, until all that remained of the fiend were piles of ash.

Darkness and quiet descended around them once more, but Aedon remained still and watchful, suppressing a start with every passing animal noise.

I shall not sleep here again.

He blinked the grit from his eyes, rubbing them with the back of his hand and yawning widely. Now that the rush of fear had faded, he felt crushingly tired. Beside him, Lief stared into the dark night, unspeaking.

After several moments, she stood and gestured to him to follow. He raised an eyebrow in question, but she had already turned away, climbing up the tree at her back with practised agility, despite her fatigue and injury.

Aedon eyed the tree with trepidation. As Lief climbed, it unfurled, straightening from the position it had taken to protect her, its limbs wide once more. With another look at the blackened ash upon the ground, he swallowed his fear and climbed up the tree after Lief.

To Lief's surprise, she slept, the overwhelming fatigue clawing her into slumber, despite her fear. The soothing, low groan of the tree around her was an unspoken comfort, lulling her. She knew the forest would not allow her to come to harm. Not after it had protected her earlier.

The sun was already high when she stirred, cracking open an eyelid.

Aedon watched her from a neighbouring branch, worry creasing his brow. He silently handed her the waterskin.

"Thanks."

The liquid was cool relief as it slid down her throat. Her entire body hurt, aching with a ferocity she had never encountered before. And at her neck, the wound festered and burned, a constant agony. Lief resisted touching it, knowing it would only worsen the pain.

Aedon continued watching her without a word.

"What?" she said irritably, though a part of her regretted her tone. After all, it had not been his fault they were attacked.

"You endangered us both," he said quietly, staring at her with steadfast reproach.

If his tone had been accusing, she would have railed against it. But as it was, with the sun high and the terror of the previous night so close, the blackened remains on the ground below them in stark contrast to the greenery surrounding them, she swallowed instead. It was still too raw.

Once more, the memory of those gleaming, black eyes in a pale face, the terrible, black veins, and the fetid stench overwhelmed her. The way those sharp, gore-covered teeth had loomed, moist, putrid breath washing over her. Yet in that same moment, darkness had surged through her, urging her to rip…tear…kill. She shuddered. Lief did not want to admit that to Aedon.

"Lief?" Worry laced his voice.

She blinked back to reality, breathing in the clean, sweet air, feeling the warmth of the sun upon her skin, the rough bark beneath her hands. His eyes were fixed upon her chest.

"What is this?" she whispered, glancing down at the black veins now trailing across her collarbone and shoulder.

Aedon sighed. "Something beyond either of us," he admitted, his attention lingering on the darkness.

They were weeks from Emuir. *Do I have weeks?*

The insidious thought plagued her. Already, the blight had spread, weakening her, corrupting her… Lief clasped her hands together so tightly her nails bit into her own skin.

Weeks might indeed be longer than she could afford, and it was clear she was in no fit state to hurry, or even defend herself, her strength and clarity of mind fading. Even the forest's defences had limits, and she did not want to see the edge of them – or beyond.

"How did they find us?" she asked suddenly, fearing the answer. Her fingers traced the spidering vein on her shoulder, the skin cold to the touch.

Aedon's eyes dropped to her wound. "I think we both suspect the same…"

"What happens if…if they find us again?" She fought to control her rising panic.

"I don't know. But…" He sighed. "Lief, your actions could have gotten us both killed." At her frown, he clarified. "Restraining me. I was defenceless. It was pure luck that saved me…saved us both."

Lief clenched her jaw. He was a thief, a prisoner. She had every right to restrain him, but she could not deny that he was correct. Doing so had endangered them both. She hated to admit it, but one fact remained.

I need him, if I am to survive.

"I will not do so again, unless you give me cause to," Lief forced out. It was as close to an apology as he would get. From his cooling sympathy as he withdrew, leaning back against the tree trunk on the thick branch he perched upon, she gathered he knew it, too.

"If you try to run, I will see you do not get far," she added, her voice level as she met his gaze, unflinching. She had no idea how, with her ailing strength and magic, she could hunt him down – but he did not need to know that.

The forest will help me, she reassured herself, even though she was not certain of it.

He regarded her coolly and inclined his head. "I'm stuck

with you just as much as you are with me, Lief," he said with a humourless chuckle. "I can hardly escape Tir-na-Alathea. First, I haven't the faintest idea where I am, and second, I know all too well what happens to those who betray your Queen and your living forest."

She could not miss the bitterness in his voice, betraying his desire to be free. She could understand that. Whatever his crimes, he had been a prisoner long enough to miss whatever his former life and freedoms had been. Lief supposed she would feel the same in his position.

No, she admonished herself. *He's a thief, a criminal. We're nothing alike.*

"I must alert my Queen to what has transpired as soon as possible. Unfortunately, it's still weeks of trekking," she admitted, biting her lip. "I may need your...*assistance* to make it. This is beyond my healing, and I can feel it sapping my strength." It irked her to have to admit any weakness. To place herself at *his* mercy.

But she had no choice. She felt weaker than the day before, her magic fading, and after the encounter with the creature, the darkness coiling within the recesses of her mind was no illusion. It had been drawn out of her, forming thoughts she had never before possessed.

"Well then," he said more lightly than she had expected. "I have no desire to be lost, wandering in this forest until it eats me alive, and I'd rather not leave you at the mercy of those beasts...or that ghastly injury. So, for the foreseeable future, I suppose we find ourselves unlikely and reluctant allies."

SIXTEEN

Vasili did not finish cleaning. He returned to the cave above the outpost that Icarus called home and waited long into the dark for his companion to return, with nothing for comfort in the carefully hewn, smoothed by age rock cocoon but a flame conjured to warm him and his own thoughts.

Eventually, the thud of returning wings heralded his friend. Vasili eased to his feet, groaning at the stiffness of his limbs. Wind battered the wide entrance of the cave as Icarus slowed to land. His claws crunched upon the stone as he alighted, and he ducked into the cave, folding his wings to his side.

"Fair skies?" Vasili asked by way of greeting, raising a hand to stroke Icarus's warm, smooth muzzle.

"Mmm," Icarus hummed appreciatively. The dragon, twice Vasili's height, had to angle down his body to reach the back of the cave, where a circular nest of woven grasses awaited. "We flew north, high and fast. The air is deliciously refreshing."

"Did Ycini have anything interesting to say?"

Vasili waited until Icarus had curled himself up in the nest, his wings folded to his side and tail wrapped around his body, the tip draping just over the edge, before he slid into his favourite place and curled up next to Icarus's warm belly.

He could hear the comforting gush of Icarus's huge breaths inside his chest. Feel the strong, rhythmic thump of his heart. Smell his unique musk. Vasili never felt as safe and at home as he did with Icarus. Dragon and bonded rider were close. Twin souls joined. And as he sank back against his companion, his back resting against Icarus's side, Vasili felt as one.

The dragon chuckled, a deep, throaty rumble as he curled his head to lay with his giant eye facing Vasili. "No. She never does, though. As you say, she is more taciturn than the elf who rides with her."

Vasili grunted noncommittally. "Well, I have news. The general would not come without good cause, and good cause she has, it seems."

He opened his mind, sharing the memory of his eavesdropping on Tristan and Elyvia.

Icarus watched him, unblinking, as the moments passed and the memory finally faded. "The Order of Valxiron, eh?"

"Yes." Vasili's jaw clenched. It was impossible not to feel anything but animosity to the Order that had caused the kingdom so much strife – and nearly destroyed his family. "Tristan will order a hunt. I know it."

Icarus bared his teeth in a grin. He did not need to ask to

know Vasili would join that hunt. Be the first, if he could. To enact vengeance for his family's suffering. And redemption for them all. He could not cleanse the blackness from his family's name until the Order was no more.

"We will hunt," Icarus said slowly, with grim relish. He had no personal quarrel with the Order, but it was in his nature to meet any challenge before him.

"We will hunt." It was a promise.

Vasili did not return to his quarters that night, the small, basic dormitory in the outpost that he shared with three other riders. The cold wind did not permeate the sheltered cave nor the warm pocket of air around them heated by Icarus's own inner fire.

Yet as Icarus descended into rumbling snores, his double-lidded eyes closed, Vasili remained alert long into the night, kept awake with thoughts of the Order that he had vowed, upon entering the ranks of the Winged Kingsguard, to defeat once and for all.

An air of grim expectation hung over the training square, where the dozen riders of the outpost had assembled in full leathers, their dragons saddled and ready to ride. The wind seemed particularly bitter that morning, with dawn late and reluctant. Vasili huddled into his fur-lined cloak, grateful for Icarus's warmth between his legs. He had thought about casting a charm to warm himself, but they all would have precious little energy to spare for such vanities over the coming days, so he sat, shoulders hunched, the fur of his collar meeting the fur lining of his hat and keeping out the worst of the chill.

General Elyvia sat upon her dragon, surveying all those gathered before her. She showed no signs of cold. At breakfast that morning, a sombre Tristan had briefed them about the missing patrol and the potential threat of the Order of Valxiron.

All of the riders shared the same nervous anticipation Vasili felt, judging by the way they shifted upon their saddles. That same sickly, swooping mix of excitement and fear of the unknown. Yet the dragons were eager to be off, their wings flexing, claws crunching as they kneaded the stone, longing to launch into the air.

Icarus shifted beneath Vasili, too. Vasili's gloved hands flexed upon the pommel grips. Dragons had no need for reins, like horses. They were not dumb beasts the rider had to steer.

"Steady, my friend. Not long now."

Icarus huffed.

Vasili's lips twitched into a smile. His dragon companion never did have the same trepidation he felt on new ventures. *I wish I had his confidence.* For Vasili's bluster was entirely fake, a wall to hide his insecurities behind. He did not think a dragon knew what it was to feel doubt. Icarus threw himself into all things with a gusto Vasili could only admire.

Before them, beside Elyvia, Tristan mounted his violet

dragon. As the captain of their outpost, it was his duty to lead them, but he looked towards Elyvia expectantly, superseded by her rank.

"You all know what is at stake." Her voice was quiet, but clear. Not a dragon moved, not a rider shuffled. Every word rang crystal clear across the crowded training square. "We must find our fellow riders."

Alive or dead, Vasili filled in at her pause.

"We must see if there is any truth to the rumours that the Order of Valxiron may be closer than we think. Search your assigned areas thoroughly, then return three days hence."

A snigger came from next to Vasili. He did not need to look to know it was his fellow scout ranger, Nikolai. Vasili glanced towards him and scowled at his smirk.

"We might see your uncles. Won't that be a lovely family reunion?" Nikolai grinned.

Vasili bared his teeth at Nikolai for a moment before forcing himself to turn back to Elyvia. He would not shame himself by reacting. He settled for imagining pummelling Nikolai instead, but it was not nearly as satisfying. Icarus was rigid beneath him, sensing his tension. His claws gouged into the stone in silent anger.

No matter that they all trusted each other with their lives, Vasili's fellow riders knew where to hit below the belt when it came to him. His family's past association with the Order had plagued him since the day he joined the Winged Kingsguard. Since they had announced him as the son of Dimitrius of House Ellarian and

Harper of House Ravakian. Hardly a more cursed name could there be.

He had hated his father for the fact his record had been blighted, through no fault of his own, before he had even set foot inside the Winged Kingsguard, whose ranks he had longed to join since he was a boy. Now, he channelled that anger into determination and a thorny exterior.

Vasili sat up straighter as Elyvia donned her thick, fur-lined hat and settled into her saddle.

"Fair winds, comrades."

"Fair winds," came the reply from all of them. Elyvia launched into the air first, followed by Tristan. Rank after rank took flight behind them, until it was Vasili's and Nikolai's turn – the youngest, most inexperienced at the end of the line.

"I'll tell your uncles you said hello," said Nikolai, grinning viciously.

"Go *sard* yourself," cursed Vasili, gesturing rudely at him.

Nikolai only laughed, returned the gesture in kind, and wheeled away.

It was not long before they were all scattered to the winds, and Vasili and Icarus were alone in the skies. They had all been assigned their quadrants to search. As the youngest, most inexperienced riders, Vasili and Nikolai had been given the territories directly surrounding the outpost. It was not the glory Vasili sought.

The mountain range spread below them from north to south, barren of all life, unless one knew where to look. Grey peaks jutted through thick snow, and already, the glaciers fattened for winter. As they flew, white-furred beasts, camouflaged for winter, shot across the snow below them, darting for cover amongst the rocks or the sparse evergreens.

Yet nowhere did they see any hint of the Order of Valxiron

Vasili scoffed. Icarus huffed in disgust.

"This is pointless," growled the dragon. They could still see the highest tower of the outpost between the peaks as they soared from one valley to the next.

"Agreed. As if the Order would be hiding right under our noses."

"We were not sent here to search for them. Not really."

Vasili knew it was true. He, Nikolai, and their dragons were simply the scouts to ensure the outpost was manned to some capacity, no matter how slight, over the next few days, whilst the rest of the outpost was on the true hunt farther afield.

A questioning tendril from Icarus caressed him. The desire to rebel, ignore their orders, venture farther than they ought.

Vasili could not help but grin. "This be damned. Let's hunt, Icarus."

Icarus rumbled in pleasure beneath him. The dragon had no desire to prove himself like Vasili, but he never turned down a chance for adventure. He tipped his wings to one side and wheeled away to the southeast. Gradually, the outpost was far behind them, a maze-like expanse of jagged, stone teeth rising into the sky before them.

Vasili whooped, as Icarus roared their challenge for the hunt.

SEVENTEEN

As much as Lief needed rest, her body dull with exhaustion, she forced herself to move on. Urgency drove her, a sense that she was running out of time…from the blight that weakened her, the dark fiends that were hunting her, and the evil that had infiltrated Tir-na-Alathea.

She could not bear to dwell on Lune's fate. Nausea roiled through her at the thought of it, at the nightmarish memories of what had attacked them.

Aedon walked in silence beside her. He did not offer his help as they ascended a ridge, for which she was grateful. She wouldn't have accepted it, even if she did need it.

They paused at the summit between two peaks to rest and drink from the dwindling water supply.

"Shall we make camp here?" Aedon suggested. With their late start, the sun had already slipped towards the horizon. They stood upon the saddle of a pass between two peaks. "It offers us a good vantage point."

Lief turned on the spot. He was right, but it was too exposed for her liking, with nowhere to retreat to if–

She stopped the thought before it could coalesce. Thinking of being attacked again was too much.

The rocky crest was bare of trees, but as the trail wound down the far side, she knew shelter would be a little way farther. "Follow me."

They scrambled down a small scree slope to where the hill dropped away. She could hear the faint rumble of the waterfall. Aedon followed without question as she traversed the incline towards the source.

The cave was just as she remembered it. Its entrance hidden behind the silvery sheet of water, the faint musty smell from infrequent use. A narrow ledge above the pool into which the cool water tumbled was the only entry, a ring of trees surrounding it as the forest continued below the ridge, far into the distance.

As she led him inside and to the small cot upon the woven floor mats, Aedon looked at her, eyebrows raised.

"An outpost," she explained to his unspoken question. "I thought it would be nicer shelter than the open hills, and we still have a view of the forest below. We won't be surprised here, and we can have a fire, too." She pointed to the ring of stones in the corner of the cave, tucked away from the mouth, that would allow them to build a small fire that would not be seen from outside. The area inside the circle was filled with cold ashes, and a blackened, metal pot sat beside the rocks.

"Luxurious." Aedon grinned. "And running water to boot."

"Which you need." She wrinkled her nose in mock disgust.

He rolled his eyes. "Charming."

"I'll forage. I know the plants. You collect firewood. Fallen wood only," she warned, pointing at him. "Don't touch the trees."

"Noted."

"And have your wits about you. Whilst you're with me, the forest shall not harm you, but there are beasts here that will see you as a tasty morsel, never mind that you need a wash."

Aedon winked at her. "Extra flavour."

Lief clamped down at the smile that threatened at his unexpected humour. She would not give him the damned satisfaction. "Ugh…"

They parted ways, returning soon after, Aedon with his arms full of wood, Lief with berries and a small bird. As she plucked, skinned, and butchered it with expertise, Aedon built, then lit the fire with a mere word, before grabbing the cooking pot and walking to the waterfall, leaning out precariously from the ledge to catch it, despite Lief's hissed chastisement at his risk.

Soon, the fruity sauce bubbled, its delicate aroma twining with the smoky scent of the meat cooking upon spits over the flames.

"If only we had a fine wine to add to this," Aedon murmured as he stirred the thickening, crimson sauce.

Lief snorted. "That can be arranged. Wood elves like a

decent vintage as much as anyone else. We never leave these places unstocked." She reached under the edge of the cot, into the pile of soft moss that formed its springy mattress, and dug through until she grasped hard, cold, smooth glass.

With a triumphant smirk, she pulled the stoppered bottle out with a flourish and offered it to Aedon first. It was only half full, but it would be enough to warm their spirits.

He took a swig and grinned. "Mmm," he said appreciatively, then passed it back to her.

The bubbly, sweet liquid was a welcome refreshment after the constant blandness of water that day. She set it down between them so they could freely sip it.

After a few moments of silence, he looked up, seeing her staring, head cocked.

"What?" he asked.

"I was just wondering… What did you do that was so terrible our Queen imprisoned you for so long?"

Crime was unheard of in Tir-na-Alathea, for the realm had no poverty or injustice. It was a true utopia. Only outsiders were foolish enough to venture in with nefarious intent.

Aedon rolled his eyes. "I *stole*. I'm a thief, remember?"

Lief pursed her lips. "Obviously, but *what* did you steal? No offence, but you don't really strike me as wanting jewels–" She had already noticed he did not wear a single embellishment, "–and you already have magic."

Aedon looked back at her thoughtfully and ceased his stirring, leaving the twig in the bubbling liquid. "It was intended to be a trade, but your people refused, so I was left with no choice. I offered a favour–"

Lief's eyes widened. "A *favour*?" she interrupted. *Does he know how foolish that is?* A favour could be used for anything the holder wished…

Suddenly, it all made sense. A wood elf never asked for a simple favour, like the mending of a cloak or the cooking of a meal. No. If no stipulations were made, a wood elf would, quite within their rights, ask for years of a life or someone's magic.

"I was desperate," he said with a rueful smile.

"For *what?*" she pressed. *What could be so valuable he would give up so much in return?*

"Tir-na-Alathea is the only place I know of where the *aleilah* plant grows."

"*Aleilah*?" Lief wrinkled her nose. "It's a weed."

"Yes, but a rare weed, and when carefully distilled becomes a powerful potion of incredible healing properties. Even in its raw form, it can stave off a variety of ills. Your people have perfected the art of making distilled *aleilah* like no other, but they keep it a closely guarded secret."

That was not the answer Lief had expected. *Who is this strange elf who steals weeds?*

"You stole medicine then? For whom?"

"There was a sickness in a Pelenori village. At the time, the king did not care about helping paupers, and without our help, many would have died."

"*Our* help?"

Aedon's face closed as he gazed into the distance. "I did not work alone."

He said no more. Lief opened her mouth, but hesitated. Lines of grief were etched into his face, and for a moment, he looked older than his young visage suggested, as though he carried a great burden within him. She sensed it was not the time to press him further.

"Did you take the *aleilah?*" Lief had never heard of anyone escaping the living forest alive for such a crime.

Aedon straightened. "I did. We escaped and cured the villagers." There was a hint of pride in his tone.

Lief gaped. "How?"

"How did we escape?" Aedon's slight smile faded. "One of my companions possessed…gifts that surprised your people. He was an Aerian, one of the winged men of his people. A finer warrior, a braver heart, a more loyal companion you could never find in all the kingdoms. He flew me out of the living forest, much to the chagrin of your people and the *dhiran.*"

He speaks in past tense, as though…

"How did he die?" she whispered.

A muscle twitched in Aedon's jaw. "In battle."

Lief swallowed, the grief on his face palpable. She needed to turn the subject away from his fallen friend. *Perhaps we'll get into that story another time.* Given the length of his captivity, it had to have been decades ago, yet he still felt the pain of loss. She could not imagine caring for someone so much that she would feel the same after so long.

"So, if you escaped, how did you come to be in Tir-na-Alathea again – and Lune?"

He shrugged. "I came back of my own volition."

Lief gawked at him, dumbfounded. "Why?" she blurted. *Why would anyone be so…foolish?*

Aedon smiled wryly. "Yes, quite. Well… It was time to face up to the consequences of my actions. So here I returned. The rest, as you probably know, is not very interesting. I've been here a while." He lifted his hands in a shrug.

"Don't you miss your old life?"

Aedon regarded her thoughtfully. "Yes, but when I returned here, that old life was gone anyway. I can never get it back, so either way, I had to start again."

"You're an enigma, Aedon Lindhir Riel," Lief mused.

He chuckled and took a swig of wine before offering it to her, his fingers lacing together across his knees in insincere carelessness. *Don't pry*, his closed body silently told her. "If you think so."

Lief took a sip, mulling over what the Pelenori elf had told her, but she suspected there was so much more to his story.

"What of you, Lief na Arboreali? Who are you?" At her silence, he tilted his head. "Come now. I've told you mine. It's only fair. Besides, it'll be very boring if we're not to talk at all for the weeks we're stuck together."

Lief shrugged. "Very well. I'm a ranger of the Queen's Forest Scouts. I was raised in Lune and serve their guard now. That's it."

"That sounds very dull."

"Maybe to an outsider. For us, our forest is enough. What more could we possibly need or desire?"

Aedon snorted. "You're a strange folk. I never did understand you."

"Have you known many wood elves?"

"A few, and that was too many. We don't have a good relationship, as you might imagine."

"I wonder why."

Aedon ignored the jibe. "Don't you ever get bored of summer, though? Surely you long for cold, winter snow, rain, the fiery colours of autumn, the freshness of the first buds of spring pushing through the frozen earth."

She looked at him blankly, not willing to admit that what he described sounded enticing. "No. The leaves are always green, the flowers ever blooming, and the sun's bounty constant. Our woods are life embodied, never dying or withering away. All else pales to this realm."

"Have you ever left Tir-na-Alathea's borders?" At her silence, he smirked. "Then how would you know?

"I read and I hear things," she retorted.

Aedon rolled his eyes. "Incredible."

"What. Like *you* know everything?"

"Well, I've certainly done my fair share of travelling. From the arid, rolling deserts where water is a precious trading commodity, to the frigid northern lands where nothing grows. From the great dwarven halls hidden under mountains, carved with such finery that is rarely seen above ground, to the plains of the Indis where the very grass itself is an ocean."

Lief had to admit, if only to herself, that such places sounded enticing. "Good for you," she said instead, then leaned across him to stir the pot once more. The sauce was ready, dribbling thick and slow from the stripped twig they used as a makeshift spoon. "Supper's ready."

Aedon offered her the two pieces of bark, lined with leaves and piled with berries, and Lief carefully extracted the skewers of meat from the fire, placing them down before drizzling over the rich sauce. Taking a bite, she licked her fingers, smacking her lips as the rich, fatty juices tingled upon her tongue.

They ate in silence, appreciating the richness of the flavours – the smoky, moist meat, the tangy, sweet sauce, atop the crisp, fresh salad.

"Ah." Aedon leaned back and patted his stomach. "That was exquisite. I haven't had a meal so nice in, well, twenty-five years," he said with a wince. "If you keep feeding me like this, I fear I shall have no choice but to ask for such fare when I return to the Queen's custody." He raised the bottle and nodded to her before taking a sip and offering her the last mouthful.

"You can't mean that," Lief said, taking the bottle, but not drinking. "Surely you want to be free."

When Aedon looked away, she frowned. "What is it?"

"Nothing."

Lief saw how his face fell as despair crept in. Aedon's hand passed across the flames, and suddenly, the licks of fire before her transformed, rising up and carving off into little birds of flame no bigger than her palm that fluttered away from the fire.

Lief's gaze followed them, filled with wonder, as they flew to the roof of the cave and disappeared into nothing. "They were beautiful," she murmured. She had never seen anything like it. Fire was not a common element in the living forest.

"But they were not truly free," Aedon said, smiling sadly. "Their freedom was simply an illusion, as it so often is."

No matter how much she knew that thinking of him in any other way than a prisoner would do her damage, she could not help but wonder at his past and wish to know more. To know how this once vivacious elf had lost his spark for life, desiring little else but his captivity.

EIGHTEEN

Pages rustled behind Venya, then quickly flipped. Suddenly, with the iron tang of magic, a great shadow towered over her and launched itself. As it sped through the air, it morphed into fur, and claws, and teeth.

The force as the two creatures connected shook the room. The aisle became a tangle of scything claws and flashing teeth, and amidst the snarls and shrieks, fur flew through the air. Shelves rocked as the creatures tumbled into them, locked in a fight so fast and vicious, Venya could not tell where one ended and the other began.

At the disruption, grimoires launched themselves off their shelves as far as their chains would allow, gnashing, screeching, howling, snapping.

Yet it was the distraction she needed. She shrank back as the beasts surged past her. Venya took one look at the beasts, still intent on each other's destruction, scrambled to her feet, and sprinted for the door, and the relative safety of the stairs outside, hoping the brighter light would expunge the nightmare from her mind.

Venya skidded under the lintel and fumbled for the librarian's seal, frantically waving it at the empty doorway as the sound of snarling and yelping emanated from within. The door materialised into being once more, immediately cutting off the noise.

Venya heaved a dry sob of relief as she slumped, trembling, against the wall. Not daring to linger, she sprinted up the stairs, her burning legs taking them two at a time, until she reached the welcome, bright, safe halls of the Athenaeum.

Her stomach ached, for it was past dinner time, but Venya did not go to the dining hall. Instead, she took the stairs to her dormer room, thankful the rest of the Athenaeum dined and the halls were empty.

Venya unlocked her door – passing through her own magical wards, which none of the other junior librarians knew of – and illuminated the room in a bright fae light to banish the nightmare she had just witnessed.

With the door closed and locked behind her, she leaned upon it heavily, strengthening her wards, as she breathed deeply, allowing her thundering heart to settle. *What was that?* She shuddered and blinked away the image of its cruel teeth and long claws reaching for her.

One by one, she peeled off Beatrix's borrowed gloves, her belt, and her tunic, throwing them onto her bed. She paused at the uncharacteristic thump of the latter hitting her mattress. She frowned.

What… She reached into the folds of the robe.

Her fingers touched an unmistakably familiar, coarse fur. Barely breathing, she slowly glanced inside.

Venya cried out.

The Book of Beasts was in her pocket.

Venya pulled her hand back as if it had been bitten, then flung the tunic to the far side of the room, backing into the opposite corner until she bumped up against a stack of books. The grimoire remained, peeking out of the pocket, as though it were nothing but an ordinary book.

But Venya suspected it was far more. What else could have produced a beast to protect her in her moment of need? The grimoire would not be archived within that vault without good cause. Perhaps she had stumbled upon the tome's power by accident, though she had no idea why it would defend rather than attack.

She stilled, still glaring at it. *Does this mean that the creature is dead? The creature that wore Beatrix's skin…*

Venya shuddered, feeling nauseous. She swallowed and stared at *The Book of Beasts*, watching, waiting for it to do something suspicious. Waiting for a beast to tear out of its pages and rip her to shreds. It did not move.

With no clear idea what she ought to do with it – returning it to the vault was definitely out of the question – Venya donned the gloves again. She cautiously walked over to the book, gingerly picked it up, then opened the door to her wardrobe and tossed it in. Slamming the door, she warded it heavily with every protective magic she knew until the worn wood hummed and glowed with spells.

She peeled off the gloves once more, but kept them scrunched in her hand, then sat on her bed and backed into the corner, glaring at the wardrobe door with trepidation. With her windows shuttered – she had not bothered to open them that morning with the late dawn and early dusk – the darkness outside was kept at bay, yet even with her blankets wrapped around her, she could not relax. Venya tried to read, a simple book of poetry she enjoyed, but her eyes jumped over the same three words repeatedly, each time flicking to the wardrobe door, which she was almost certain kept opening a crack. It was a trick of her mind. Eventually, as the night bell tolled, she set the book down beside her with a sigh.

A sharp rap on the door made her jump.

"Vee, are you in there? Are you all right?" Beatrix's muffled voice came through the door.

Venya's heart thundered in her chest, flooded with adrenaline, and for a moment, she was back in the vault, watching Beatrix's face morph from warm and kind into a cruel, horrific predator.

If I'm quiet, she'll go away. Think I'm sleeping.

"I can see your light on. You didn't come to dinner. Are you ill?"

"I'm fine," Venya forced out, half-expecting that terrible beast to tear through the door any second.

"Why didn't you come to dinner?"

Venya swallowed and pulled her blanket up to her shoulders, knowing the cold chills crawling down her spine had nothing to do with the temperature. "I… I worked late."

"Want me to get you some leftovers?"

Venya drew her knees up to her chest and rested her forehead on them with a soft groan. Why did Beatrix have to be so kind? It only made Venya like her more. "No, thank you. I'm not hungry, Bea."

A long pause. "Are you sure you're okay?"

"I'm positive." Venya forced warmth into her voice. "I'll see you in the morning. Night."

"Okay…" She sounded uncertain. "Good night."

Venya could see her shadow under the door as she dithered. At last, her soft footsteps padded away.

Venya relaxed, then immediately stiffened once more, flinging a glance at the wardrobe. Half of her wanted to open it, to check the book was still there. Check it hadn't morphed into some terrifying beast. The other half of her never wanted to open the wardrobe again…ever.

The last bell sounded. Time for lights out. Venya had never disobeyed it before, but she had no intention of extinguishing her faelight. And, as much as her tired body ached and stinging eyes drooped, she knew she would not sleep that night.

So, she sat long into the night, until she felt stiff from her stillness. She stared at the wardrobe, plotting ways she could rid herself of *The Book of Beasts* – hide it, destroy it, return it – until the door blurred before her and she drifted off into unwitting sleep.

The Book of Beasts remained in the wardrobe for the rest of the week. Venya did sleep again, but only fitfully, and with the lights on, becoming so exhausted that Nieve reprimanded her for not paying attention and carelessness, much to her shame – and the amusement of the rest of her cohort.

Beatrix hovered over her, watchful and worried, but after the encounter in the vault – with her terrifying doppelgänger, and how it had enticed Venya to lower her impenetrable barriers – she avoided her as much as possible.

After the first week, Venya collapsed onto her bed with a groan. That morning, in desperate need for clean clothes, she had finally dared to open her wardrobe to find *The Book of Beasts* exactly where she had left it. It had not harmed her, and she resolved to get it out of her closet.

Then I'll be able to sleep comfortably again.

She stifled a yawn and stood. With her last shift as a temporary librarian looming, she slipped the book back into her large tunic pocket and, heart hammering and palms sweaty, returned to the librarians' lounge to put it back where she had found it.

Overwhelmed with relief, good spirits broke through her foggy exhaustion and she finished the day with a spring in her step when she noticed the book had vanished from the lounge. Some other soul had put it back then. She shivered, hoping they had not encountered the same beast she had. But such news would have spread like wildfire through the library. Her secret was safe for now – and hopefully forever.

That night, after her first vaguely sociable dinner in a week sitting next to Beatrix, though she let the other woman do all the talking, Venya retired to bed with relief. She had managed to suppress the awkwardness of being around Beatrix, separating her friend and mentor from the beast in the vault. The nightmare was over. There was no reason to dwell upon it a moment longer.

Venya opened her door, illuminated the faelight...and stopped dead, muffling a cry.

The Book of Beasts lay in the centre of her bed.

She stumbled backwards out of the door, nearly bumping into the rest of her junior cohort as they returned from dinner.

Is this a cruel joke? Which one of them put it there? How did they know?

Yet as she looked at their blank, cold faces, her eyes wide and face drawn with fear, she saw none of the gleeful spite they would wear if they had done it.

She scrambled back into her room and slammed the door.

A moment later, their steps continued down the corridor.

"Freak…," she heard someone mutter.

For once, she ignored it, her attention focused on the grimoire.

She opened the door once more, checking to make sure the hall was clear, before she darted to the bed, grabbed the book, and stuffed it into her pocket. Hurrying to the latrines, she locked herself in a cubicle and shoved the book down the opening, where it would drop into an intricate pipe system below. She heard a faint splash, and relief surged through her. There was no way it could return from that.

Yet when she returned to her room, there it was on the bed once more, wet and stinking.

Venya gagged and swore.

One of the shutters was ajar, gently banging open and closed, allowing a cold gust to spill into the room, but Venya hardly felt it.

"What do you want?" she asked it desperately. "Why won't you leave me alone?"

A warm breeze blew through the room, banishing the cold, bringing with it the smell of wet fur, cut grass, and summer flowers – a welcome relief from the scent of excrement. The book shuddered on the bed. Venya tensed, not sure if she was getting ready to fight or flee. Suddenly, it bulged and changed before her eyes, growing legs, a head, and a tail, until a tiny puppy with curly brown hair, floppy ears, giant paws, and warm, chestnut eyes sat upon her bed. The only sign of the beast within was its slitted, gold-rimmed pupils.

Venya was frozen, not even daring to breathe. "What are you?" she whispered.

"I am whatever I want to be," the puppy said, cocking its head and blinking up at her, "and whatever my master needs." It spoke with the voice of a boy, yet its timbre held age and wisdom.

"How did you get back in here?"

The puppy frowned and harrumphed. Venya had never seen such an oddity. "I don't much appreciate being disposed of, let alone down a latrine–" Venya flushed, "–so I did not deign to stay. I took on the shape of an otter to swim out of the pipes, then the form of a bird to fly back here."

Venya's mouth hung open, aghast.

"Yes, it is rather incredible," the puppy said with no small amount of smugness.

"And… And you… Was that…that beast that protected me in the vault…*you*?" Venya stuttered.

"Yes, mistress. You needed my help, so I became what you called for in that moment."

She gaped. Teeth, claws, shaggy fur, wild eyes… Yet sitting before her was the softest, most innocent looking puppy she could have imagined. A prickle of unease niggled at her.

What have I gotten myself into?

The cold now seeped into her. Venya crossed the room, keeping an eye on the puppy, which just watched her, to secure her shutters once more. She stood by the window, arms wrapped around her body to try and banish some of the chill.

"What was that…*thing*?" she asked.

"An old grimoire, a very unpleasant one, that ought not to be loose," the puppy replied quietly.

"It… How did it look like Beatrix?"

"Who?" The puppy wrinkled his nose. "I cannot see what you saw. The grimoire appears differently to each person, showing them the source of their desire, whatever form will most torture them at that time. Such glamours allow it to draw close to its prey until…"

Venya drew her finger across her neck.

"Exactly."

"What did you see?" she dared to ask.

"Hmm… This and that."

It…*he* did not want to answer her. *Interesting.* Venya examined the creature again. Still, he appeared as nothing more than a puppy.

"Did one of us unleash it?"

"No. The magic binding that one was old and faded. It's been biding its time for a couple centuries now. You were just unlucky to be the first being it encountered when it managed to unsnap the shackles, both physical and magical, that restrained it."

"W-what should I call you?"

"Whatever you like." The puppy lifted his hind leg and stretched out his neck to scratch just behind his ear. "I've been called a lot of things – plenty of which I shan't repeat in such polite company – but I prefer Nyxastriatamun."

When she just blinked at him, he repeated slowly, "*Nicks-ah-stree-ah-tah-moon*." At her furrowed brow, shaking her head, the puppy sighed. "You can call me Nyx."

"Nyx," echoed Venya faintly. "Right."

NINETEEN

When Lief awoke and looked around, she sat up quickly. Aedon was gone. Sunlight filtered into the cave entrance, and the hum of insect, bird, and animal life was a drone against the rumble of falling water outside. But of the Pelenori elf, there was no trace.

Lief swore and leapt to her feet, any trace of drowsiness gone in an instant. She grabbed her bow and knife and dashed from the cave, her heart hammering. This was it. Her life would be as good as over when her grave failure was discovered.

Damn it! she admonished herself. *I shouldn't have trusted him. I let my guard down, and now he is gone. Fool of an elf! What imbecile loses a prisoner? Allows them to simply walk away?*

Lief groaned as she thought of the implications. She would be ruined. Everything she had worked so hard for, and earned on her own merit, would be wasted.

I'll be damned if I let a blasted thief ruin my life.

She rounded the curtain of water and halted, the cool spray misting upon her bare arms. In the pool far below, a figure stood, his back to her.

Aedon…

Her stomach swooped with relief that he had not run, that she was not ruined. But she did not call to him. Instead, she stood and watched, transfixed by his bared body.

Oblivious to her presence, he ducked his head under the surface of the cold pool before standing again, water cascading from him. As he shook his head, like a hound, droplets flew in all directions, glinting as they caught the morning sun before splashing into the pool.

But it was not that which captivated her.

His tunic and trousers lay discarded on the rocks nearby, and the water only came up to his hips. His back, which she could tell had once been muscled, had wasted away after years in captivity, the far leaner muscle riddled with scars. The pale lines criss-crossed his olive skin, stark silver against the warmth.

Who did that to him? She knew it could not have been her people. Torture was rarely sanctioned, though she knew the Queen liked Her rather more cruel games with those who displeased Her. Yet those old wounds looked *brutal.* Deep and rough, they sliced across him with merciless savagery.

As Aedon turned and strode from the pond, naked, Lief retreated behind the curtain of the waterfall, cheeks warming. Heavens forbid he should catch her watching and think anything of it. He had not run off this time, but it had been a reminder.

I should not trust him, no matter how charming he may seem.

Yet beside the pond, neatly stacked, were two clean bark plates and a cooking pot. Lief swallowed. *Maybe I've misjudged him.*

"*Aleilah* might help you, you know," Aedon said, glancing at Lief, who strode beside him.

They had barely spoken. She seemed flustered, though he could not fathom why. He had thought their conversation the previous night had gone a long way to calming the hostility between them. Despite their differences, he had no desire to spend weeks in close confines with nothing but animosity.

It had been a long time since he had felt the companionship of another, around the fire, after a day's travelling. It brought forth fond memories, yet they were painful to recall. His former companions were scattered to the winds in life and death, never to meet again for a game of *chatura,* or a sparring session, or an ale.

Aedon had not realised quite how much he still missed all of it. All of them. He wondered fleetingly how those still living fared, before Lief answered.

"Hmm?"

"If we can procure some of the plant, we may be able to use it to slow the progression of the poison."

Her fist clenched at the word, and his eyes rose to her shoulder. Her sleeveless tunic no longer concealed the spreading darkness, for it had now begun snaking down her upper arm and across her neck.

Aedon had never known of anything *aleilah* could not help, and despite their differences, his old nature still endured. He felt duty-bound to see she did not suffer, regardless of the misery her kind had inflicted on him.

Blasted conscience.

Lief slowed to a halt, Aedon stopping beside her. "Are you sure?"

He heard the unasked question.

Can I place my faith in a cure?

"Well… No," he admitted. "But it's worth a try. Where does it grow? Perhaps we might find some on our way to Emuir."

From the way she bit her bottom lip, looking away from him, he knew she was considering whether or not to tell him the details of her kingdom. He suppressed a sigh at her caution.

"We could take a detour," she finally said. "It wouldn't take us too far out of our way, and we are likely to find *aleilah.* If you think it will help, I suppose it's worth it." She straightened, wincing as her tunic grazed the still open, festering wound.

Aedon noted the way her chest heaved with shallow, rapid breaths, as though even their leisurely trek was exhausting.

"I think it would be wise. Lead the way."

Lief glanced at the sky through the breaks in the canopy, then checked the bole of the nearest tree for some sign of bearing that Aedon did not understand and gestured. "It's this way. Come on. We're still a few days away…give or take." Her mouth tightened with the pain of even that as she strode off into the trees.

Aedon followed, watching her carefully. Was it his imagination, or did she seem slightly off balance? Before, she had been nimble and agile with the customary unearthly grace of an elf. Now she shuffled, sometimes stumbling over hidden roots. Lief seemed in control of her mind, despite the blight so clearly affecting her physical wellbeing. Yet he could not help but shudder at the memory of the dead elves and their predatory nature.

Would her amber eyes turn black? Would her tanned skin fade to deathly white, her scattered freckles replaced by black veins? Would he have to fight her off to survive? Aedon could not shift the pit of foreboding in his stomach. He subtly fingered the dagger hidden inside his boot on the pretence of adjusting his footwear, making sure it was secure and still concealed by the hem of his trousers…just in case.

Despite Aedon's acceptance of his fate, his sense of self-preservation was not entirely extinct, and being attacked by the dead was not how he wished to perish.

They had long ago climbed down the ridge where they had camped in the cave and returned to the forest, following one of the trails – a path of pale, crushed stones that wound into the shadow of the trees ahead.

"These trails are a marvel. The rocks are transported from a particular place in Tir-na-Alathea. When messages must be delivered, they remain visible even in the darkest night, so one does not become lost in the endless forests. Of course, one must still know the way. Only we and our messenger creatures know the full network of these trails," Lief explained at Aedon's questioning look as he watched his feet crunch on the ground, puffing out her chest in pride at her people's ingenuity.

"Fascinating," Aedon murmured, but his encouragement did not entice any further secrets of her people from the taciturn wood elf. His boot struck a big stone, kicking it ahead on the path, where it landed with a *clack*.

Aedon halted. *That is no stone…*

Lief rushed forwards and squatted to examine it. Long, smooth, straight, and picked clean – scored with hundreds of criss-crossed lines. *Teeth marks*. She reached for it, but stopped just short, turning back to Aedon, her eyes wide with horror, her mouth ajar.

"It's an elf bone," Aedon whispered. He had seen enough bones upon battlefields long ago to know mortal and elf from animal or beast. "Specifically, a shin bone." He swallowed past the lump in his throat, and the nausea that threatened, and glanced around them.

Not far away, in the overgrown tangle of forest, more white gleamed. He drifted closer. A shattered pelvis. Aedon looked up into trees around them.

"How…"

It was only when he jumped at how unnaturally loud Lief's voice sounded that he realised just how deathly silent the forest had fallen. A tingle of fear curled along his spine.

"Where does this road lead, Lief?" he asked quietly, slowly turning as he scanned their surroundings.

"To an isolated area in the mountains. There are some settlements beyond that I know of, but they are many days away. We will go to the mountains, then divert away again to Emuir." Lief fingered the hilt of the dagger at her hip, before unhooking her bow from her shoulder and nocking an arrow. "Stay behind me."

He was slightly offended. "I can defend myself." Then Aedon raised an eyebrow. "We should set wards before we go any farther." *We have been lax in not doing so.*

"I know this forest far better than you. I know which beasts are friend and foe."

"I think these beasts are clearly foe," Aedon muttered, but if Lief heard him, she did not respond.

Instead, the wood elf suddenly moved with grace again, despite her injury, walking forwards, her bow clutched in front of her, pointing at the ground, but ready to draw and loose at a moment's notice. Aedon gritted his teeth, having no choice but to follow.

The shadow was silent as it dropped from above, the only clue to its presence the almost missed crunch of its clawed feet upon the gravel.

Aedon whirled around, eyes widening at what he saw. Standing on long, muscled hind legs, the creature was taller than him by several heads with black, shaggy fur, black, gleaming eyes, and a dripping maw full of jagged teeth set in a long muzzle. Aedon dove aside as it lunged and passed above him, the stench of wet, soiled fur and rotten breath rolling over him, then the metallic tang of dark magic slapped him as physically as its bushy, tangled tail.

Aedon crashed to the ground and rolled, ignoring the pain in his shoulder as he leapt to his feet. He fumbled with the hem of his trousers as he wrenched the dagger free. A poor weapon against a beast with serrated black claws as long as the blade he wielded, and yet, as the beast advanced on Lief, its huge, shaggy head bowing to scent her and hunt her, Aedon charged.

Lief raised the bow with a cry, jolting at the pain of her injured shoulder. She loosed an arrow at it, but one was all she had a chance for, and with the involuntary wrench of her muscles, her arrow only struck the beast in the thigh. It snarled at the impact and swiped at the protrusion, snapping the shaft, the point still embedded in its leg.

Lief raised her hands, magic blooming…and stuttering, before it waxed anew…blasting the beast. It howled in agony and fell back, right into Aedon's magical attack, which seized it whole and sent pain writhing through it. Aedon made swift work with his dagger, slicing through the tendons in the back of its legs. It crashed to the ground with an ear-splitting howl. Aedon swore and took several steps backwards as the creature dragged itself across the ground, its dark eyes fixed upon him with unbridled malice.

Lief was a blur as she nocked the bow and loosed.

Grunt.

At such close range, the arrow drove clean and deep, right into the base of its skull. The beast shuddered as its eyes dulled and it sank to the ground, lying still.

Howls emanated from the forest all around them. Aedon swore again as shadows blurred through the trees. Somehow, the light seemed darker, as though a storm were coming, but Aedon knew the taint of dark magic – the iron tang upon his tongue, the smothering despair he felt deep in his soul.

"Run," he growled, grabbing Lief's arm and tugging her along with him.

"Where did you get that dagger?" she asked as they ran, dodging trees and jumping over exposed roots.

He glanced at her incredulously, before returning his attention to the precarious tangle of roots before them as they strayed from the path. "*That's* what you're bothered about? What are these beasts?"

But Lief only threw a wide-eyed glance over her shoulder before she redoubled her pace.

Aedon's heart sank. *She either does not know or does not want to say… We're in trouble.*

Around them, the woods drew in, becoming more dark,

gnarled, and tangled with every step. Moss covered the ground, hiding treacherous rocks and crevices that would turn their ankles if they weren't careful. The tangle of branches drew closer and closer, until they had to slow in order to clamber through. Still, the chilling howls behind them continued.

"We can't…outrun them," Aedon gasped, quickly tiring. After decades in captivity, his stamina was no longer what it had been. He could not see an escape, an end to the ghastly forest that seemed to constrict upon them. Even the daylight was gone, kept at bay by the thick leaves and tangled branches above, until all they could see before and behind them was a murkiness.

The very air around them seemed heavy with ancient malevolence, and Aedon's limbs grew more sluggish with each step. Despair filled him as the crashing sounds behind them drew closer and louder, the beasts ripping apart the forest to pursue them.

Just ahead, Aedon saw a break through the trees and heard the dull rush of water. Trusting Lief's instincts, he followed her as she veered towards it. He chanced a glance back…and immediately regretted it. At least a dozen beasts followed them in a great, arcing line that easily tore through the trees. They would soon be surrounded on three sides.

And then there will be no way out.

The woods opened before them. Aedon yelled in alarm, quickly grabbing Lief's arm. They both skidded to a halt amidst the mossy boulders and tangled brush atop a giant ravine. Water rushed far beneath them, between its sheer sides.

Lief glanced behind them, eyes widening, before she looked at him. "If you want to live, elf, jump!"

Aedon looked over his shoulder and swore.

The beasts were five paces away.

Four…

Three…

Grasping hands, Aedon and Lief leapt into the void.

TWENTY

Scything claws whistled past them as the beasts reached them – a fraction too late.

The drop felt endless as Lief's terror engulfed her, the churning water below rushing up all too quickly.

At the last second, Lief remembered to take a quick gulp of air before her feet broke the surface. The freezing water knocked the breath from her lungs, and the water ripped her this way and that until she had no idea which way was up. Her only anchor was Aedon's hand firmly gripping hers, and she clung to him as her lungs burned.

There was not a moment to worry whether the foul creatures would follow them. *I need air!*

Stars danced across her vision as blackness threatened, and then she was yanked up, her head breaking the surface. Aedon put an arm around her waist and held her close, holding onto a rock with his other hand, his teeth gritted against the relentless pounding of the water.

Lief gulped in grateful breaths, not caring that he took such liberties. She clung onto him, her hand fisting in the billowing fabric of his tunic as her other arm snaked around him. Her heart thundered in her ears, as loud as the water crashing around them, but the howls of rage from above cut through it all.

They both glanced up. The beasts prowled on the edge of the ravine, shrieking, howling, growling. Without the shadows of the forest to hide them, their full dread was exposed.

Their black, rot-stained, gnashing teeth caught the light, as did their gore-covered, serrated claws and dark, gleaming eyes, which were fixed upon the elves far below as they prowled back and forth, as though trying to determine a way to reach them.

"Can they get down here?" Aedon shouted above the crashing of the water around them.

"No. I don't think so," Lief replied. If the beasts had not leapt in after them, it meant they would not, much to her relief. *They are averse to water.*

She tucked the information away as she looked around them, a disquieting realisation hitting her. There was no way they could climb out of the river.

"We'll have to let the river take us, Aedon," she groaned.

He regarded her for a long moment, then glanced up at the creatures above. *He's deciding if he wants to trust me.* She could understand that. The river was an unknown, but the alternative was no choice at all.

"Don't let go of me," he warned. "Try to stay afloat on your back." She saw his throat bob as he swallowed hard and glanced back up at the beasts that now leaned over the cliff's edge, raining pebbles down upon them as they fixed their hungry eyes upon their prey below.

With that, Aedon relinquished his grip on the rock. With an alarming tug that wrenched a slight cry from both of them, the river swept them away. Feet first, they plunged down the river, holding tightly to each other. Sky became water, became sky, became water, as they plunged down the river, the churning water tossing them around.

Howls rang out above them. When Lief glanced up, blinking water from her eyes, the beasts' dark shadows were a blur as they followed them along the cliffs.

They rose and fell with the undulating bluff as the precipice above them gradually sloped downward. Lief could not help but wonder what would happen should the banks drop away to shallows and they came close to the beasts. She shuddered at the thought of those great claws reaching eagerly for them.

She trembled with the cold, clinging tighter to Aedon. His lips were blue, and she supposed her own were, as well. With every rapid they crested, the cold water battered them.

After what felt like hours, the river grew less violent, and the ravine receded, the cliffs falling away to high banks. With every bounding leap the beasts took beside them, easily keeping pace as they floated away, their howls grew more cacophonously triumphant as they sensed their prey coming within reach.

The cold sapped Lief's resolve, and her resilience gave way to despair. They could not float away forever, yet they did not want to leave the relative safety of the river.

Ahead, water parted around a small islet. It was little more than a bar of rock with a few trees, but protected by the rushing water to either side, it was as close to a haven as they were likely to find, especially if her theory of the beasts' aversion to water was indeed correct. She hoped so. Their lives depended upon it.

Letting go of Aedon, making him cry out in alarm, she struck out for the islet, painfully slicing through the water as best she could with her clumsy, frozen limbs and injured shoulder. Aedon splashed beside her, his stroke only marginally better than hers.

We must make a fire, whether the forest approves or not. Otherwise, we might not live another day. Although that thought was still a more pleasant alternative than being shredded by the claws and teeth that awaited them. Besides which, fire would keep them safe from such denizens. She hoped.

They dragged themselves through the shallows. Lief gritted her teeth as the jagged rocks scraped and punctured her skin. At last, her fingers sank into moss and grass. With one last surge of energy, Lief pulled herself up and free of the water, shuddering with relief. She collapsed upon the ground, her chest heaving with each breath.

Angry snarls forced her back to her hands and knees, and

she scrambled farther up the small islet and beneath the shelter of the few gnarled trees. With an apprehensive glance over her shoulder, Lief almost expected to see them wading through the river towards them, or feel a clawed hand close around her ankle at any moment. The terror of that screamed through her, and she almost wrenched an ankle in her haste to scramble away from the shallows behind her.

Yet the creatures did not advance. Over a dozen of them crowded onto the riverbank, snarling, yelping, howling, but not one claw did they put into the water. Relief surged through her. She did not feel safe, for they were still too close for comfort, but knowing there was a barrier between them was a slight comfort.

Aedon turned and sat with a grunt, leaning against the trunk of a wizened tree, Lief doing the same. Her eyes slipped shut in momentary relief.

"Th-thank the skies y-you knew about the r-river," Aedon said through chattering teeth.

Lief lolled her head to the side and groaned, "I didn't."

She could see Aedon's rising misgivings in his horrified expression. "You m-mean we're alive d-down to luck and n-nothing more?"

Lief nodded tiredly, the rush of fear and flight receding in the face of sheer exhaustion, her body trembling.

Aedon glanced at the creatures prowling relentlessly on the riverbanks, and dark anger clouded his vision. "You can't be serious," he growled, then blew out a breath. "Do you not know the meaning of the word caution?" he snapped with sudden vigour. "I said we needed to stop, place wards upon ourselves. They could have kept us safe, concealed from those foul beasts!"

Lief drew up, filled with indignation at his judgment. "I don't need your approval, and I sure as roots won't take your chastisement, elf."

"Then what the heck were you thinking? You should have told me so I could take the necessary precautions if your magic was not up to the task."

"How dare you," she hissed. "I may be injured, but I am not so weak that I need your protection."

His stare bored into her, eyes narrowed. "Could have fooled me."

"Ugh," Lief scoffed. "Well, I'm not buying your contrite 'woe is me, leave me to rot in my punishment' rubbish, either."

"You don't know the first damn thing about me, wood elf."

Her hands balled into fists at her sides. "You don't get to speak to me like that. Why don't you just lay down and die, since you have so clearly given up on life?" she spat at him, her fists shaking.

He rose and stalked closer, glaring at her. "At least I'm not stupid enough to *die* rather than accept help!"

That stung. She shot to her feet, but still, she had to look up at him. "Like I'd want help from a prisoner, a *thief*, and a liar," she retorted scathingly, her cheeks heating. It was a low blow, but she had no defence against his accusation…because it was true. She worked alone. It was better that way.

If I don't rely on anyone, I can't be hurt again. Finarvon's betrayal still hurt more than she cared to admit. She did not owe Aedon an explanation.

His face paled and closed, his jaw clenching.

She did not offer any apology.

Neither did he.

Instead, Aedon kicked a stone into the river, with a barely concealed grimace, and turned away. He began to collect wood – fallen twigs and other detritus that would burn, being careful not to touch the trees – as though she did not exist, as though he were not drenched in icy water, as though there were not fiends mere feet away baying for their blood.

Lief sank onto the rocks once more, keeping vigil over their hunters.

There was precious little fallen wood on the tiny island, yet it seemed to take him an age to collect it. *He deliberately delays.* He refused to meet her eyes as he returned with the sad quantity, placed it upon the ground, and ignited it with a quick flick of his wrist.

Aedon stripped down to his sodden undergarments and squeezed out his wet clothes, then sat and pulled off his boots, tipping out the water with a grimace. He donned his clothes again, save for the boots, which he hung upon long sticks wedged between the rocks near the fire. A warm breeze blowing over her, Lief watched in fascination as he closed his eyes and concentrated, his clothes drying within minutes.

It was magic she had never seen but thought she could replicate…had she the strength. Her entire shoulder throbbed painfully, both from the wound and the cold, and she knew her own magic would no longer be strong enough to use for such seemingly frivolous ends.

She clenched her jaw to stop her teeth from chattering and scooted closer to the fire. Evening drew close, and the sun had almost fallen below the horizon. With it came the cooler climes of night.

Lief would not show weakness before the Pelenori elf. Instead, she drew her knees up to her chest and wrapped her arms around them, turning towards the paltry warmth of the fire.

"You don't have to sit and freeze, you know," Aedon said gruffly, glancing at her from beneath lowered brows.

A peace offering. It was more generous than her stubborn nature would have allowed. She would have sooner sat there and frozen all night than beg him for help.

And yet…

Lief nodded once, biting her lip and looking away. It was hard to humble herself – impossible to do so enough to actually *ask* for his assistance – but if he offered, she reasoned she ought to accept. When the alternative was to spend a night wet and cold, making her even more tired and weak, she would be a fool to refuse.

"Please," she forced out.

A few minutes later, Lief sighed in relief as the dry textiles caressed her skin, her hair blowing lightly, which was far more pleasant than it dripping cold wetness down her back.

"Thank you," she said quietly.

Aedon inclined his head in acknowledgment. Then he fixed his attention on the creatures prowling on the other side of the river. In the encroaching darkness, they seemed more shadowy and terrifying than before…and they were foul enough in the light of day. Each time the breeze picked up, the scent of death and rotting, fetid meat drifted to them.

They had ceased their snarling and howling, thankfully, now loping back and forth incessantly, trying to find a way across. Lief did not know what kept them from entering the water. Their aversion to it must have been powerful to overshadow the allure of fresh prey.

"They shouldn't be here," Lief murmured. "I've never seen creatures like that before."

"They are imbued with dark magic. At least in part." Aedon looked at her, shooting troubled glances at the beasts, as though he expected they would take to the river at any moment.

"That's not possible," Lief muttered. Dark magic had no place in the living forest, nor had it ever.

"It must be. The taint of dark magic is unmistakable." Aedon's anger had cooled, as had hers, in the face of the far greater threat that taunted them.

"But how?" Lief frowned. It ought to have been impossible, yet the proof lay across the river. She could not help but wonder.

"We are in the heart of your realm, no?"

Lief nodded. She supposed she could admit that much. It was not betraying her people.

"Hmm..." Aedon scratched his chin. "For them to be so strong in the middle of your realm ought to be an impossibility. I can only surmise there is some darker force at work here."

"What do you mean?"

"I'm not sure. I... I have not felt dark magic like this for a long time," Aedon said softly. "Twenty-five years ago, in fact..."

She waited, breathless, for him to say more, but a guttural roar from across the river made them both start. Their attention snapped to the source.

"We cannot hope to defeat them. That much is certain," Aedon admitted, his face grim.

Lief raised an eyebrow. "We must outrun them?"

Aedon grimaced. "Either that or outsmart them..."

They both fell silent, appraising the beasts once more. While they watched, one of the creatures dragged over a log, which was large enough that it would have taken five elves to move, grunting as it dropped it into the shallows with a splash, where it lodged amongst the rocks.

Still crouched, it looked at them, tongue lolling out as it panted from the exertion of its task, and seemed to grin wickedly.

Aedon and Lief watched with rising dread as the beasts dragged boulders and logs towards the river with inexorable determination and a surprising amount of coordination.

"They're making a causeway," Aedon murmured. "Soon, they'll be able to cross."

TWENTY ONE

Another sleepless night followed as Venya lay in bed, her blankets pulled up to her neck, as if they would be any protection, staring at Nyx curled up in the corner of her room until her eyes stung. Yet she did not dare close them for fear that the beast she had seen, or worse, would materialise.

Never trust a grimoire, Nieve had said on their first week as trainee librarians.

I didn't imagine one would look like a puppy, though…

Venya stifled another yawn. She was so tired, so cosy, perhaps a little sleep would not hurt…

She woke with a jolt. It was light. *I fell asleep!* She sat up hurriedly, blinking the sleep from her eyes and casting about for a threat, expecting a beast to be looming over her, ready to attack. Her heart thundered.

Venya frowned. In the corner of the room, on a pile of clothes that had been folded and were now decidedly *not*, the puppy lay sprawled on his back, the golden curls of his belly rising and falling gently with each breath. His head lolled to one side, paws flopping, and Venya could hear the slightest snore.

She blinked a few more times as she stood, but the puppy did not vanish.

"Nyx?" she said softly. No response. "Nyx?"

The puppy grumbled and groaned, cracking open one eye. "What?"

"It's time to get up. I have to return you to the library."

Nyx scrambled to his feet, whining as he looked at her with his giant, brown, watery eyes. "I don't want to go back on that stuffy old shelf! Please don't make me! Can't I stay with you?"

Venya cleared her throat. "Absolutely not. If you were in that vault, it was for a reason. And that reason is way above my pay grade, as are you."

The puppy pouted and sat on his haunches. "I don't want to go back. Do you have any idea how mind-numbingly boring it is to spend decade after decade on those forsaken shelves?"

"You're a grimoire. It's where you belong."

"Says who?" Nyx retorted with a growl.

"Says…" *Who did decide that?* Venya wondered. She shook her head. "It's just the law."

Nyx cocked his head at her. "I think you don't believe your own words, Venya. Do you ever stop to question anything, or do you just do what you're told?"

She drew herself up with indignation. "I don't know what you mean."

"You're clearly too scared to do anything out of the ordinary. I think I will call you *Mouse*."

Venya's cheeks heated, and she gritted her teeth. "You don't know a thing about me, book, and…and…if you're going to resort to names, then I'm going to call you what you are, Mister Book of Beasts – *Bob*!"

Nyx growled and sprang to his feet. With his movement, the shadows seemed to lengthen and the light filtering in through the shutters drew back.

Though quivering inside, Venya did not shrink away, bracing herself.

"My name is Nyx!" the puppy insisted, his voice deepening. His legs lengthened, head and body growing, until a hound as tall as her waist, with shaggy, grey fur, stood before her, baring his sharp teeth.

"And my name is Venya," she insisted, though she yielded a step at the sight.

They glared at each other, until Nyx huffed and abruptly sat, hanging his head, his voice softening. "Please don't make me go back, Venya. I don't belong there."

"I have to…," she said quietly, hating the sound of despondency in his voice. "I'll be in so much trouble if I don't. I'll lose everything I've worked so hard for."

Nyx sighed. "If it's really that important…"

He glanced at her slyly then. Her stomach filled with unease as she reminded herself that an otherworldly creature lived behind those innocent eyes.

"What of the monster?" Nyx asked lightly. "Surely you have factored that into your plans. If you return me, you will have to face it again."

Nausea roiled through Venya at the thought, and she sank down onto her bed once more. *I cannot face that creature again.* She was only a junior librarian, after all. She had no place in that vault, and despite the power of her magic, the creature had outmatched her with ease. Venya had no doubt that if she returned to that vault, she would die.

"I have to find some way to right this," she murmured, more to herself than Nyx. *Nieve and Beatrix trusted me with this responsibility… I cannot let them down.* She balked at telling Nieve. Imagining the stern woman's ire was terrifying enough.

"All right…" Venya sighed, her shoulders slumping. "I guess you can stay whilst I figure out how to fix this mess."

"Wonderful!"

Nyx suddenly burst into flight, the giant, shaggy dog shrinking down into a jewel-coloured bird smaller than her palm, his wings no more than a blur. He flitted around the room, cavorting and wheeling through the air, chirping a jaunty tune.

Venya could not help but smile a little, distracted for a

moment from thoughts of the beast prowling the vault a thousand feet below them, and the impossibility of how to bind it once more.

TWENTY TWO

Over the following week, Venya's life became a strange mockery of the semblance of normal, for a junior librarian, mixed with the presence of Nyx, until she did not wake up each morning feeling as though it had all been a terrible dream.

Each day, she went about her duties in her usual solitude, for all intents and purposes, but with a stowaway companion. Nyx, typically in the form of a small mouse, curled in her pocket each and every day. She had never felt so refreshingly social, and Nyx became a far more interesting conversation partner than any of her peers, save Beatrix. He was a constant source of amusing chatter, yet never when others were around, but also a font of knowledge about the grimoires she shelved.

"How do you know so much?" Venya mused, hand in her pocket, stroking a delicate finger down Nyx's soft fur.

Nyx leaned into her touch – he continually confused her with his snide, acerbic nature that paired so closely with animal instincts and domesticated pet behaviours – and seemed to hum against her finger. "I've been around a while and have spent plenty of time not locked up in a library. Have you ever thought about exploring the big, bad world?"

Venya baulked at the suggestion. "No, I'm quite happy here, thank you very much."

Nyx chuckled. "You're a home bird, all right."

"I know what I like, so why change it?" Venya said, withdrawing her hand from her pocket.

Nyx snorted. "That's not a good excuse. You have no idea what you're missing out on. The joy! The wonder! Ah, the world is a large and colourful tapestry of life and nature. What I wouldn't give to see it again."

Venya's interest piqued at his wistful tone. "Where are you from, Nyx? How did you come to be here? How old are you?"

"I'm as old as I can remember," he mused. Venya frowned at the vague statement. "If you measure by the way you pass time, at least a dozen centuries. Maybe twice that. Or thrice. It's been so long I can't recall. I came…was brought here some centuries ago, and here I have remained since. I much prefer to be out in the world." His voice held a bitter tang.

"Why were you placed here? You… You must be dangerous, or forbidden, to be archived where you were."

Nyx growled from her pocket; the sound far bigger than the form he wore. "Says who?" The mouse leapt out and scrambled up her chest to rest on her shoulder. "Just because someone *says* something is dangerous does not make it so."

"*Are* you dangerous?" Venya halted, twisting her neck awkwardly to look at the tiny mouse quivering indignantly upon her shoulder.

"Well… Yes, but that's not the point! My point is you ought not believe everything you are told, Venya. You really need to learn how to think for yourself, else you'll go your whole life living by someone else's rules and end up never really living at all."

Venya frowned and continued walking, down into the darkness of the vaults.

"I can tell you don't understand." Nyx sighed. "In time, you will. Life is meant to be lived to the fullest, Miss Venya. Don't keep your heart and soul trapped in a vault your entire life."

And with that, he was gone – leaping down to the ground and scampering away.

"Nyx?" she hissed into the darkening gloom. Suddenly alone, she felt strangely vulnerable without him.

A low growl sounded ahead.

Fear rushed through her. Heart hammering, Venya bloomed with magic, calling forth her power in case she needed to defend herself.

Two eyes glowed in the darkness, reflecting her faelight, then Nyx, in his shaggy hound form, padded into the light.

Venya let out a deep huff of relief, calming her frazzled nerves.

They delved this deep into the vaults every day, between the last bell and dinner, so they could steal away, undetected, to Nyx's vault to check it still remained firmly sealed, with the creature safely inside. Venya had already surrendered the librarian's seal back to Beatrix. She could no longer enter the vault – not that she wished to.

Each day, she expected to see the carved door sundered. That distorted form looming from the shadows. Feel those teeth closing around her limbs. Those long, serrated claws slicing into her.

Venya raised her faint faelight to illuminate the door just beyond its sphere. She did not dare brighten it further, scared to see what the light might expose.

"I smell dark magic," growled Nyx.

"What is it?" Venya's reply was a mere whisper.

Nyx padded to stand beside her, his tall body a warm, reassuring mass against her legs. His ears up, alert. His nose forward, straining. "I'm not sure…" He slowly crept forward. Venya moved with him, reassured by his presence, but at the same time looking twice at every pooling shadow on the twisting stairwell.

She could feel the stinging, iron tang of magic. Fresh magic, not the slumbering, faded, bound kind she was accustomed to within the Athenaeum. Magic that had lain for centuries, layered on top of older spells. Worse still, she recognised its signature, for it was laced with familiar terror – hers.

"It's breaking free, isn't it?" she whispered, her hand resting on the scruff of Nyx's neck.

"Yes, it is." His voice was devoid of his usual sardonic mirth.

Venya would have closed her eyes with the despair of it were she not so afraid of the yawning darkness around them. She could not deny her desire to just forget what had happened. But she knew she could not in good faith do so, for as much as Venya had no idea how to contain the beast, she also knew she could not rely on the vault never being opened again.

One way or another, a librarian would enter, and the beast would have a fresh, unsuspecting victim. Unless she intervened, someone would eventually get hurt.

Venya shuddered as another thought entered her mind. Was it possible for the beast to escape? To roam the halls of the Athenaeum, living in the shadows, picking them off one by one? Yet as she leaned closer to the door, it was unmistakable.

Whatever magic the creature, the grimoire, possessed seemed to be slowly eroding through the wards, layer by layer, one by one. She could feel the oldest had already disappeared, probably burning bright and quick, like old paper set alight. The newest held firm, although singed around the edges, and she could feel some patches weakening faster than others.

I'm going to have to fix this, one way or another.

Strengthening the wards would be the first step, at least to prevent it getting out. Venya was not sure, however, what she could do to stop people from going *in*. She sent a silent prayer to the skies far above the mountain to keep her fellow librarians safe. That it was such an infrequently used vault no one would pass there.

Slowly, hesitantly, Venya raised her hands, palms facing the door, but not quite touching it. She did not dare, lest the vault think she was trying to infiltrate it. At the very least, it would smite her. She did not want to find out what kind of injuries, and pain, that would inflict. At the worst, it would suck her into that dark and terrible place once more.

With a deep breath, she called forth her magic and pushed it into the door, imbuing it with fresh energy to shore up the ailing wards, rejuvenating them. She felt them bloom under her fingers, like plants starved of nourishment, then coaxed back to life by sun and water. For a moment, the warmth of the magic banished her fears and worries, and her mouth curled into an unconscious smile.

Beside her, Nyx's nose rose, and he huffed a deep breath onto the door. A different kind of magic, wild and ancient, coated hers, sending a shiver through Venya – anticipation and fear mingled with awe at the strange feel of it.

When they were done, the door hummed with energy, almost glowing.

"Will this hold?" Venya basked in the feel of it, but she was not complacent enough to assume it had worked.

Nyx cocked his head. "As well as any other hope we have

right now."

That's not very encouraging.

Yet it was the best they could do at that moment.

The warmth of magic faded, leaving only cold dread as Venya and Nyx turned away and began the long ascent to the land of the living.

TWENTY THREE

By the time the sun had fully set, the gloom of night settling in, the fell beasts were halfway across the water. It would not be much longer before the gap had closed enough for them to leap across. The fire had dwindled to embers, and though Aedon had set wards of protection upon the island, she could sense his resignation to the fact they would do little to keep the fiends at bay.

Lief stood, unable to sit any longer, even though she could think of nothing else to do except pace relentlessly, consumed by fear and anxiety. Would they have to fight for their lives? She could see no other way. Yet they faced beasts that would not hesitate to rip them to shreds. Lief shivered at that thought. She did not want to end her days feeling teeth cutting into her flesh.

"Aedon?" she whispered and looked over.

She had not heard him stand, but he now stood in the shadow of a tree, watching the fiends, an idle spark of fire at his fingertips.

"I have an idea," she added.

With a last look at the river, seeing little more than giant, hulking shadows with glittering eyes, Aedon retreated to her side. "Yes?" He grabbed a stick and stabbed at the hopeless remnants of the fire, but the embers only glittered and faded. There was no more loose wood upon the islet, and neither of them would harm the trees to obtain more. He muttered a curse.

"Aedon, listen. If we could leave this island without them noticing, perhaps we could escape to the other bank."

He frowned. "Swim across?"

"I don't see any other way."

"Beasts like this are bound to be able to see in the dark. And then they will follow." Aedon gritted his teeth in frustration at the hopelessness of the situation.

"What if we could conceal our movements, our scent?" She crouched and trailed a finger through the cold ash around the fire. *The magical equivalent of rubbing mud all over ourselves to conceal our scent, with a little extra to make us unseen.*

Aedon cocked his head to one side, regarding her with a curious, albeit doubtful, frown. "What do you have in mind?"

"Well, we wood elves are experts in glamours." A smile of pride curled her lips. "What if we conceal our true selves under your wards to prevent them from seeing, hearing, or smelling us, then escape. In our place, we leave glamours of ourselves to distract them."

Aedon's eyebrows rose into the messy waves of his tousled

hair. A moment later, he flashed a grin. "That's incredible. Yes, that could work." Then his smile faded. "Are you sure you can manage that?"

Lief hesitated for a moment. *No.* But the alternative was too terrible to imagine. "Regardless, we have little other choice. If we wait here, they will end us. This way, at least we stand a chance."

Aedon considered for a moment, looking out towards the beasts. He shuddered. Lief followed his gaze. In the darkness, the waters were opaque, unwelcoming and dangerous…and probably even colder. Yet it was a better alternative than staying upon the islet to meet their fate at the claws of the beasts.

"Well, I had resigned myself to end my days in this forest," he said with a rueful smile, "but I'd rather not be ripped apart. Come to the far side of the islet where we are concealed. Then you can start on the glamours, and I'll craft our wards."

Lief followed him, though it unnerved her to lose sight of the beasts, which howled in annoyance that their quarry had left their line of sight, and frantically pulled on her magic. Making glamours always had been as easy as breathing for her, yet with her injury sapping her strength and magic, the flow felt sluggish and weak.

She gritted her teeth against the beginnings of a pounding headache and continued drawing on her magic. The glamours would be rudimentary. She had neither the time nor strength to craft true likenesses, down to the finest hair and smallest stitch upon clothing. But it would look and smell like them. More importantly, it would provide enough distraction for them to make a hasty escape – she hoped.

"The wards are ready," Aedon murmured into her ear.

She had already felt them washing over her like a warm tide.

"I don't mean to rush you, Lief, but they're getting closer...," he said.

She bit back a cry of despair. She was nowhere near finished.

Suddenly, a rush of magic engulfed her, lending her strength. She threw a grateful glance at Aedon, but his attention was fixed behind them. Hungrily drawing in his power, the glamours stepped from nothingness into reality, sitting near the embers of the fire.

A sudden howl of triumph, and bloodlust.

"We're out of time." The whites of Aedon's eyes gleamed in the dark. Without waiting for her to respond, he grasped her hand and tugged her towards the water.

Behind them, howls erupted, then the crash of heavy paws against the rocks, scrambling up. The fell beasts had bridged enough of the water to leap onto the island. A moment later, they heard the soft crunch on gravel.

Expecting to feel their claws slice through her, hot breath on her ear, teeth at her throat at any moment, Lief did not dare look back and leapt into the water with Aedon.

Thankfully, Aedon's wards muffled their splash, as well as her gasp as the cold water punched the breath from her for the second time that day. She braced against it, gritting her teeth, and swam into the centre of the channel, where the water flowed fastest and carried them away from the islet.

Behind her, vicious snarls erupted. The fell beasts had discovered their deception. With relief, she severed the weakening flow of magic, and whatever was left of the glamours far behind her disintegrated. Lief looked back. Dark shadows, little more than blots of obsidian in the shadowy night, roamed upon the island, hunting for them.

A few moments later, the river turned, whisking them out of sight. She revelled in the warm feeling of Aedon's magic spreading through her, banishing some of the chill. Neither of them wanted to be in the water, yet it seemed the safest place to be, especially when dark creatures roamed the forest.

A furious howl chased them down the river.

TWENTY FOUR

Vasili and Icarus did not recognise any of the peaks or valleys below, far outside their usual patrol range, but Vasili did not fear becoming lost. Like a bird, Icarus's internal compass would always guide them home.

Vasili could not still the quivering excitement within him at their rebellion against orders and the possibility of discovering the Order before anybody else. Yet Nikolai had planted the seed of another thought within him, one that gnawed at him.

He had never met his uncles, his father's brothers, one of whom had died in the battle against Valxiron twenty-five years ago, alongside Vasili's grandfather. The other two had escaped from their life-long imprisonment to atone for their crimes during that time. Never had they been seen again.

Vasili knew it was a sore subject for his father, who had let the realm mete out justice, though he had wanted to obliterate them himself. They seemed to have disappeared, but Vasili knew the truth. His penchant for eavesdropping had discovered they were now amongst the Grandmasters of the Order of Valxiron. Those who held highest command. Those who followed Valxiron's teachings most fervently.

"If we find them, I will stand beside you, to whatever end," Icarus promised, having sensed Vasili's unguarded thoughts.

Vasili did not reply, instead focusing once more on the terrain below them. From the gradual incline of the land and the wide spaces between pockets of evergreen forest, Vasili could tell the mountains here held larger valleys that were filled with meadows in the summer.

During Tristan's briefing that morning, when the entire garrison had pored over a sprawling map of the mountain range, Vasili noticed there had been a gap in the patrols along the tangent they now flew, not having quite enough bodies to fly all the space of the mountain ranges.

He had felt the seed of the idea to deviate from their instructions rise in Icarus the moment he shared the memory of the map, the layout of the patrol grid, with the dragon. Why had Tristan and Elyvia missed the sliver of land? The more Vasili thought about it, the more he wondered whether it was an accident or deliberate.

There is nothing there. Elyvia and Tristan would never make such a mistake.

He pushed the thought away, not willing to acknowledge that he might be chasing the whispers and shadows of his imagination.

"Or perhaps there is something," Icarus countered his thought, able to see the wordless depths of his rider's mind. "Tristan's patrols, even with Elyvia and Britte's assistance, are too few to cover every area of the mountains. They will have chosen the places they think the missing patrol *may* be, but they might be wrong. There is just as much chance they could be in the cracks between his search area. We are giving them a better chance of being found." Icarus sounded self-righteous.

A smile tugged at Vasili's lips. "You're incorrigible."

"The very best, I know."

Vasili flicked Icarus's neck in a fond chiding. Icarus turned his head to snap at Vasili with careful precision, not to actually wound him.

They followed the winding valleys southeast, Icarus needing no nudging to readjust his course, using Vasili's knowledge of Tristan's map from that morning.

They flew without rest long into the day. Icarus was strong enough to fly for two days without sleep, if necessary. Vasili had slept in the saddle before and, when the need arose, was well practised at eating and drinking there, as well. He did that day, clutching his waterskin tightly and carefully buckling the saddlebags so none of his precious supplies were lost to the heights.

As they rode along the air currents that funnelled through the valleys, the wind chased them as the mountains closed in on either side with the narrowing of the valley. Caves dotted the mountains here and there. Icarus drifted across the valley, and Vasili could taste what his dragon smelled. The rocks here were cold, dead, and devoid of life, though in the sheltered valleys carpeted with trees and mostly free of the thick snow that blanketed higher ground, they could both feel the tug of life. A brightness in the otherwise bleak landscape.

The caves, however… Vasili examined them as they passed. They looked so similar to those of the outpost, Vasili wondered whether riders or other peoples had once inhabited these, too. Neither his childhood lessons of history nor his knowledge of the riders gave him any answers.

Looking long abandoned, they were smooth with age, the wind having scoured all definition from their entrances, some of which were small enough to pass for human doors, others that were big enough for a dragon to pass. Far above the valley floor, they would have been unreachable on foot, but Vasili had seen more precariously balanced outposts. Bridges could be built to link caves, or tunnels inside the mountains could offer passage.

Ahead, the valley narrowed, cliffs closing in on either side above a rushing course of white water, but beyond, where the cliffs parted and above the partially frozen waterfall that cascaded into the valley bottom, Vasili could see the mountains open, cradling a high valley.

Exploring that would have to wait, though. Darkness fell, and Icarus descended to the valley bottom, gliding lower and lower, circling above a narrow meadow where there was room enough for his wings. He landed running, soon slowing to a halt, before scenting the air. He stood there, poised and still, assessing for any threat. Vasili cast out his awareness as far as he could reach.

Beasts, small and large, roamed the forest around them, but there was no other trace of life, save for the slow, sonorous pulse of the trees around them. Ancient, gnarled evergreens stretched tall above, blocking out the large expanse of sky they had flown through moments before.

It was constricting after the openness. Vasili pushed away the feeling of being stifled and unbuckled his legs from the saddle. He slid down Icarus's side and dropped softly to the ground, crunching the hard crust of snow that remained there from the last snowfall that had partly melted and refrozen.

Side by side, they walked through the meadow to the rushing water at the base of the valley. White and fast, it tumbled down over rocks, creating vortexes that whirled in deep pools carved by the force of its charge down the valley. The faint rumble of the waterfall at the head of the valley became the only noise around them as the forest hushed with their arrival, a giant predator, Icarus, in its midst.

Icarus crouched low over the bank, dropping his head to the water below. Vasili slid down the bank and opened the waterskin to refill it from the glacial water. He took a sip – refreshing, yet so cold, it made his teeth ache – before sealing it once more and clambering back up so he could have a clear view of their surroundings while he waited for Icarus to finish. That had been one of Tristan's early lessons. The forest grew silent in the presence of predators. Yet that did not mean they were the *only* ones out there. Vasili scanned their surroundings carefully as he silently retraced his steps through the meadow.

It remained quiet and deserted as Icarus finished his long drink and crunched up the hill to stand next to Vasili. The sky, filled with grey clouds that threatened snow, had already started to darken for dusk.

"I don't want to rest here," said Icarus, voicing Vasili's thoughts.

"The caves will be perfect, yes?"

In answer, the dragon lowered his belly to the ground. Vasili leapt into the saddle, slipping his legs through the loops but not bothering to tighten them for such a short journey. Moments later, they were airborne and rising quickly to the deserted, ancient caves above. Icarus chose one that could easily fit his bulk. Vasili was pleased to find it wormed its way back into the rock face to a comfortable nook, worn smooth by the passage of those who had come before, where both of them could sleep, out of sight and the elements.

Vasili dismounted, unsaddling Icarus to give him some small relief after a long day of flying. In the narrow confines, the dragon stretched, groaning in relief. He flexed the long, supple line of his spine. "I need to hunt. I'll fly the way we came, back to the larger meadows. I'll be able to find something there. Want anything?"

Vasili wrinkled his nose. He might no longer think whatever game the mountains could give him as distasteful, but he still had boundaries. A half-eaten dragon kill was drawing the line. "I'll make do, thanks." Though he wondered if the hard breads and dried meats and fruits he carried with them for his own sustenance were any more appealing than Icarus's offerings.

Icarus rolled his shoulders – his equivalent of a shrug, one of the few elven-like behaviours he had learned – and turned to leave, his scales scraping the stone walls with a hiss. "Your loss."

"Fair winds, my friend. Don't stray too far…"

Icarus huffed. "Don't start worrying like an old woman, elf. It doesn't become you."

Vasili slapped him on the rump and laughed, retreating a few steps as Icarus launched himself into the darkening skies. The elf lingered to watch him go, his emerald scales dull and dark in the fading light. As he watched, the first flakes of snow fell from the clouds. Fat, heavy flakes that quickly obscured Icarus flying into the distance.

As the snowstorm rolled in, soon all Vasili could see was white that quickly thickened to grey, then darkened to black as night fell and the storm closed in.

He retreated into the cave. Knowing the storm, as well as the twist in the cave, would offer him cover, Vasili lit a faelight that blazed with the warmth of a fire. It hovered before him, and he enjoyed the feeling as he pulled off his thick, leather gloves and held his cold, aching hands out to the magical warmth, feeling the stiffness melt away in moments.

It was a long evening as he sat hunched on the ground with his hands around his knees and cloak wrapped around his shoulders, the faelight slowly bobbing before him. His saddlebags lay an arm's length away. Vasili had already raided them for a meagre meal, fishing out the battered tin cup last of all. He used the faelight to heat water within, which he then steeped with dried fruits and spices for a warming brew that made him feel slightly less cold and hollow.

When the cold and the stiffness of the day had worn off, his belly at least half-full with the small meal, Vasili stood, stretching his arms overhead, his fingertips brushing the sloping ceiling of the cave above him.

He moved through a training regimen, first at half speed, then at full speed, from one form to another, stretching out every muscle in his body as he moved with a grace belying his usual rigidity. It was more to pass the time than hone his body, but he found it centred him in a way few other things could.

As he finished with a final stretch up, he wandered to the cave mouth. It was pitch black outside. The precipitous drop below was invisible in the night. Snow had piled in the cave mouth as he had sheltered, and there was no sign of Icarus. He could faintly feel the dragon at the periphery of his awareness. Icarus was focused as he hunted, not open to casual chatter. Vasili withdrew the tendril of awareness to leave his friend to it, hoping the dragon returned soon – for warmth, safety, and conversation.

He was about to turn back to the solitude and relative cosiness of the now warmed cave when he heard the tell-tale thud outside. It took a moment longer than usual to register that the sound was dragon wings, for Icarus was far beyond the reach of his hearing. But if he had any doubts, they vanished with the powerful rumble that shook the very stone.

Deep. Guttural. Old.

Vasili froze.

Wingbeats thudded closer, then faded, as did the echoes of the rumble.

He knew the call of every dragon in the Dragon's Nest. It was not a single one of them.

"*Icarus*!" Vasili pulled on the bond between them as nervous energy flooded through him. Possibilities crowded his mind, his thoughts tumbling. *Is it the missing patrol? A wild dragon?* And the darkest possibility. He was one of the few who knew the truth of the Order of Valxiron's forces. *Is it one of the Order's dragons?*

TWENTY FIVE

Their daring escape had awoken something within Aedon, a fire long extinguished. The ember of it only grew, like he had been starved of air and drew breath once more. Now that it had reignited, he did not want to let it go.

He wanted to live again. To see more than the rough walls of a prison for the rest of his days. To no longer be at the mercy of the woodland Queen. To be any shred of the elf he had once been.

Even if he did not deserve it, Aedon *wanted* it again.

And as he held Lief's hand while they plunged down the river, their eyes met and they shared a giddy smile, soaring with relief and the rush of freedom at their daring escape. He could not remember the last time he had felt anything other than crushing emptiness and grief.

The river slowed as it flowed over a ford, and their feet dragged on the pebbled riverbed. They clambered out of the shallow depths – on the far side, hoping the creatures would not pursue them further – and used the light of the moon to guide them along the uneven ground.

It was a fraught few minutes as Aedon used what magic he could spare to dry them off, though he could not afford the time to air their boots, so each step they took squelched unpleasantly. Eventually, they stumbled upon a game trail through the woods and followed it a ways before diverting to find somewhere to shelter for the night, both of them utterly exhausted.

Still warded, Aedon risked a small faelight that bobbed ahead of them, like an eerie will-o'-wisp in the darkness. "Where are we?" he whispered, not quite trusting that his wards would shield them from the dark denizens of the forest.

"I don't know," Lief admitted.

He groaned.

"It's all right. Once the sun rises, I will be able to determine our location and the direction we ought to go to get back on track."

Aedon nodded. He was drained, and he could not imagine how much worse she felt with her wound and the spreading blight.

What else might hunt us? Aedon wanted to ask, yet did not want to voice it. Not when they were so vulnerable.

Lief's eyes roved over the dark forest. "There are circles of trees where we can shelter. They are enchanted bowers by the grace of our Queen, scattered across the kingdom. We can find them when we need to, or a safe space to rest, if one is not close by. They… They sing to us. I can sense one not too far from us," she added after a pause.

Aedon frowned. He had no idea what she spoke of, but Lief moved with greater purpose, no matter that she was so tired and weak. He followed her without question. The trees here were silent, but the creatures in the canopy above and the tangle of bushes around them were not. He strained his sight and hearing, but he could not discern anything approaching. If nothing else, the nocturnal life reassured him. If the beasts of the forest made their presence known, it meant nothing prowled nearby.

A cluster of small trees stood ahead, creating a clearing in the forest that looked out of place. As they stepped into it, pushing aside branches, Aedon felt the magic brush over him. Light and careful, it was comforting, welcoming. The noise of the forest outside dropped away, as though muffled, and at the far end of the clearing was a small, bubbling spring, the water trailing outside the safety of the bower.

Lief's sigh of relief carried across the clearing. She pulled off her boots and tipped them upside down. Water splashed out. Aedon followed suit. His toes curled gratefully into the thick, springy, mossy carpet beneath their feet.

"We're definitely safe here?" He looked around. The moon hung overhead, illuminating the clearing. The trees and bushes encircling them hid the forest beyond. But Aedon could not shake the unnerving feeling of being watched.

"Definitely," Lief replied without hesitation. "These *boma* are sustained by the magic of the forest and my Queen."

"All right. I'll take the first watch." His stinging eyes were heavy, but he did not trust the forest, or Lief's word, enough to sleep.

She shrugged. "As you wish. Wake me when you tire."

With a sinking feeling, Aedon realised he had left his dagger on the small islet. He groaned, cursing himself silently. Despite his magic being a far greater weapon, he always felt that bit safer with steel upon him.

"What's wrong?"

"I lost my dagger," Aedon sighed.

"We are safe here."

At his silence, eyes darting around, Lief sighed, too. After a long moment of hesitation, she pulled out her own dagger and held it out to him, hilt first. "Here."

Aedon took it from her automatically, eyes wide. He had not expected that. Not from the elf who had refused to arm him before and called him a thief and a criminal.

She nodded at him in silent understanding of the trust she placed in him to protect her, to not betray her. The action spoke more to him than any words she could have said. It was an apology. A peace offering. And for the first time, he was inclined to take it.

"Thank you, Lief."

"Good night, Aedon," she said and retreated to the far side of the clearing.

Aedon watched as she selected a particularly lush patch of

moss beneath a weeping willow, which seemed entirely out of place given the huge, leafy trees that seemed prevalent in that part of the forest, and laid down. Within minutes, Lief was still, her chest rising and falling steadily with the deep breaths of slumber.

Aedon settled across the clearing from her, his back against a tree. He set the dagger down beside him and glanced at Lief. *She trusts the forest enough to sleep without fear. Interesting.* He had no such faith.

Hours later, when his eyes refused to stay open any longer, he woke her, then curled up in the soft moss to sleep, grateful for the warm, still, summer night.

TWENTY SIX

When Aedon awoke, the sun was high and Lief stirred across the clearing. Anger flashed through him that she had fallen asleep, but he suppressed it, albeit with difficulty.

I must learn to trust her, too, he reminded himself.

After the previous day's nightmare, one thing was clear. To have any chance of succeeding, they had to trust each other. If she said they were safe in the circle of trees, he had to believe her. And nothing had disturbed them in the woodland glade overnight. Looking around the clearing, the balmy warmth of the sun bathing his face, the gentle babbling sound of the spring, he could not help but feel a sense of peace wash over him that was entirely at odds with the terror and despair they had felt the previous day.

Lief stretched with a giant yawn and sat up, rubbing the sleep from her eyes. "Good morning."

"Good morning." He mirrored the small smile she gave him, unable to be anything but grateful for the fact they had survived.

"Thank you," Lief said quietly.

He cocked his head. "What for?"

"For helping me. I… I wouldn't have been able to survive that without your help."

Aedon could see what it cost her to admit that…and the fact she saw it as a weakness. He wondered why she was so reluctant to lean on anyone else. He inclined his head. "You're welcome. But I owe you my thanks, too. Neither of us would probably be here now without your glamours."

Lief laughed, a humourless chuckle. "Look at us cooperating."

He smiled. "Who'd have thought it." He had forgotten what camaraderie felt like. That thought was enough to sour the current of contentment filling him, smile fading.

"What's wrong?"

His lips twisted. "Nothing. I just… I remembered something I have not thought of in a while."

"Oh? Want to talk about it?"

He hesitated. He had carried the memories and the burden for a quarter of a century. It still seemed too raw, too painful to share with a stranger, no matter what the two of them had already endured together.

"You don't have to tell me if you don't want."

From the wrinkle in her brow, he could not tell if she was frustrated or disappointed.

Aedon shifted his weight on the ground, forcing out a smile. "I wouldn't want to bore you."

"Nonsense. How about this. I suggest we rest and recover today, then strike out tomorrow at dawn. We're safe here, and I think lying low for the remainder of the day is sensible. There's little chance we will find anywhere this safe in the few hours we have before evening. These shelters are often a day's walk apart. I don't want to be out in the woods in the dark if there are more of those beasts roaming around." Lief shivered.

Aedon nodded. "All right." When his stomach rumbled, he gave her a genuine smile. "But I think we ought to find something to eat first. Then we can talk."

"It's a deal."

Lief directed Aedon's magic to the small mound at the side of the spring. Easier than either of them digging out the earth with their hands.

"It really would be easier if you just told me what I was doing, you know."

Lief smirked with a hint of mischief. "Where's the fun in that?"

She had already had him lift off the flat stone that marked its location and set it carefully to one side. She then washed it off with water from the spring and started butchering the small *tiral*, a mammal the size of a large rat, which was a delicacy in Tir-na-Alathea.

"There you go," she said, pointing to the hole, where a basin of carefully arranged stones sat under the final layer of soil.

He furrowed his brows, still not understanding. "Okay…"

"This is a lesson in Tir-na-Alathean cooking, Aedon of Pelenor. You have never tasted anything so fine as an earth-baked *tiral*."

Aedon wrinkled his nose.

Lief laughed. "There's no need to be rude. I admit, this won't be half as nice as from the Queen's own table…after all, we're making do with what we have…but I'm *starving*. I reckon that'll make up for the rudimentary situation we currently find ourselves in. Although I've not been able to find half the herbs I need to make this properly…"

Indeed, Lief was making do with hardly anything – a few acorns crushed into paste and mixed with a scattering of whatever mushrooms and herbs she had been able to find around the glade. She had not strayed too far, just in case, even though the open, sun-dappled woods were the picture of innocence and light.

"What now?" Aedon asked.

"Heat the stones to as hot as you can manage."

"Ah." Understanding dawned.

Heat, an uncomfortable blast in the warmth of the day, roiled over them both as Aedon directed his fire magic upon the stones. The pale stones soon glowed, like cherries waiting to be picked.

"Okay. Now, carefully cover those with a layer of earth as thick as two fingers," Lief instructed.

When Aedon had finished and smoothed out the sandy earth using a fallen branch and its leaves as a makeshift brush, she nodded and rolled the meat around the nut paste and herb mixture, wrapped it in several layers of leaves, then placed it in the middle of the rocks.

"All right. Cover it up. A palm's depth, please."

Once done, they sat in companionable silence on either side of the earthen oven. Lief tried to appear casual, but her arm ached and stung, and the creeping, niggling pain had started spreading down her back. She glanced down at her arm…and wished she had not.

She swallowed. One snaking vein wound its way towards her elbow, and she knew more would soon follow. Bending her neck to glance at her shoulder, she saw it covered in them, and the bite at her neck was too painful to even consider touching. It pulsed, hot and angry, a burning, constant pain. It exhausted her, so she was glad of their extra rest that day.

"How far are we from the *aleilah*, Lief?"

Aedon's voice pulled her from her thoughts, but it was muffled, as though he spoke through something. Dread filled her.

The blight is affecting my senses.

"We ought to reach it tomorrow, or perhaps the day after, if we have strayed farther than I thought." Lief rubbed a hand across her forehead, though it did little to banish the dull ache.

Maybe some food will help. Yet her own reassurance rang hollow in her mind.

"Are you all right?" Concern laced his voice.

"Y–" Her natural aversion to ask for help almost caught her again. "No," she admitted, hating the simple word for its weakness.

"Is there anything I can do?"

"No." She sighed. "I just hope you're right and this weed will cure the blight." *Before it's too late.*

"Lief, forgive me if this is too personal, but…" He furrowed his brows. "Why are you so averse to accepting help?"

She raised an eyebrow, caught off guard. "I…" He waited, not apologising for his frankness. She swallowed and looked away. It was painful, even now, as much as she hated to admit it. "I didn't always used to be this way," she said softly. "Before, I was…*involved* with somebody. I thought he would be my mate and we would share our lives. Unfortunately, he was not as honourable and faithful as I. It made me realise that I had been stupidly naïve, and I promised myself I would never make such a mistake again as to rely on anyone else." She still could not decide whether she hated Finarvon or herself more for it.

"I'm sorry, Lief." Aedon's voice was low, and the pity… Skies above, she despised it.

"Don't be." Her reply came out more harshly than she intended. She scowled, more at herself than Aedon. "I've learned my lesson."

"Not everyone is like that. I promise you. I understand it, though. It's a natural response to the grief and pain. I've been there, too, though for different reasons."

"You?" She could hardly believe it. He seemed so taciturn, but as the cracks of wit and humour had begun to show through, perhaps she could understand it after all. Perhaps he was running from his own pain, too.

"Yes." He smiled wryly at her disbelief. "Before I entered your realm, I led quite a life."

"Will you tell me about it?"

Lief was definitely curious. She knew so little of him, and what she thought she knew, she was no longer certain of after their few conversations. Her attention lingered on the shaggy hair that rested upon his collar, the haggard face that seemed so at odds with the twinkle she had begun to see at times in his eyes.

Yet he was no pauper. Well-spoken, accent soft and lilting, and the way he carried himself, even after twenty-five years in captivity, spoke volumes about the status he had once held. He was so different from Finarvon's swaggering arrogance that she could not help but be drawn to him.

Aedon cocked his head, regarding her with narrowed eyes that brimmed with curiosity. "I think I am interested in your tale, as well, Lief na Arboreali. How about a deal?"

"Oh?"

"After we serve up this delicious smelling meal, how about a question for a question?"

Lief smiled wryly. He was more sly than she gave him credit for. They were both tight-lipped when it came to revealing too much of themselves. But it was enough of a draw for her. "Deal."

She prepared and served the hot, dripping, flavoursome meat upon the flat slab that had concealed the cooking pit, sharing from the one platter and picking morsels off the hot carcass in turn. As they ate, Aedon began.

"Before I came to your lands, my reputation preceded me." Aedon's lips quirked with mirth…and a hint of pride, Lief suspected. He spread his hands out with a flamboyant flourish. "Lief na Alathea, I am Aedon Lindhir Riel, the legendary Thief of Pelenor."

Lief could not contain her snort of mirth. She quickly covered her mouth as hot juices from the meat dribbled down her chin. "*Legendary?*"

"Oh yes, young miss." Aedon winked, his eyes twinkling. "Do you know, of all the criminals on the continent, I had the highest bounty on my head?"

Lief raised an eyebrow. "A fact you're very proud of, aren't you?" she said accusingly.

"Of course! Do you know how much work that takes?"

She shook her head in disbelief. "Surely you cannot be proud of being a criminal."

Aedon rolled his eyes. "Have you learned nothing of me, Lief na Arboreali? The term *criminal* is somewhat debatable."

"The *law* is not debatable."

"Oh sure, sure. But the morals of those who make it?" He raised an eyebrow and paused. Lief scowled. "Questionable, to say the least. I was many things, but I was not a bad elf. Everything I did – *we* did was for the benefit of others. Namely those who could not defend themselves. We did everything, from liberating stolen goods and gold from greedy lords to return to the rightful owners, to stealing *aleilah* from your Queen to cure the ills of innocents."

Doubt curled within Lief. Damn the elf. He was far more complicated than she had ever given him credit for. Indeed, those did not sound like crimes of a heinous nature, no matter that they were forbidden in the laws of the land. Yet if his story were true… That would mean he had been imprisoned for a quarter of a century all for wanting to cure a sickness.

The treacherous thought caressed her. *That is unjust.*

Lief banished it just as quickly. To think ill of the Queen's judgment was to think ill of the very Queen Herself. Queen Solanaceae would not have acted without just cause…

Aedon could well be lying to her. He would have to be an accomplished liar, she reasoned, yet Lief could not banish the niggling doubt. The elf sitting before her had been nothing but honourable since the first moment they had met, even going so far, despite the risk to himself, as to warn her of the danger of returning to Lune.

"They were the best of adventures, and I treasure all those memories," Aedon said quietly, his gaze falling to the ground.

"You said that, when you came here, your old life was over," Lief said, equally softly, the food now lying forgotten between them upon the sun-warmed stone, "and that either way, you had to start afresh. What happened?"

"The world changed. Do you know what happened twenty-five years ago? The rising of the Dark One of Altarea?"

"Of course. Everyone knows what happened."

"To some degree," Aedon corrected her. "I was in the thick of it, right from the start. The *aleilah* was just the beginning of that saga." He paused and glanced up at her with a rueful smile, those green eyes of his dark and subdued. "Perhaps one day, once we have the luxury of time, I will tell you the full epic in detail, as it deserves. For now, I suppose the brief version will have to suffice."

Lief waited as Aedon cleared his throat and stretched out his legs before him, facing her across the hot stone.

"On my way back into Pelenor from stealing the Queen's *aleilah*, I bumped – quite literally, and in the same manner we met, which is rather ironic, I suppose – into one Harper of Caledan."

Lief gasped. "*The* Harper of Caledan? From the stories?"

Aedon smiled. "There is only one Harper." His voice held a

fond warmth to it, and Lief wondered on that as a small, stray breeze lifted the wavy locks of hair from his forehead.

"That means… You're *the* Aedon from the tales – from the *Chronicles of Pelenor*?" She looked at him with fresh vision, unable to associate the elf before her with one of the heroes of the epic saga. He had given her his full name when they had met, and yet, in the midst of their terror-filled flight, she had never even dreamed to associate the shaggy haired convict with the legendary warrior of old.

He inclined his head. "And thereafter unfolded everything you probably already know in some small detail.

"Saradon, the accursed half-elf, arose from his banishment and quickly seized control of Pelenor. Unbeknownst to us all, the true darkness inside him was not his own, but that of Valxiron, the Dark One of Altarea.

"There were many battles and huge loss of life. I wonder if Pelenor is recovered even now, a quarter of a century later." Any hint of mirth was gone, replaced by the sober reality of his memories.

"In the end, Pelenor mustered the nomad warriors of the Indis tribes, along with the dwarves of Valtivar. The last wave of the alliance was your own people and the living trees of Tir-na-Alathea. Truth be told, your people turned the tide. The cost was great, but our alliance bought Harper of Caledan time to strike the fateful blow. Valxiron was cast down. You probably already know that much, yes?"

Lief nodded, riveted.

"Then perhaps you will understand why the life I had led was over. My companions were scattered to the four winds in life and death, and we could not go on as we had. Pelenor needed to rebuild, but I had no place in it. Instead, I chose to fulfil the oath I had given to Solanaceae. That when all was said and done, I would pay for my crimes."

Aedon chewed on his bottom lip. "If I am being honest, the pain of loss was so great at that point that perhaps I hoped your Queen would end me, put me out of my misery. Alas, She had other ideas. Perhaps She knew keeping me alive would greaten my suffering."

Lief swallowed at the raw grief he held back. She could hear it in the tightness of his voice, see it in the way he clenched his jaw, as if to stop the emotion from spilling forth. "I would love to hear more another time, if possible."

She shook her head. "I must confess, I do not understand who this Dark One truly is. Could anyone be so powerful?" It sounded as though even her own Queen's power was far eclipsed by him, and she had never thought it possible. In Tir-na-Alathea, Queen Solanaceae was all-powerful and all-enduring.

"Yes. There are far greater powers out there than any of us little insects realise." Aedon's attention had strayed to a tiny beetle scuttling over the moss beside him.

He forced his lips into a tight smile and lifted his attention to her once more. "But that shall have to wait until another time. You have asked *two* questions now, so by the rules of our game, it's my turn."

Lief sighed, but nodded. If he asked them quickly, perhaps she could get back to his tale. Though now, she realised, she was entirely at his mercy; she had promised to answer *anything* he asked. Her stomach swooped.

"All right then, Lief na Arboreali…" Aedon chewed his lip as he contemplated. "Can you… Will you teach me how to make a glamour?" He cocked his head and raised an eyebrow, his eyes twinkling with a hint of spirit that tried to burn brighter with each passing hour, despite their dark predicament.

Lief had not known quite what question to expect, but relief washed over her that he had not pried into her personal affairs. "Of course," she said swiftly. Wood elves were proficient in glamours, and Lief prided herself on being one of the finest in Lune. She gestured around the clearing. "Why don't you choose an object?"

Aedon pushed to his feet, searching until he found a small flower tucked into a tangle of vines. Its lavender trumpet was delicately veined with dark violet, the fringes of the thin, crumpling petals fading to white. The flower pulsed open and closed, revealing the amber-coloured heart within.

"This."

He plucked it and returned, handing it to her. Their fingers brushed as she took it gingerly, and she jerked away at the spark of contact. He sat opposite her, their crossed legs bumping.

Lief pushed through the barrier to her magic, momentarily alarmed by the presence of any resistance. It felt like walking through a viscous liquid. She swiped the worry aside, for she did not have the heart to address it just then.

"May I?" She placed the flower on Aedon's knee and reached across the stone, nodding at his hands. "It's easier to feel it than explain it."

He rested his open palms atop his knees, and Lief slipped her slender hands into his. Aedon closed his fingers around hers, and she hesitated for the barest moment, her breath hitching. It had been so long since she had permitted anyone to touch her that even this felt too intimate.

Lief fought the urge to pull away, that fierce desire to protect herself, and swallowed, trying not to think about how warm, smooth, and comforting his hands felt. Finarvon's hands had once felt the same. The pool of hurt opened once more.

Aedon closed his eyes, and she did the same, grateful for the absence of his scrutiny. At the periphery of her senses, she could feel the powerful pool of magic pulsing from him. It feathered at the edges of hers, teasing and withdrawing, as their minds tentatively opened to each other.

Lief tightly wrapped up her fear and pain at that, for the action was far more intimate than holding hands. It had been a year since she had opened her soul to someone else. Since *him.*

"*Are you okay?*" Aedon asked into her mind, opening his eyes once more.

"*Fine,*" she ground out, though she regretted the harshness of her tone. Her past was not Aedon's fault.

Aedon watched and felt as she crafted the glamour of the flower, teasing and coaxing the magic to form the matrix of the petals, the anther, the stamen. She layered the delicate veins into the petals, nudging and shaping them just so, leeching the colour from their tips so they were edged with white, leaving the rest a pale lavender. It only took mere minutes.

Beside the original flower upon Aedon's knee lay another bloom, indistinguishable from it. As they watched, both flowers pulsed open and closed in time with each other.

"It is exquisite," Aedon breathed, extracting his hands from hers to gently cup the flowers. He looked between the two. "I cannot tell which is the original."

Lief smiled with pride.

"May I try?" He glanced up at her from under those dark brows, his eyes alight with curiosity.

"Of course. Best of luck, elf." Lief grinned, which he returned, competition sparking between them.

Aedon settled, examining the flower closely before he cupped it in his palm and closed his eyes.

Lief watched as his brow crinkled, his mouth twisting in

concentration, his eyes scrunched shut. She examined him, realising he was finally getting some colour back to his skin. After years of captivity, a few days in the sun had brought a tinge of healthy warmth to him, which made his green eyes twinkle even more. He could have almost been handsome, if not for the haunting grief that dogged him.

Not wanting him to catch her staring, Lief dropped her eyes to his palms. Ever so slowly, matter coalesced in his other palm, swirling together. Lief caught the pale purple colour of the petal.

Too pale.

As she examined his creation, purple veins spidered up the petals. *Too thick and clumsy.*

"Not bad for a first attempt," she said generously.

He opened his eyes to look, wincing.

She held up the original flower, twirling it. "You really have to tune into the finest details. Only once you have captured every little grain of what you are trying to glamour, understand it intimately, can you truly recreate it."

"You managed to recreate me on the islet," Aedon said, cocking his head. A playful smile danced across his lips. "Do you know me *intimately*?"

She sucked in a breath. "No! I didn't mea–" When he laughed at her easy rise, she growled and thumped him on the arm. "Those were crude likenesses. Thank goodness it was dark. All I had to do was make sure they appeared a similar size and shape, smelled like us, and vaguely resembled us. With such little time, I wouldn't have been able to create a glamour the likes of this for you." She gestured to the intricate flower she had created.

"If you want to get to know me better, you only have to ask." Aedon winked at her.

Lief rolled her eyes and scrunched up her face in disgust.

He laughed again. "Gee, thanks!"

"You're not my type," she said with venomous sweetness, pushing away all thoughts of those warm hands enveloping hers, those green eyes twinkling, those lips quirking in that infectious smile…

"Luckily for me," he replied with equal relish, grinning at her.

Lief could not help but choke out a laugh. She gestured at the remnants of their meal. "Come on. We cannot let fresh *tiral* go to waste."

They picked over the rest of their meal until it was just bones, washing it down with refreshing, sweet spring water, then sat in companionable silence.

"I think this is what I first imagined the living forest would be like," mused Aedon.

"What do you mean?"

"Magical, I suppose. Benevolently enchanting. More…" He gestured around at the green leaves gently rustling in the stray breeze, the setting sun in the rich, clear sky, the hum of life around them, "*this*, and less living trees that can rip you limb from limb."

Lief snorted. "If you're a wood elf, the forest is always the former." She raised an eyebrow. "The forest protects its own. If you belong here, there is little in the forest that would do you harm, thanks to the Queen's own magic."

"Little except those hideous creatures that chased us." Aedon grimaced.

"Yes, I suppose so." *They were definitely an unsettling anomaly.*

Lief shifted, trying to adjust her stiff body. She winced as pain lanced through her, a wave of dizziness making her reel.

Aedon was at her side in a moment, steadying her with his hands upon her arms. "Are you all right?"

"Fine," Lief forced out, along with a smile that Aedon did not look the least bit convinced by. "It's fine, Aedon. Trust me."

She saw a flicker of something in his eyes, before it was gone. "Hmm… You must tell me if you take a turn for the worse. Can't have you collapsing on me. I'd be lost in here forever, not to mention I'd miss your unique charm."

Lief chuckled. "Charm is a very polite way to put it."

Aedon's eyes twinkled. "I thought I had better be kind, seeing as I'm at your mercy, Lief na Arboreali."

"If I were at my full strength, you would be," she said with mock sternness. He drew away, finally convinced that she would not collapse.

"I have no doubt," he said seriously, but she could not tell if he were teasing.

"Come on," he said more lightly. "We ought to get what rest we can before we set off tomorrow. The sooner we find the *aleilah*, the sooner you will be at your best again and can keep me in line."

She could not help but smile at his infectious charisma, or contain her genuine happiness that was caused by more than a full stomach. Despite the fear and uncertainty that had chased them so relentlessly, there was a bubble of peace in that clearing that she did not want to burst.

For the first time since they had met on that ghastly night, thrust together and chased by nightmares, Lief felt as though they could do it all – find the *aleilah*, stem the blight within her, and alert the Queen.

"I agree. We can travel fast and light–"

"A small perk of losing what little we had." Aedon raised his eyes skyward and shook his head.

"Quite. But we do have two things going for us – my knowledge and your magic."

Aedon grinned, that tentative fire within him seeming to burn brighter at the challenge of what lay ahead.

No matter that they faced darkness and the unknown. For the first time in a while, Lief felt the call to adventure, with someone beside her she could possibly trust.

TWENTY SEVEN

Lief's low moan awoke Aedon. He froze against the mossy ground, senses searching for any threat. However, the clearing was still, empty, and safe. The only movement was from Lief. He sat up.

She had fallen asleep nestled into the cushion of moss, curled upon herself. Now her limbs were spread as she thrashed. Once more, her low moan rang out.

Aedon rose and crossed to her upon swift, silent feet. He dropped to his knees beside her. She shook violently, shivers wracking her body, and her teeth chattered, as though she were freezing cold.

"Lief?" he called softly. "Lief? You need to wake up."

She mumbled, her response so incoherent he could not be sure it was directed at him.

He placed a hand upon her bare shoulder, where her sleeveless tunic gave way to olive flesh, and gasped. She was freezing.

"Lief?" He shook her gently, then more insistently, but she did not awake ready to fight, as he would have expected. Instead, her eyes slowly opened a crack, glazed and unfocused.

"Lief, can you hear me?" Aedon's palms cupped her cheeks as he bent close, nose wrinkling. She smelled…*wrong.* The taint of dark magic, the tang of metal and darkness, clung to her skin. He swore softly.

"So…c-c-cold…," Lief mumbled.

"I'm going to help," Aedon said, though he didn't know if he were reassuring himself or her. He called forth his magic and wrapped her in warmth, but as he sent searching tendrils through her, he could feel the core of dark magic within repelling him, resisting. Only physical warmth might work. Yet he could light no fire and had no cloak.

Aedon swallowed. "Lief? I need to warm you, but my magic won't work. I'm going to try and share my warmth with you, all right?"

She did not reply, but her eyelids fluttered and her hand grasped his tunic briefly before dropping to the ground.

Aedon swore under his breath – at her state, at his predicament, at the whole situation – before he lay on the moss next to her and tucked her against him. He wrapped his arms around her and pulled her close, hoping it would help.

She would be furious if she realised how I am holding her. Aedon had no doubt about that. Yet in her current state, he could only hope that come morning, she would be herself enough to *be* mad with the liberty he took.

Aedon froze as she nestled her head under his chin, winding her tremoring fingers in the fabric of his tunic.

"Aedon…"

Her whisper was barely audible. Had he imagined it?

He swallowed and rested his head upon hers, wrapping his arms around her and hoping it helped.

He lay long into the night, awake and unmoving, as the stars watched from above. Eventually, her shivers and her fitful tossing subsided, and Aedon drifted off, holding Lief close.

Lief woke, taking a long moment to gather her senses. She blinked blearily in the rising dawn, trying to shake the strange feeling of being wrapped in another's arms. She glanced around. Aedon was nowhere to be seen.

Lief groaned and propped herself up on an arm. It had been a horrible and strange night, filled with nightmares at odds with the warmth, the safety she had felt as her chills subsided. Had she imagined that Aedon had held her close, a burning sun against the freezing dark? Was it nothing more than a feverish nightmare?

What happened?

Hearing soft footsteps nearby, she looked over. Aedon strode into the clearing with pockets full of berries and plants.

"You're awake," he said, his shoulders sagging as he smiled.

Was that relief?

Lief swallowed, her mouth dry. "Morning."

"How are you feeling?" Aedon deposited his foraged finds beside the spring and crossed to her, dropping down upon a knee before her. He held out the waterskin, and she took a grateful swig.

"Like a bear trampled me," she groaned. Her head felt thick and fuzzy, a headache threatening. Her arm was stiff and tingled with numbness as the black, spidering veins spread past her elbow, the wound itself an oozing, burning, throbbing mess.

Aedon's lips quirked. "I can promise you, no bear did such a thing last night." His smile faded. "But you were rather unwell." And now his eyes were deep pools of pine green, filled with concern for her.

Lief shoved past the tremor within her at that, at his proximity, his care.

"You were freezing cold. I tried to wake you, to no avail. Do you remember anything?"

"Nothing more than snatches and flashes of dreams mixed with reality and…" Lief shivered, "nightmares." She closed her eyes, trying to shake off the memory of the dark beasts that prowled her dreamscape, then opened them again on the sun-dappled clearing. Aedon watched her, worry shadowing his face.

"I'm fine, Aedon."

He nodded, not looking at all convinced. "I… I had to keep

you warm somehow," he said tentatively. "My magic didn't seem to work. The darkness in you repelled it."

Lief's stomach fluttered with unease, and something else that passed too fleetingly to name. *It was not a dream.*

"I'm sorry. It was forward of me, but I did not see any other way."

Lief nodded jerkily, refusing to meet his gaze, trying to suppress the coil of unease in her stomach. She had worked so hard to erect the walls around her heart, had been so fastidious at not allowing anyone to come close enough to breach them, yet Aedon… He had slipped right through her defences. She missed being held, though she had tried to deny it. Somehow, in the dark of nightmares, Aedon had provided her comfort, and it had felt *right,* soothing her. The thought scared her. Never would she open her heart to that hurt again. Never.

She slowly pushed to her feet. "We need to move on."

"I foraged." Aedon gestured to the berries. "Not sure if any of them are edible, but I figured you might know."

Lief nodded and staggered slowly across the clearing, wincing at the aches that tore through her muscles. *We were right to divert for the aleilah, if he thinks it can help.* Lief felt the blight spreading through her. *I would never have made it to Solanaceae without him, but unless we find this miracle cure, it shall all be for nought.*

She busied herself sorting out the edible berries, but it did not dispel the fear swooping within her at the thought of her own mortality at the hands of something she could not fight. They ate the berries in silence, which seemed awkward after the previous night's companionable experience, drank from the spring, then tidied up all signs of their presence before they left.

At her request, Aedon shimmied up a tree to check their bearings, shouting down to Lief so she could realign their direction of travel. Then, as they hovered upon the edges of the clearing, Aedon halted.

"Oh, I almost forgot. Here." He held out the dagger she had given him for the previous night's watch.

Lief swallowed. By rights, she ought to have taken it from him already. If she were being honest, she ought to have never given it to him in the first place. Yet Aedon of Pelenor no longer felt like a thief and a criminal. He was a companion and…

Shock hit her when she realised something she hadn't experienced in a long time. She trusted him.

She met his gaze. "Keep it."

Aedon blinked, sucking in a breath. "Y-you mean it?"

"Yes. I have my bow and a small knife. That will suffice."

He regarded her for a moment, a flicker of understanding crossing his face. Her gesture was a token of faith, of friendship, of trust. A few days prior, such a thing would have been inconceivable, yet with what had happened since, Lief knew with an instinctive certainty that she had not made a mistake. Aedon had proven himself to her.

He inclined his head. "Thank you."

She felt the warmth of the clearing's magic brush her skin as they left its protection, then the tingle of Aedon's wards descending over them. With that, they strode into the forest, shoulder to shoulder.

TWENTY EIGHT

Venya woke to the morning sun filtering through the cracks in her shutters. It took a moment for her to realise that for the first day in weeks, the winter sun shone, and strongly...*and* on her day off.

She sprang out of bed with more vigour than usual, throwing open the shutters and the window. The frigid air chilled her skin, but she savoured the freshness of it, the brightness of the light, after so many weeks spent in the dull murk of seething, winter storm clouds – or the dark, sunless depths of the Athenaeum's vaults.

On the floor in the corner, atop a spare blanket Venya had purloined from the dormitory's shared cupboard in the hallway, Nyx stirred. It seemed he preferred being the brown, curly-haired puppy most of the time, but Venya had no problem with that.

Sometimes she even forgot he was some strange, magical construct about which she knew disconcertingly little and thought of him as an innocent puppy. One that talked back. One that turned into all manner of strange beasts when they walked the vaults alone each day.

"Well, that's a bit different," Nyx remarked as he jumped up onto the windowsill to survey the landscape before them. What had been dreary, dark plains yesterday were pristine, white rolling hills, an ocean of snow as far as the eye could see.

Venya sighed. "It's beautiful. We hardly ever get snow at home."

Home was far away to the north and east, on the coast, where balmy air crossed the sea, warming it beyond normal temperatures. But here, in the heart of Pelenor, within its capital city of Tournai, the winter snows came low each year.

From the Athenaeum, near the top of the city in the wealthiest district, amongst the public buildings and former royal palace, which was now High Court of Pelenor, Venya had the finest view in all of Tournai. From her dormer window in the eaves of the Athenaeum, she was as high as anyone could get in the city without venturing within the old royal palace.

The squares below her already bustled with market stalls and locals perusing wares, the calls of traders hawking their goods and the raucous din of haggling rising faintly to her. Below the market squares, tier after tier of buildings fell away, the order of the city with them, until the streets became a warren near the walls, filled with all manner of craftsmen and commoners.

"I don't like snow," huffed Nyx.

Venya raised an eyebrow.

"It's *cold*, and *wet*! Then it freezes. Most unpleasant to walk on, you know."

Venya giggled. "Want me to make you some shoes, Bob?"

Nyx rounded on Venya and headbutted her, which only served to amuse her, for the small puppy was no real adversary physically. "You know I hate it when you call me that, *Mouse*."

She only stuck her tongue out at him. Truth be told, she was growing rather fond of his nickname for her, even if she would never admit it.

A knock at the door made her jump. Before she could move, it opened, and Beatrix's tousled head emerged around it. Venya's heart leapt into her throat, but as she whirled back to the windowsill, Nyx was gone. To cover her anxiety, she closed the shutters, wincing as they slammed shut with a mighty *clack* from the force of her motion, and turned back to the door, forcing a smile onto her face.

Beatrix raised an eyebrow in bemusement. "Who were you talking to?"

"I-I wasn't talking." Venya's cheeks burned.

"All right… Thought I heard something. Must have been next door." Beatrix's frown deepened, then she shrugged. "Listen. It's our day off, it's beautiful outside for a change, and…" She swallowed and licked her lips, looking uncharacteristically awkward. "I'd love it if we could take a walk together, then perhaps warm up after with tea and nibbles in my quarters?" She looked at Venya through lowered lashes, her usually smiling face serious.

"Yes," Venya blurted before she really had a chance to think about it.

Beatrix's shoulders relaxed as she straightened, a wide smile stretching across her face. "Great! Wonderful! I… I mean, good. I'll get my cloak. Come on. Hurry up and get dressed!"

Beatrix closed the door behind her. Venya heard her footsteps barrelling down the hallway to her own, rather more generous librarian quarters. Venya hurried to dress, pulling on grey leggings and a knitted, cream jumper that would keep her warm. She quickly braided her hair to one side, snaking it over her shoulder, not minding that it was rough with a few flyaway strands. She hardly noticed them, so filled with thoughts that she would get to spend time with Beatrix outside of their jobs as friends…even though she wished it could be more.

Venya admonished herself for even thinking it. She had no idea whether Beatrix liked her as more than a friend, so Venya had decided long ago that friendship would do her nicely. To rock the balance was to risk losing her friend altogether if she did not feel the same. A risk she did not want to take.

Beatrix met her under the great stone arch of the main door. The protective magics of the Athenaeum ended there. Once they passed under the portal, the warmth of the archives would simply…cease.

Venya walked through the door, sighing with happiness at the cold, refreshing air that met her. Beatrix linked arms with her, eliciting a flutter deep in Venya's stomach, as they descended the wide, stone stairs to the cobbled square.

Usually empty in the winter, save for the statue of a previous King and Queen of Pelenor standing tall, their upraised arms shooting out jets of now frozen water, the square was a tangle of market stalls that wound up and down the streets of Tournai for the monthly trading day.

Venya and Beatrix strolled leisurely through the maze of stalls, basking in the noise and bustle, the smells and sights, from spiced sausages and mulled wines, to textiles and clothing, to weapons and trinkets. Scarlet-cloaked Kingsguard patrolled the streets, too, though Tournai – and the Kingdom of Pelenor as a whole – had been at peace for a quarter of a century, and crime was low in the city.

Venya slowed by a stall of books, examining the variety of tomes…all second-hand, some with strange, flowing script upon their covers and spines that Venya did not recognise. It opened a yearning within her to learn more.

"From Roher, this one," said the stall holder eagerly. "All the way from across the great seas and the realms without magic." With a flourish, he picked up the book and passed it to her.

Venya took it reverently, savouring the rough, warm texture of the cover as she opened it, relishing the audible *crack*, and breathed in the scent of aged pages, softly laced with the scent of cinnamon. Across the pages, right to left, flowed a beautiful, slanted script in an alphabet she had not seen before.

Roher…

She had heard tales of it from her mother, Harper, for she had spent her early life in Caledan, a realm just to the north of Roher, lands almost devoid of magic. She could hardly imagine it. The tales had seemed so fanciful she was not quite sure whether her mother had made them up.

"Just five silvers for that, pretty lady," the seller crooned, leaning forward with a persuasive smile and waggling his bushy eyebrows.

Venya swallowed, then gently closed and laid the book back on the stall. Junior librarians did not carry money like that. It did not matter that her family was wealthy. The reason she had chosen to stay in the Athenaeum instead of the luxurious townhouse her parents resided in while they conducted business in the city was the same reason she had rejected any financial support from them. Venya would pay her own way…even if it took a good while longer.

Besides, she thought glumly, *I don't have space in that tiny dormer room for any more books.*

"Perhaps another time."

The seller scowled, nodded, and stepped back, already

scouting the crowd for his next customer.

Venya glanced back at the book longingly. *Maybe I can save up for it.*

"We'll get it next time, Vee," Beatrix said, hooking her arm through Venya's once more. "Ooh, look over here!" She dragged her to a stall filled with quills and pens, which was laced with the sickly-sweet stench of perfume from the stall next door.

They came away with two matching quills of firebird feathers as long as their forearms, the bright orange and red sparking with magically enhanced embers that the stall keeper had promised were "for effect only".

"No doubt they'll wear out by next week," said Beatrix, nudging Venya and giggling.

They wandered down the winding streets and back up again, stopping here and there to examine leather satchels, decorative letter openers, hand-painted artworks from across the mountains, and last of all, the sweet treats of a baker's stall.

Venya breathed in the scent of warm, fresh bread appreciatively. It was layered with honey, pastry, candied fruits… Her stomach rumbled loud enough that Beatrix burst into laughter.

"I suppose we've been wandering long enough. Come. What do you prefer? My treat."

Venya smiled shyly, meeting Beatrix's smiling gaze for a second before her cheeks warmed and she dropped her attention to the pastries.

Soon, they were on their way, with a paper bag filled with pastries and sweet nibbles, back to the Athenaeum.

Both red-cheeked from the cold and the long ascent to their quarters, Beatrix opened the door to her own and beckoned Venya inside.

Beatrix opened the paper bag, and the smell of sweetness wafted through the air.

"Mmm," Venya hummed appreciatively.

"I may have sneaked a crumb already," Beatrix admitted with a wink.

They sank onto the threadbare but comfortable couch. Beatrix, as a librarian, was privileged to have her own small sitting room, complete with fireplace, adjoining her bedroom. Like Venya's room, Beatrix's was stuffed with books, though hers were neatly stacked on shelves. Every time she visited, Venya wanted to ascend to Beatrix's rank even more, if for no other reason than the bookcases.

"Tea?" Beatrix broke through her reverie.

"Yes, please."

"Cook's finest orange and lavender tea, paired with almond and honey pastry folds and plain pastry crescents."

They sat in companionable silence as they ate, Venya savouring the rich, buttery taste and the flaky, light texture. The room was far warmer than Venya's, with the fire fully stoked and piled with coal – a cosy guard against the chill outside. Beatrix's rooms looked over the mountains behind the Athenaeum and the city of Tournai. Grey, rocky, and somewhat barren, it afforded incredible views of a now frozen waterfall that plummeted from unseen clifftops far above to dash on the rocks that swept around the valley.

"Are you all right, Vee? You've been somewhat distant of late. I'm worried about you." Beatrix reached over to give Venya's hand a light squeeze.

Venya swallowed. She longed so desperately to tell someone, but it would be to her professional ruin if she did, even if she shared it with Beatrix. Perhaps *especially* her. Beatrix, like her, would be duty-bound to alert Nieve.

"I'm fine," Venya lied. "Work has been so busy lately that I fear I'm becoming somewhat tired."

"Why don't you request an extra day off from your annual leave?"

Venya smiled. "You know I can't. I'm–"

"Saving it all up to go home. I know," sighed Beatrix.

"You're welcome to come with, you know. There's plenty of room, and I think you'd like it. There's an excellent library."

"I should have known a bookworm like you would have a well-stocked library. I bet it's huge." Her voice held longing.

"Come with me then." Venya felt as though she had turned

to madness, to be so bold.

Beatrix grinned. "You had me at 'library', Vee. If there are books, I'm there."

They shared a laugh, and Venya's heart caught at the way Beatrix looked at her, so open, so warm, her attention lingering…

"You have a crumb… Let me get it." Beatrix leaned closer, so they were almost touching, her green eyes sparkling, her wavy, chestnut, chin-length hair seeming to create a veil that blocked out the rest of the world for a moment.

Venya's heart thumped, a thrill racing through her body. She could not help but lean closer.

Beatrix slowly lifted a hand, her gaze rising from Venya's jawline to her eyes. She cupped her face – Venya closed her eyes and melted into the touch – and softly brushed away the flake of pastry from her lips with a thumb.

"You're beautiful when you smile," Beatrix breathed, their breath mingling. "You ought to frown less and smile more."

Venya swallowed, unable to speak, her throat closing at how much she was both thrilled and terrified about what might happen next.

"I really like you, Vee. I have since the moment we met. There's something different about you. Something special. I can't stop thinking about you and…and how much I want to…kiss you. I don't want to resist anymore…if you'll let me." Beatrix moved closer, slowly, tentatively, watching Venya's reaction for any sign she did not want the same thing.

Panic flooded Venya. It was everything she could have hoped and dreamed of, but she was terrified of what might come next – the unknown. Terrified of the lingering memory of the beast in the vault. How similar their words were, even though she knew this was the *real* Beatrix. Before she could sink down a rabbit hole of panic, Beatrix's soft lips were upon hers.

Her entire body flamed as their lips met, anticipation, fear, and attraction mingling. Beatrix's kiss was tentative, chaste, as though she, too, feared Venya's rejection. Even though terrified, Venya tilted her head up, desperate for more.

A soft moan escaped Beatrix, and she drew closer, their chests bumping, as her arm snaked around Venya and they sank into the plump cushions, a tangle of limbs. Beatrix's tongue teased her lips, and she parted them on a gasp as Beatrix's other hand caressed her hips, waist, back, pulling her into a closer embrace.

Venya trembled with attraction and anticipation, fear still warring within her. She had never had any intimate encounters, and the thought of her painful inexperience paralysed her. Beatrix's eyes were closed as she slipped her tongue inside Venya's mouth, a moan escaping her, louder this time, and Venya sank into the moment until she was certain she had no physical form and was only fire and lust.

The lack of control thrilled and terrified her in equal measure. *More.* She wanted more, though she did not know what that meant. She only knew her core lit up with desire, desperate to free herself from the usual shackles of her reserved nature.

As they kissed, tea and pastries forgotten on the table, they sank lower onto the couch, Beatrix hovering over Venya. She broke their kiss, her breathing ragged, her eyes dark and hazy with lust as she looked at Venya. "I cannot tell you how long I have wanted to do that."

With that, she dove in for more, kissing more forcefully now, as Venya dared to rest her own hands upon Beatrix's body, grasping the soft fabric of her top, revelling in the slim, firm body upon her own, as their legs tangled together.

They had never touched as more than friends – an embrace, a light touch upon the arm. Yet Venya had thought of it often, never dreaming it might happen. All thoughts of the vault, the beast, were gone. It was finally happening. Her heart's desire was coming to pass, and in that moment, nothing else mattered.

Beatrix pulled away, but only for a moment, before lowering her mouth to Venya's neck, kissing, licking, sucking. Venya gasped in surprise, heat spreading through her at the new sensation. Beatrix moved lower, softly kissing her collarbone, and Venya instinctively arched into her.

Clang… Clang… Clang…

The bell far below rang out three peels, the sound reverberating through the very stone, humming with power and age.

They froze at once.

One bell for the time.

Two bells for a gathering.

Three bells meant *danger, come quickly*. Everyone knew it.

They sprang apart and scrambled up, breathing heavily. Beatrix's hair was even more tousled than usual, and Venya smoothed her own self-consciously. They shared a stricken, speechless look, neither able to speak for a moment.

"Let's go," said Beatrix raggedly.

Venya followed her at a run, the pair pausing at Venya's room to collect her seal. They were mandatory to carry in the library, bringing protection to their owners, should the need arise.

In a heartbeat, gone was the lust, the excitement, the distraction. In its place, terror.

Only tremendous danger would cause the bells to ring out thrice…and Venya knew of only one thing that could risk the library's safety.

The beast from the vault.

TWENTY NINE

Blood splattered the stairwell. Silent, sombre librarians lined the stairs on either side. All made sure to not step in the blood that trailed in ghastly, dragging lines where Beorn had hauled himself up, stair by stair, as his life ebbed from him. Venya could imagine the desperation within him in those moments, wondering whether he would live or die.

Venya stood with Beatrix, grasping each other's hand, almost painfully, in silent horror at what they saw. Now, there were no shadows in the spiral staircase that led down into the depths of the Athenaeum's vaults. Faelights burned brightly, illuminating every crack and corner.

"No trace of the attacker has been found," the murmur passed up and down the stairs. "They're certain it was a magical beast, though."

Beorn lay unconscious in the infirmary, unable to attest to what had transpired.

As they had all gathered in the atrium in answer to the bell, Nieve had told them Beorn would live. Her mouth had been a thin line, her pale face and rigid posture the only testament to her fury at what had happened. That, on her watch, a librarian had been harmed in the Athenaeum.

"Henceforth, until you are told otherwise, no one will walk alone in the Athenaeum. You will go in pairs everywhere – your superior will assign you your partners – until the source of this attack is found." Nieve's voice had rung out over the silent mass huddled in the giant, vaulted space. Light streamed in through the ornate, glass roof, but it was cold upon them all, casting a pale, baleful glare across the space.

Venya did not dare look down the stairs, towards the vault hundreds of feet below. Surely it was too neat a coincidence. She dreaded having to behold the vault's portal again, yet knew she had to. Knew she had to see the truth of it for herself. She expected the protective magics on the door, her own included, to be corroded, burnt to ash, the beast free to roam…

Venya shivered. Beatrix, standing a step higher, released Venya's hand and snaked an arm around her shoulders, pulling her close. If they were no longer permitted to roam alone, Venya would have no opportunity to steal to the vault to find out if her suspicions were correct. And, with the beast loose, she was not sure she wanted to, or dared to, as much as it was her duty.

This is my fault.

Venya felt sick to the pit of her stomach. She ought to have found a better way to contain the beast. Ought not to have shied away from her duty as a librarian, junior or otherwise. Ought to have told a superior. But now she could never admit to it. Not to Beatrix, not to anyone. For her to have known a grimoire had broken its bonds and not said anything was unforgivable enough, but now that it had gravely injured someone, it was beyond salvation.

Venya knew she ought to be thinking of Beorn…poor, kind, innocent Beorn, who had borne the pain and suffering of her lapse…but all she could feel was sheer terror at the thought of being discovered as the reason the creature had been able to free itself. The reason it had not been safely bound once more.

I will lose my job. My career. My reputation… But is that worth someone's life?

The question did not even need to be considered.

Venya knew right from wrong.

Yet did she have the courage to stand up for her convictions?

THIRTY

Once they discovered the road once more, Aedon thoroughly checked it, deeming it safe to pass. Nevertheless, they remained warded. Lief could tell from his agitation that Aedon did not trust the forest, no matter how pleasant and innocuous it seemed. Every crunch had him twitching, eyes darting here and there to evaluate any threat, and he walked with his hand on the dagger at his hip.

Yet she revelled in it – the easy simplicity of being able to walk around unguided, the warmth of the sunlight. It was a much-needed distraction from the curse upon her, despite the fact that every step pained her as the aches lanced through her body.

The sun alleviated any awkwardness between them, too, and with every step serenaded by birdsong, the ease between them grew once more. As the road wound through the trees, their conversation flowed.

"I used to love a game of *chatura*," Aedon admitted with a smile.

Lief's eyes widened. "*You* played *chatura*?"

He sniggered. "Yes, but I wasn't very good at it."

She gasped in mock horror. "Are you being modest, legendary Aedon?" She squinted at him. "Or are you trying to lure me into a false sense of security? We wood elves invented *chatura*, you know."

"I think the dwarves would dispute that."

"They can dispute whatever they like. I'd still wipe the ground with you."

"I'd like to see you try, wood elf."

"No cheating, *thief*," Lief replied, but her insult was accompanied by a warm smile.

"I would never!" insisted Aedon with mock contriteness, but her gaze snagged on the glimmer of mischief within his eyes, tempting her – the same as Finarvon had – to let go, to succumb to the capriciousness of the moment.

With that, she recoiled back into herself and her mirth died. Lief increased the distance between them as they continued along the road, silently.

Towards mid-afternoon, they passed a flower-covered mound beside the road, then came upon a beautiful, tiny village set high in the giant trees above.

Aedon halted, wonder spreading across his face.

"Incredible," he breathed.

Despite her earlier anxiety, Lief could not help but smile as she watched him. She supposed it was strange to outsiders, but to her, this was how her people lived.

The trees themselves had flowed without cessation to create hollows, dwellings shaped by the magic of her people that had stood in the giant boughs for hundreds of years, if not longer. The bark bulged to form stairs around the giant trunks, lined with slender railings of vines and flowers, that linked the dwellings. Branches intertwined high above the forest floor to make bridges from tree to tree. Birds darted through the sky, and squirrels chased each other from bough to bough.

"It's beautiful," Aedon murmured.

Lief agreed, mainly because it hopefully meant a safe place to sleep that night, as well as being able to clarify how far away they were from the much needed *aleilah.*

She called out a greeting in the Tir-na-Alathean tongue, and heads popped out far above, shouting in return. Elves appeared in the canopy and swiftly descended, converging upon them in a babble of interest, for visitors were probably seldom seen in their part of the forest.

"Common Tongue for my travelling companion, please," Lief said, smiling and gesturing to Aedon.

A dark-skinned, dark-haired wood elf with bright, amber eyes stepped forwards. "Greetings, friends. What brings you here?"

"We make for the mountain pass, but were thrown off our trail by dark beasts," Lief replied.

The elf's face clouded. He glanced at his people, who clustered around them. "Dark beasts, you say?"

"Yes. Far from here, so I hope they will not darken your doors."

Again, the wood elves shared a heavy look, and unease stirred within her. Aedon inched closer to her. *He senses it, too.*

"Let's talk elsewhere," the wood elf said, glancing around at the forest. Lief noticed the way his gaze snagged, as if evaluating for threats. Yet what threats could there be?

The village seemed innocuous and pleasant. Another corner of the sprawling forest realm she called home. Another corner of a realm she felt entirely safe within…until a few days ago.

Lief and Aedon fell into line in the midst of the elves, who led them into the trees and up into the canopy using a clever system of ropes, pulleys, and lifts.

Lief shared pleasantries with the wood elves in their native tongue, only listening half-heartedly as she eavesdropped on several of them gushing over Aedon, for Pelenori elves were a rare curiosity in the heart of Tir-na-Alathea.

"Common tongue for my…" She swallowed, having stopped herself before she said *friend*, "companion, please?" Lief smiled tightly.

The elven females chuckled and switched to Common

Tongue. "Look at his *ears*? Have you ever seen such a thing?!"

One had the audacity to reach out and flick a slender, dark finger across the pointed tip of Aedon's ear, so different from the long, tapered ends of their own. Aedon shied away with an easy smile and a throaty chuckle.

"Please, at least tell me your names first," he said with a smouldering gaze, his grin widening.

They giggled and continued their babbling in the tongue of the wood elves. Lief blushed and ducked her head to hide her crimson cheeks at the impropriety of their words, hating how uncomfortable it made her. Fortunately, Aedon did not notice as he looked around, drinking in their surroundings, unaware of the fuss.

The platform swung to a halt beside a giant bough worn smooth from years of elven passage, and Lief followed the wood elves, glancing over her shoulder to make sure Aedon was behind her.

"What brings you here…" The male wood elf paused.

"Lief," she supplied, then raised an eyebrow in question.

"Kat'har," he replied smoothly and inclined his head.

Lief glanced at Aedon, his head craned back to look at the flower-covered canopy above them. "Aedon and I travel to Emuir on the Queen's business." Lief said nothing more. She owed it to no one. Not to mention she had no desire to explain why she travelled with a prisoner of her Queen, unrestrained and as an equal…not to mention armed.

She suppressed a groan at the ridiculousness of the whirlwind that had been the past few days. The strangeness of her growing familiarity with Aedon, the nauseating fear and grief at whatever plagued her, the horrors she had witnessed.

Kat'har frowned slightly, glancing at Lief as he walked beside her upon the silvered wood. "Where did you say you are from?"

"I did not." At his expectant silence, she offered reluctantly, "Lune."

"Lune? You are off the beaten track. Did you become lost?"

Her tongue darted out to wet her lips. "Not exactly. There was, uh… We were attacked by a creature. I was injured." Kat'har's eyes widened as she turned to show him the full horror of her arm and shoulder. "We seek a cure from the mountains – *aleilah* – then we will make our way to Emuir."

"Ah." Kat'har nodded, his lips thinning with sympathetic understanding. "You would be welcome to our stocks, but I fear we have none left ourselves after the attacks."

Unease curled in Lief's belly. "Attacks?"

"You must take care, Lief." Kat'har paused for a moment, and Lief halted beside him. He fixed her with serious, amber eyes. "These past few weeks, dark creatures have ventured down from the mountains. Creatures the likes we have not seen before. The likes of which have no place in Tir-na-Alathea." His brows furrowed, and Lief could sense his worry as Kat'har scanned the forest floor below.

As if he could hear the unasked questions crowding her tongue, Kat'har gestured for her to cross a slender bridge to another wide bough. "Come. Let us speak of this in private."

"Can I come, Papa?" A young female darted forwards, slipping her hand into Kat'har's.

Kat'har gave her hand a squeeze, then let go. "Not this time, Mirielle. Go play now, but stay in the trees." Although he smiled, Lief could hear the tight edge of worry lacing his words. He watched his daughter run off, before turning back to them and leading them inside.

Lief stepped under the intertwined branches that cocooned a cool, muted space. The tree flowed smoothly around them, creating an organic, uneven room with slanted walls, shafts of afternoon light tumbling in through natural chinks in the tree's formation.

It felt small after days in the wide-open forest and was nothing like the giant dwellings in the mammoth trees of Lune. This was more humble, though no less special. Lief noted the handwoven rug upon the ground, the chairs and smooth, flowing table made without a single tool, sung from the trees themselves.

"Sit, please." Kat'har gestured to the chairs as he took one himself. A younger male slipped in with a crystal jug of cool, sweet water, then poured it into tall, slim, wooden cups.

Aedon and Lief drank it immediately, then refilled and drank again.

Kat'har cleared his throat. "I do not wish my daughter to hear any of this. The beasts are terrifying enough…" He swallowed, lowering his voice, "and my son is already dead by their claws."

Now, Lief now understood the thin, harsh line of his mouth, full of unspoken, barely contained, bitter grief. Understood the fresh barrow they had passed upon the road. Her heart ached for him, just as it ached for the friends she had lost, perhaps by the same dark magic.

"Creatures reeking of death and darkness pass through the forest in the night. We have not seen their like before. We are too few to defeat them. Not one have we managed to slay, and we have not dared since…" His throat bobbed with a hard swallow. "Since Matteo was taken from us.

"They are poisonous in nature, their claws and teeth bringing infection and death. I fear for us. Here, we are far too remote and too few to warrant the protection of the Queen's rangers." Kat'har threw a troubled glance at Lief's dirtied uniform, hardly recognisable after days of rough travel. "We sent for help, but my brother did not return."

Lief fought back a surge of shame at her appearance. She ordinarily took such pride in it, but lately, survival trumped having clean clothes.

"Where do they come from? When did this happen?"

Kat'har shook his head. "We have not discovered the source

of their spawn. They come from the direction of the mountains, so perhaps there. It's been several weeks now. We have abandoned the forest floor and now remain in the trees, where it is far safer. As yet, they have not seemed able to climb. The attacks always come at night. Always sudden, always deadly. Any creature that gets in their way meets a grisly end." Kat'har visibly shuddered and his lip curled, exposing a finely pointed canine.

Lief and Aedon shared a dark look. "It appears we have been lucky then," Aedon said quietly, looking to Kat'har again.

"Dark creatures chased us from Lune," Lief explained, carefully avoiding the whole truth. How could she explain that it seemed as though her comrades had been killed and risen from the grave to fight anew, with darkness animating their corpses? "I had not seen their like before, either. Like great, shaggy wolves that walked upon two or four legs as they chose, with deadly teeth and claws as long as my hand."

"They were clever, too," Aedon interjected. She knew he recalled the way the creatures had bridged the water to attack them on the small island. "You ought to leave. Before they figure out how to climb trees."

Kat'har paled. "We cannot leave. This is our home! Where would we go? Besides, even if we left at the first sliver of dawn, we could not reach safety before night fell, when the risks are even greater."

Lief shivered, recalling the sheer terror she had felt at being chased by the dark beasts. "Is there a *boma* nearby where we could stay the night?"

Kat'har shook his head. "I'm afraid not. You will stay here. I insist. I would not see any of our people or our friends…" He nodded at Aedon, "harmed when we have safety and shelter."

Lief smiled faintly, relieved that they would not have to spend a sleepless night fearing each and every shadow was imminent death. "We would be most grateful. Thank you."

"It is our pleasure," Kat'har insisted. "I'm afraid we only have one spare hammock, but it is rather large. You should both be comfortable there."

Lief's heart stuttered, warmth flaming up her cheeks. "I… I beg your pardon?"

Aedon chuckled. "How romantic. A night cuddled up together under the stars, Lief. Doesn't that sound lovely?"

She growled and swatted at him, annoyance sparking at her embarrassment, especially as he laughed. "Not a chance, *thief*," she hissed.

"Thief of your heart," Aedon crooned, smouldering at her through his eyelashes in the way only he could. When he winked, Lief was so angry she could not speak.

Kat'har looked between the two of them, bemused. "I'll show you to your bough, and you can wash and eat, if you wish."

"No," Lief forced out, wrenching her attention away from Aedon's infuriating, widening grin, which she dearly wanted to punch off his smug, insufferable face. "We will work for our keep, Kat'har. I insist. We'll scout the area whilst it's still light, see if we can find any signs of the beasts or where they come from."

She did not wait for Aedon's acquiescence before she stood, bowed to Kat'har, and walked out. The slight creak of wood heralded her confounded companion doing the same.

THIRTY ONE

Lief and Aedon spent the rest of the day circling the hamlet in ever increasing loops, taking careful note when they found unusual tracks laced with the hint of dark magic. Giant claw marks were gouged into the earth. The meandering trail led straight in the direction of the hamlet, but they had not found any by way of return.

Lief suppressed an uneasy shiver and glanced around, but she could not see, hear, or sense anything.

They remained silent all afternoon, their ears straining for any sound of something untoward. As Aedon watched, Lief dropped to the ground and placed her slim hand inside one of the beast's prints.

"*This is no small creature to trifle with*," Lief murmured into Aedon's mind.

He shot her a troubled glance, his eyes dark and lips thin, and nodded. "*We should head back. Before nightfall.*"

Lief glanced around the innocuous looking forest. The

reassuring hum and chatter of creatures was a constant background noise, lulling them into a sense of security in the sun-dappled forest. But Aedon was right. Tir-na-Alathea was a dangerous place to those who did not respect it – even a wood elf.

With the sunset nipping at their heels, the warm, innocent vibe of the forest began to fade, too. The tang of dark magic, metallic and sickening, made Lief's head pound in time with her injured shoulder. She fought it down as they returned to the hamlet in silence. She would have wondered what Aedon pondered had she not been so focused on putting one foot in front of another amidst a wave of dizziness.

They were welcomed back with shouts and cheers that rang through the trees. Kat'har greeted them, his daughter, Mirielle, hanging from his arm, an eager but shy smile gracing her bright, young face as she watched them with awe.

When Aedon gave her a wink, the girl's cheeks bloomed bright red. But Kat'har's attention was fixed upon Lief, whose grim visage had not wavered. His own merriment sobered. "Mirielle, tell your mother our guests have arrived. You and your cousins can serve the meal at once. We'll be along shortly."

As she disappeared into the canopy above, Kat'har turned back to Lief, waiting expectantly.

"There are traces of dark magic in the forest," she said.

"Tracks of great beasts. We saw nothing of them, but the evidence of their passage is clear. You would do well to stay in the trees when night falls. Even when day dawns, I would advise constant caution. Whilst we are here, we will lend our strength to yours." She did not look to Aedon, knowing he agreed. If two of their small number had already fallen victim to the beasts, the isolated family needed their help.

Kat'har swallowed as his gaze drifted to the forest floor not that far below them, the long shadows that yawned across it from the setting sun passing through the trees. "I thank you both. Come. Let us speak of this no more for now. My family has prepared a feast in your honour. Guests are so rare in these parts, and your aid is most appreciated."

They followed Kat'har to a higher bough, seeing a long trestle table and benches, which seemed to flow from the very branch itself. Upon it lay the bounty of the forest – bowls of fruits and berries, salads, fresh-baked bread, rich, golden butter and cheeses. Around them, faelights bobbed in the trees, illuminating the scene in a golden glow as the sun's light faded, like the stars had fallen from the sky to light their meal.

They were welcomed warmly as they sat. Lief could not help but smile, for it brought back memories of her childhood, though it had been years since she had graced her father's halls on the other side of Tir-na-Alathea. It was a reassuring sense of normalcy, of family, that she had craved for so long. She missed it. Missed laughing with her brothers whilst her mother braided her hair, her stern father reprimanding the boys for their mischievous antics.

I need to visit home, she thought with no small amount of guilt. Her arm throbbed in response. Lief swallowed. There were more pressing matters to attend to first. She hoped her family was safe.

Blinking as she returned to the present, an eager, young elf shoving a plate of cheese under her nose, Lief smiled and took her share of a creamy block, murmuring her thanks as she slid it onto a thick slice of honeyed bread. She bit into the soft, gooey cheese and moaned, savouring the springy, still-warm slice of bread, the tingle of her tongue from the burst of tangy flavour. Lune's food, as an outpost of the Queen's empire, was usually far more basic. There was no fine fare made by loving hands. Just the simple food needed to sustain them on patrol.

They treated Aedon just as finely as they treated her, the females plying him with sweets and delicate flutes of golden and claret liquids in their efforts to flatter. They seemed utterly charmed by the mischievous smile that irked her, but she did not complicate matters by revealing his true nature. Though she was beginning to think of him less and less as her captive or a thief. Had he somehow wormed his way through her best efforts to stay aloof? Lief narrowed her eyes at him thoughtfully.

Aedon caught her looking and grinned. He brimmed with mirth. She could not help but smile in return, though her own was more muted in the face of what they had come to do, and she did not partake as eagerly from the intoxicating liquids they were offered, no matter how sweet and moreish.

After dinner, with full bellies and fuzzy heads, conversation flowed, from Aedon's past life, to the family's adventures in the forest, to Lief's own life with the patrol of Lune – through she was careful to not mention Finarvon. No one needed to know of her shame there. Or her anger. She would not cloud such a happy place with her grief and regret. Instead, she watched as Aedon flourished his hands, a charming smile upon his face as he told of past exploits filled with dragons, magic, and adventure.

With a start, Lief realised he was definitely *the* Aedon from the Chronicles of Pelenor…which meant he had been a dragon rider at one time. One of Pelenor's finest, if the tales were anything to go by.

More and more, she wondered at him, for he seemed like a lake – calm on top, but with hidden depths lurking below. It disconcerted her; how little she truly knew of him.

In short order, a few *chatura* sets appeared, the pieces lovingly carved and well worn, and before she knew it, they were both roped in to play, Aedon bragging about his proficiency playing the board game with its complex set of rules and pieces. He beat Mirielle – though Lief could see how he held back, claiming just a slim victory – whilst Lief drew with Kat'har, though Kat'har gave her the victory, claiming he would rather watch. Beside them, a crowing, whooping victory emerged from one of his nephews.

Aedon faced one of the nephews next, and Lief took her turn with Mirielle, giving an apologetic smile as she wiped the floor with the girl.

"Brutal," chided Aedon with a twinkle in his eye.

"You're next," she warned, grinning viciously, the drink finally getting to her enough to ease her usual standoffishness.

"Bring it on."

It was a painful reminder of all he had lost, for had Aedon closed his eyes, he would have sworn he was back around the campfire with his former companions before his imprisonment in the living forest. They had spent many a night dining, drinking, and playing *chatura*, an ancient game.

Yet as he watched Lief laughing, swiftly capturing her opponent's pieces with enthusiastic competitiveness, and winning with no small hint of modest pride, he could not help but be brought back to his lighter side, watching her, for the first time, actually have *fun*. It was strange to see her so unfettered by the walls she kept around her at all times. He could not help but wonder what had cut her so deeply that she would not choose to be so happy every day.

Finally, it was their turn to spar. Anticipation tingled within him as he met the challenge in her gaze. "Ready?"

"You bet. I'll even let you take the first move."

"Ladies first," Aedon insisted.

Lief arched an eyebrow. "You'll regret that."

"I shall never regret chivalry, m'lady," Aedon said with a mocking bow, to the merriment of the giggling elves around him.

In twelve moves, Lief had him cornered.

Aedon gaped as she captured his king and declared victory, spluttering as he tried to put his indignation into words.

She let out a delighted peal of laughter. "I've never seen you so lost for words! If I knew all I had to do to get you to hold your tongue was to trounce you at *chatura*, I would have started before now."

Aedon snorted. "I let you win!" he protested feebly, but she shoved him.

"You got beat by a *girl*," she said smugly. "Isn't that something you Pelenori folk are ashamed by?"

Aedon drew himself up in mock outrage. "We are never ashamed to lose to a worthy adversary."

"Now, now," Kat'har chuckled. "Save your competition for another time."

After Kat'har handed her a fresh set of arrows for her victory, he dispersed them all to bed with full stomachs and fuller hearts.

Aedon grumbled good-naturedly all the way back to their bough, whilst Lief pointedly ignored him, a smug smile creeping across her face as she examined the smooth, dark, straight arrows with their reddened fletchings.

Once they entered, Aedon bowed and gestured to the hammock…nearly falling over in the process. "M'lady, it's yours. I could not take it and leave you without."

She stared at him, lips pursed. "How much have you had to drink?"

Aedon only giggled and waggled his eyebrows.

Lief groaned. "I won't be held responsible for you rolling off the bough to your death. Take the hammock, you pain."

"I can handle it!"

Aedon grinned and stumbled over to the table and ewer of water the wood elves had left for them. He lifted it and drank noisily before smacking his lips as he set it down. "To stave off any morning headaches," he explained, giving her a wink.

Lief rolled her eyes. "You're insufferable."

"You adore it."

Aedon struggled with the hammock, tipping it this way and that. Lief's heart lurched into her throat as he sat and nearly overbalanced, wildly swinging his arms to right himself.

"You're completely hopeless, Aedon Lindhir Riel!" She stomped over, holding the hammock steady so he could situate himself.

Like a giant cocoon, it enveloped him, until his head popped out of one side. "This beats the ground."

Lief pressed her lips together. "I should hope so."

Aedon pulled back the fabric, holding his arm wide. "Are you coming in?"

She faltered and swallowed. "W-what?"

He yawned. "You might be sober-ish, but I still wouldn't sleep on the branch. Doesn't look like it'll be any good for you."

Lief had to agree. The whorled, knobbled bark would make for a terrible night's sleep. Yet the alternative… She glared at him through narrowed eyes, but he only smiled at her and let out another giant yawn.

"My offer will expire shortly," he mumbled.

Lief groaned, sighed, and clambered in as gingerly as she could. The ropes holding it up creaked with the additional weight, and after a few careful adjustments, causing the hammock to sway, Lief settled into Aedon's body, her back against his front, legs tangled together. Aedon let the fabric fall over them and unceremoniously threw his arm across her.

"Night," he mumbled. Seconds later, his gentle snores whistled against the back of her head.

Yet for Lief, Finarvon's ghost was there, cradling her tense form. This was how they had fallen asleep every night, and she had not been so physically close to another male since finding out what he had done. Since wondering if that was how he had slept with *her,* too. This was too intimate, too close.

Aedon is not Fin, she told herself firmly, but it was so hard to not leap from the hammock, her skin crawling, at the thought of

Finarvon, of being so vulnerable with the male she had trusted most. The male who had betrayed her so deeply the cut to her heart had not yet healed.

Aedon is not Fin…

With Aedon's warm breath on her neck, his cheek resting on her head, his arm slung carelessly across her, it was so hard not to melt back into him, the need for warmth and physical contact overwhelming. As much as she hated to admit it, shut out any notion of closeness with others, she missed being held.

She chided herself silently, squeezing her eyes shut, as if she could block out her own thoughts. She would be foolish to mistake that simple, base need for physical attraction to Aedon. It was a lie that told her his kindness, handsomeness, and easy charm were anything more than shallow. It would be disastrous for them to be anything more than acquaintances. A thief and a ranger could never be united.

Not that I want to be, Lief assured herself. *He's insufferable. I'd sooner strangle him than sleep with him.*

Eventually, serenaded by Aedon's quiet snores behind her, Lief drifted off to sleep, the branches gently rustling overhead with the slight breeze and the scurrying of small creatures through the canopy.

It was the absence of sound that first roused her, though she did not realise it, until she heard the snuffling far below, the deep, rattling breath, scratching.

In a heartbeat, Lief was wide awake. She pushed Aedon's arm off her and slipped from the hammock with as much grace as she could manage, steadying it with a hand so Aedon did not fall out. He mumbled incoherently at the movement, but did not wake. She might have tipped him out any other time, but all thoughts of revenge at his intolerant teasing were gone, replaced with apprehension.

The breeze lifted her hair from her face, brushing it gently against her cheeks, and with it, the fetid stench of death teased her nose. She swallowed down the rising bile, fear, anxiety, and anticipation flashing through her.

She moved with silent precision, then stopped abruptly with a soft snarl at the pain in her shoulder. Lief flexed her tingling, almost numb fingers, gritting her teeth. The spidering veins spread farther down her arm, and with them, a loss of sensation.

Lief forced herself to ignore it and peered over the edge of the bough, through the criss-crossing web of branches and leaves.

Far below, a dark shadow prowled.

Lief quickly retreated to grab her bow, biting back a cry of pain as she strung it, straining her throbbing shoulder and her numb hand.

"Aedon, wake up," she hissed.

He did not respond.

Lief growled and jabbed him with the tip of the bow

Aedon groaned, and the hammock wriggled as he shifted.

Lief swore at him silently and glanced around, spotting the ewer of water. After an appreciative swig, she dumped the rest over her sleeping companion.

Spluttering, Aedon shot out of the hammock, falling from it in his haste. Lief pounced on him, clapping her hand over his mouth and hauling him back from the edge of the bough before he gave them away – or plunged to his death.

"What the heavens was that for?" he grumbled around her hand.

Lief put a finger to her lips and removed her hand. "You wouldn't wake," she whispered, then pointed below. "Look. Listen. We have visitors."

The anger drained from his face; his inebriation gone. There was no trace of his earlier merriment. He quieted as he crawled to the edge and looked down. Lief peered again, too. The dark shadow moved between the silent trees, snuffling and snorting, following a scent trail.

Should we alert someone? Lief scanned the trees, but she could see no sign of life. No sign that someone kept vigil, just in case. For all she knew, the wood elves all slumbered.

"Kat'har said they couldn't climb trees," Aedon whispered. "We ought to be safe."

The beast rose on two legs, stretching up the base of the tree next to theirs – the one where Kat'har and his family slept. Then, Lief and Aedon watching, aghast, it flexed its claws, dug them in with a crunch, and began to ascend.

THIRTY TWO

No one worked the next day. Gossip and shock tore through the Athenaeum like wildfire, growing taller with each telling, of what had happened to Beorn, as well as speculation about the unknown attacker, which had still not been found.

Venya had snuck to the infirmary – with Beatrix by her side, for Nieve's new edict forbade anyone from walking the halls alone – but the matron angrily threw them out before they could cross the threshold, cursing nosiness and gossips for disrupting her work. So Venya worried, and worried, and worried.

Beatrix, as the head of their small cohort, gathered them into her small sitting room, the mood sombre. Venya stood in a corner, whilst the others took the sofa. It was hard to not think that just a day ago, her and Beatrix had been tangled upon it, sharing a kiss she had waited two years for…until the bells had rung.

Today, the mood was different. All of them pale and drawn from lack of sleep. All of them quiet, withdrawn. All of them free of the usual cattiness and snide comments that normally plagued Venya daily.

"So, we must follow Nieve's rule to ensure we are safe," Beatrix concluded.

There was no sparkle in her eye, no smile upon her face. Today, she was solemn. Beorn had been kind to them all. Had not deserved what had happened. Guilt gnawed at Venya again.

Beatrix swiftly split them up into a group of three and one of two, leaving Venya alone. "You're with me," she said to Venya, watching her steadily, as if wondering whether she might reject her, might have had a change of heart about them after the previous day.

Venya swallowed and nodded.

Beatrix's shoulders seemed to relax as she straightened and sighed. "All of you, take the rest of the day off. But remember, outside this dormitory, you move in your allotted groups at all times. And…"

Venya sensed her hesitation. Saw the way she folded her arms across herself, as though they could protect her.

"Nieve has also ordered the Athenaeum sealed until further notice. No one goes in or out. The High Council has sent the Kingsguard to patrol the halls and vaults, as well as placed a seal upon the complex. Whatever attacked Beorn shall not escape justice."

Venya heard what she did not say. *And we are all trapped here with it, too.* She shivered.

They dispersed in a whispering group, leaving Venya and Beatrix alone.

Beatrix looked exhausted, dark shadows under her eyes. Venya had hardly slept, as well, even with Nyx's closeness, the puppy sleeping with her in bed, his warm body lending her strength and solidarity. He now hid in her pocket, a mouse once more, undetected.

"I need to go to the lounge to fetch something. Will you come with me?" Beatrix muttered.

"Of course." Venya walked across the room to give her hand a light squeeze.

Beatrix smiled tiredly and pulled her into an embrace, burying her face in Venya's neck. Venya melted against her chest, feeling the reassuring thump of Beatrix's heart against her cheek, the warm huff of her breath against her collarbone. They stood for a few silent moments, before Beatrix pulled away.

They descended to the lounge, which was crowded with withdrawn librarians filling the chairs and standing amongst the shelves, conversing in low voices. None of them paid Beatrix and Venya any heed, for which Venya was glad.

"Wait here."

Venya halted by the shelves as Beatrix darted off, trying to make herself as unnoticed as possible.

"Well, good afternoon, my darling. How are you this fine

day?"

Venya jumped at the familiar voice and spun around.

"Sylvio?" she hissed. "What are you doing here?"

Sylvio sniffed and replied as haughtily as any grimoire could. "I was retrieved for some light reading, but it appears my borrower has decided gossip is more important than the secrets of my pages. The poor fool will not know what he missed now, for I shall not open to him out of spite." Sylvio ruffled his pages indignantly.

"Yes, well… I–"

"Oh, I know what's happened, girl. *Dreadful* business." Yet the grimoire sounded positively gleeful about it.

Venya narrowed her eyes at him. "You ought not sound so pleased."

Sylvio only chuckled, his papery, rustling laugh lost amongst the quiet hubbub around them.

"Where's your lock?" Venya asked, noticing his padlock was absent, though a thin, glimmering chain tethered him to the shelf.

"Gone," Sylvio replied with relish. "And good riddance to it. I shall enjoy some breathing space. Do you know how appalling it is to not be able to air one's pages?"

He flared open, his pages flicking back and forth, fanning her with a slight breeze. Inside, she caught brief glimpses of doorways, portals, and thin, slanting, spidery script, occasionally illuminated with diagrams or strange markings she did not have time to fully see before they flicked past.

"You do know someone nearly died," Venya growled at the tome. "Show some respect."

"Why? No one shows me any," Sylvio replied airily.

"You're a *book*."

"I have never been so insulted!" Sylvio spluttered, ruffling his pages. "I am a *grimoire*, thank you very much. Besides which, I could solve the Athenaeum's present predicament in a moment, yet no one has even thought to consult me!"

"What?"

"*I beg your pardon*," Sylvio corrected. "Goodness, do they let any old rabble in these days?" He tutted.

"No," Venya hissed impatiently, leaning closer. "You said you could fix this. What do you mean?"

"Exactly what I said. Everyone is searching for this dastardly attacker, and I could take anyone right to it."

Venya stilled. "You know where it is?" She was still convinced the attacker was the beast she had seen in the vault. It was too neat a coincidence.

"Of course not, but I could *find* it. I am the book of gateways after all. I can make a door to anything or anyo–"

"Sylvio! What trouble are you spouting?" Beatrix snapped from Venya's side, making her jump. "Don't make me archive you."

Sylvio slammed shut with a huff.

Yet Venya's heart sputtered at his words. Sylvio could find

the beast? If that were true…

Thoughts raced through Venya's mind. She could defeat it, contain it, bind it, hide it… So many possibilities. All of which were terrifying, but–

"Vee?" Beatrix interrupted her thoughts. "I'm done. Let's go."

"Huh?" She looked up. "Oh. Of course."

However, as they left, she could not help but turn and stare at Sylvio, wishing she could take the grimoire with her.

That evening, in the privacy of her room after dinner, Venya stretched out on her bed, with Nyx beside her once more in his puppy form, fingering the token Beatrix had given her earlier, which was the reason for her visit to the lounge.

The silver metal, no bigger than the diameter of an eye and only as thick as a coin, was wrought in the design of a compass. Beatrix had its matching counterpart. They were paired, she had explained, to find each other.

"Should we become separated for any reason," Beatrix had said, pressing it into her palm, "these will bring us together. Promise me you will keep it with you always."

Her eyes had shone with a fervent intensity Venya understood. Beatrix did not want to lose her. She had agreed, of course, for she felt the same.

"You cannot trust him, you know," Nyx said, resting his chin across Venya's stomach and nudging her to scratch between his ears. "Sylvio is a grimoire."

"So are you." Venya slipped the coin back into her pocket, the warm hum of its magic against her skin a comfort.

Nyx huffed. "We are *very* different."

"That's not the point. It's not about trusting Sylvio. He can do this. Can find the beast. Wouldn't you agree?"

"I'm not disagreeing with you there. I'm only saying to watch him. He doesn't help anybody out of the goodness of his heart. He doesn't have one. He'd just as likely deliver you to somewhere or something that would kill you, just for the sheer pleasure of it. There is no inherent decency in him."

"What other choice is there, Nyx?"

"Leave the Kingsguard to it. Heed Nieve's orders. Sooner or later, the beast will be found, caught, and contained once more."

"But what if others get hurt in the meantime?" Venya countered. It had slowly dawned on her, the uncomfortable truth she now had to face. "This is my fault, because I did not report it. Therefore, it is my responsibility to make this right. I cannot bury my head in the sand any longer. Not after Beorn got hurt. Not when it could happen to someone else."

"There must be a better way."

"Unless you can tell me one, this is the choice I'm left with," Venya snapped. "I can take a chain and padlock from the stores. I can already bind just as well as most of the qualified librarians. Better than some, in fact."

It was not a boast, though Venya was proud of it. The power of her elven blood and her natural aptitude for sorcery gave her an advantage over many of her peers.

"I just have to get Sylvio to take me to it, then I can immobilise and bind it." And this time, she would use something far stronger than mint and asphodel to subdue it.

Nyx sighed, silent for a long moment. "Then I'm coming with you. I can protect you."

"Thank you," Venya said quietly. She still did not know much about Nyx, yet instinctively knew she could trust him. She was a fool perhaps, but even so, she would be glad to not have to enter the dark halls alone.

"We go tonight. This ends now."

THIRTY THREE

The halls were deserted of librarians, for it was far past the last bell, but crimson-cloaked soldiers strolled in pairs. Venya's mouth was dry, her hands clammy, and her heart pounding as she stole through the halls.

Nyx, who now wore the shape of a great, obsidian panther as tall as her hips, moved as silently as a shadow beside her. They used columns, statues, shelves, and walls as their cover to play a silent game of *chatura* with the moving pieces that were the guards.

This sounded like a good plan in the light and safety of her bedroom, but Venya's senses were heightened now, and the fear running through her was an ever-present reminder of the true danger she faced. She touched her belt every few steps, to reassure herself it was all still there. That everything was present and accounted for.

As she approached the double doors to the librarians' lounge, the tall, slim, wooden leaves shut, no light emanating from behind them, Venya's apprehension ratcheted up another notch.

Barely breathing, she tried the handle.

Locked.

A simple burst of magic, and… *Click.* Venya slipped inside, Nyx padding in behind her, with a last look at the hallway. It was a simple matter to return to where Sylvio had been shelved.

Venya cursed. The shelf was empty. Sylvio was gone. There was only one place he would be.

Venya swallowed. "Nyx? We have to go to the Sylvio's vault…"

"It would appear so." Nyx sighed.

On their way out, Venya selected a couple of thick padlocks and chains that she coiled up and clipped onto the back of her belt.

The darkness seemed to close in as they padded to the spiral staircase that descended into the bowels of the mountain. Each of her silent footsteps seemed too loud. But when they reached the hall leading to the stairs, Venya heard voices. She froze and pressed herself against the cool, smooth wall, as Nyx shrank into the shadows beside her.

"What do we do?" she hissed.

"Leave it to me."

In the blink of an eye, the panther was gone, replaced with a small, four-legged, furry beast too blurry to make out as it hurtled down the corridor and darted off down a fork, making as much racket as possible.

Panic rose in Venya, until she realised Nyx's intentions. The murmured conversation ceased at once. Carefully glancing around the corner, Venya saw the guards reach for their weapons, drawing them silently. Glancing at each other with a shared nod, they left their post at the top of the stairs and pursued Nyx down the hallway. Their footsteps soon faded.

Venya gritted her teeth. This was her chance. Yet she had never felt less inclined to descend those stairs. Not when she knew what lurked at the bottom. She almost expected to see it waiting for her, its eyes glowing in the shadows. However, Nyx had given her a limited window of opportunity, and she refused to waste it.

Before she could talk herself out of it, Venya bolted for the stairs.

Nyx loomed out of the shadows, once more in his panther form. Venya clamped a hand over her mouth to stifle a scream. "How did you get here?" she whisper-shouted.

Nyx only winked. Who knew what manner of creatures he had shifted into in order to avoid detection and return to her side before the guards even realised they chased nothing. "Come on, mistress."

They descended the stairs together, Venya's hand embedded in the fur at the scruff of Nyx's neck a silent comfort, the dim glow of the faint faelights only just holding back complete darkness. Too soon for her liking, yet not quickly enough, she saw the familiar door to Sylvio's vault. Using her seal, they passed inside and quickly closed the door again. Venya leaned against it, slowly breathing in and out, slowing her racing heart, her terrified thoughts.

This is just another day in the vaults, she told herself.

Holding her chin high, her magic ready to call forth, she strode to Sylvio's shelf as though nothing were amiss. As though it were not the middle of the night. As if a beast did not stalk the vaults unchecked. As if Beorn did not lay in the infirmary somewhere above them.

Relief washed over her when she saw Sylvio on his usual shelf. The grimoire snored gently, until she nudged it and cleared her throat, careful not to disturb any of the others.

"Sylvio, wake up."

Sylvio groaned and rumbled, his spine creaking and cracking. "This is most rude, junior librarian."

"Yes, well, we're all in danger, so you'll have to forgive me. I need your help. You must take us to the beast that roams these halls, the one that harmed Beorn. You will remain whilst we bind it, and then you will return us all here." She enunciated each word clearly, in detail, for she had no wish to fall prey to the clever grimoire's twisting of her instructions – or absence of them.

"And what if I do not want to?" he replied snootily.

"You are a grimoire, bound to the Athenaeum. Thus, if I ask it, you are bound to help me."

Sylvio grumbled. "Fine. You'll have to unbind me, though." His last words sounded hopeful.

Nice try.

Venya carefully released his chain from the shelving, then tied it around her own wrist. "Where you go, we go."

"One beast, coming right up," said Sylvio grudgingly.

With that, his covers sprang open and pages flipped too quickly to perceive, finally settling on a double spread of a dark portal ringed by moon-fire and runes Venya could not read. Larger and larger the portal grew, until it was bigger than the page, bigger than the shelf…

With a physical tug somewhere about her navel, the magic of the book yanked her forward. Complete darkness engulfed her for a second before it spat her out back on the stairwell, but far below Sylvio's vault, close to the beast's own haunt. Venya stumbled at the abruptness of it, flailing her arms to balance herself upon the edge of a step.

"Hmm… It *was* just here. This one is quick," Sylvio said, his voice too loud in the utter silence, but Venya did not chastise him, too busy searching the shadows for any trace of the beast.

They stood where Beorn's blood still stained the stairs, Nyx beside her and Sylvio floating before her, tethered to her wrist by the slim, golden chain. Horror crawled through Venya. *No one has cleaned it?*

She edged around the dark patches, following Sylvio as he tugged her down the stairs. She knew where he would lead her. Just around the bend, to the broken door that was whole. Sylvio paused just outside it.

Before her stood the carved wooden door that had haunted her nightmares. To the mortal eye, it looked intact and unremarkable, other than its carvings. But Venya felt the aching emptiness of it. The wards upon it were now only singed, tattered remnants around the edges. It was a door, nothing more.

She cast her eyes skyward for a second, gathering her resolve and sending a prayer to the stars – for what little good it would do her – that she would survive this. Taking a deep breath, Venya walked forward.

The door shimmered around her. Then she was inside. She didn't need a seal to enter, so corroded was the once ancient, powerful magic. That in itself was worrisome enough. They moved away from the door quickly, stepping to one side and silently passing the rows of shelves lining the vault.

Shelves and cages wrought of dark metal, each containing only one grimoire, most bound by multiple chains and locks. She had never seen them so secured. Never encountered any that *needed* to be restrained thusly. Her own knowledge of binding suddenly felt woefully inadequate.

Once more, she checked the pouches at her waist. This time, she had armed herself with aconite mixed with *papaver* – poppy essence – and salt. It would subdue the beast…she hoped.

The vault was filled with the rustling of sleeping grimoires, as well as the snarling, growling, and snuffling of those awake. Words in languages she did not understand spiked through the vault, muttered by the grimoires.

Nyx met her gaze, a silent warning passing between them. They would do well not to attract any unwelcome attention, no matter that the grimoires were bound. That did not mean they posed no danger.

They padded silently down row after row. Most grimoires slumbered as they passed, but some glared at them malevolently with all manner of beastly eyes. Snarls erupted, and suddenly, the books were no longer still, but a flurry of gnashing covers and pages, teeth, tails, and claws flashing, as the grimoires surged against their bindings – physical and magical – to attack.

Venya and Nyx ran, Sylvio in tow, dragged along by his tether. Books hurled themselves off their shelves, dangling and flapping helplessly at the end of their chains. Torn pages fluttered everywhere and dust rose, choking the air.

The vault had awoken. Venya hurtled down one long aisle after another, twisting and turning, but everywhere she ran, grimoires strained against their bindings for a chance at a piece of her, until Venya was deep in the vault, and unable to see the door.

Her pulse thundered through her ears, mixing with the cacophony around her. Venya turned on the spot, Nyx prowling around her, growling and snapping at the grimoires that fought to escape their bindings.

Panic engulfed her. There would be no way to escape this quietly, if at all. Surrounded by malevolent, powerful grimoires on all sides, not to mention a deadly beast prowling the dark vault, Venya had never felt so small, so vulnerable. There would be no way out of this. Either she would die at the hands of the beast or be discovered by Nieve and her career would be over.

A long, low, guttural growl chilled her blood, seized her mind and body, froze her into fear. Venya slowly turned to look behind her.

A great shadow loomed at the end of the aisle. Venya turned back and swore. Dead end. The shadow rounded the end of the bookshelves and turned to them as they backed down the aisle cautiously.

Even in the shadows, it was unmistakable. It had not bothered with any guise, the full horror of its stretched skin, misshapen body, and long, gangling limbs clear. It cocked its head slowly to one side. Then that terrible, tooth-filled maw opened in a wide, slow smile as it advanced, its black, bulbous eyes fixed upon Venya.

THIRTY FOUR

"No...," Lief breathed in silent horror. Beside her, Aedon swore, and she felt the tension radiating off him. If the beasts could now climb, there was nowhere they were safe. It was an uncomfortable reminder of the creatures' cleverness. Their ability to learn and adapt.

Lief whirled around to grab her bow and slung her quiver around her waist. "Let's go."

Aedon drew his dagger. It seemed so thin and small in the darkness. Too small to tackle the great shadow before them.

They hurried to clamber down the tree, but the beast was already a quarter of the way up, its breathing laboured. By the time they reached the branch below, the creature was already halfway up the tree to Kat'har's darkened dwelling.

Damn it! Lief cursed. The bridge was still too far below them. There was no way they could reach it in time. It was too high to jump from bough to bough, even with their elven agility. There were no stairs, no ladders, no pulleys, not even a rope.

Lief gritted her teeth as despair rose within her. *We cannot reach it.* But she still had her bow and arrows. It was far, with a terrible angle, but she had made worse shots. *This one needs to count.*

From beside her, light bloomed, and a roiling ball of crackling magic launched from Aedon's palm, followed swiftly by another, then another. Two blasts went wide, distracting the beast, but then they heard the unmistakable snarl and yelp as one struck home.

The beast swung from the tree wildly as it reached a clawed paw to its back, desperately trying to get rid of the magic that clung to it. The smell of singed fur was sour upon the air.

A scream rang out from above. Mirielle looked out of a window, slack-jawed in horror at the rabid beast that hung too close for comfort.

The scream pulled the beast's attention, its empty gaze snapping to her. Mirielle froze in fear. The beast snarled and lunged up the tree, claws scratching and ripping at the bark in its haste to reach her.

Other cries of alarm rang through the trees, but the beast's attention did not deviate from its prey.

Aedon burst into action, leaping into the void. He landed and rolled upon the wide bough below, immediately up and running again, bounding across a bridge and jumping from branch to branch to cut off the beast.

As he ran, Lief took aim and loosed, but the speed and jerking motion of the beast made it impossible to hit anything. *I'm too far away*. She knew her arrows would not have the force to penetrate the beast's hide from where she stood.

Not wanting to risk destroying or losing her bow to take a leap like Aedon, she growled and ran to the rope ladder, shimming down it as quickly as she could.

Lief alighted on the branch below and sprinted after him, her quiver bouncing on her hip and her bow grasped in her sweating palm. A howl of fury and pain rang out as Aedon reached the creature and stomped viciously upon its paws as it tried to find purchase and clamber up onto the bough.

One claw released, the beast swinging by only one arm, but then it swung and embedded its grip deep within the bark again. It hauled itself up, springing onto the bough. Aedon fell back, brandishing Lief's dagger before him.

He stood between the beast and Mirielle, who now stood frozen in fear against the open window of her room. Lief willed her to be quiet, for the beast's full attention now lay upon Aedon. At least he had a fighting chance of defending himself.

Lief crept forwards as the beast circled Aedon, but he did not yield. Light crackled along the blade as his magic shrouded it. The glow lit up the beast's eyes and slavering jaws. It eyed Aedon hungrily, albeit cautiously. Its wary behaviour told her it was smart enough to recognise a threat. It wanted blood, wanted to attack, but it knew Aedon was dangerous. So far, so focused on Aedon, it had not spotted her.

Lief eased an arrow from her quiver with practised fingers, only the slightest rattle giving her away, and nocked it, ready to draw as soon as she had a clean shot. Yet as she moved, so did they, and Aedon now blocked her shot. Lief bit back a curse. She could not risk shooting. The irony was not lost upon her that a mere few days ago, if it had been reported that he had escaped, she probably would have shot him and not thought twice about it.

"Try me," goaded Aedon, grinning wildly and swiping the dagger at the beast. It dodged with ease and swung at him. Aedon darted out of the way. He circled and thrust, never marking it, yet not allowing the creature to touch him with its serrated claws or sharp teeth, either.

Understanding dawned. Smiling, Lief flitted from branch to branch, working in tandem with Aedon now she knew what he was trying to achieve – drawing the beast away from Mirielle, trying to give her a clean shot.

Lief took a deep breath, raising her bow and drawing back the string until the fletchings rested against her cheek. Waiting. Holding. Her shoulder started to shake, but she gritted her teeth and held firm.

Almost…

Aedon tripped over a knot in the wood and went sprawling. With a triumphant snarl, the beast charged. Aedon shouted, a wordless exclamation. Mirielle screamed. The beast looked up, then back at Aedon, torn between its prey. Aedon was closer, but the girl, so fresh and sweet-blooded…

Lief loosed the arrow.

It struck the beast square in the back, burying into the deep fur. It bellowed as Lief nocked, drew, and loosed again. The arrow struck its side, and another its thigh. The beast stumbled and fell onto all fours. Aedon scrambled backwards, leaping to his feet and slashing at its face as the beast's jaws snapped.

Lief prepared another shot, but her shoulder throbbed with pain, preventing her from raising the bow. As she watched, horrified, the beast tried to rise, but stumbled, then Aedon rushed it.

Dagger held forwards like a lance, he drove it into the creature's chest and pushed backwards, hard. The creature tried to grab him in a deathly embrace, but Aedon deftly slipped away, and the beast stepped backwards to regain its balance – into thin air. It flailed, and time seemed to slow as it reeled backwards. Its claws scrabbled at wood and air, but it could not recover. The beast fell with a shrill cry, then a crash sounded as it hit the ground far below.

Chest heaving, Aedon fell to all fours, peering over the edge, head bowed and shoulders sagging. Lief leapt the last few boughs, dropping down by his side. Far below, a forlorn, broken body lay. The monstrous head was still, jaws open, limbs spread.

Behind them, Mirielle sobbed into her mother's arms, as

Kat'har ran a hand through his tangled hair, glancing between his daughter and the beast far below. Others joined them in silent horror.

"Are you all right?" Lief asked Aedon, resting her hand upon his sweaty shoulder.

He swallowed and nodded. "You?" He met her gaze. A quiet look of shared triumph – and exhaustion – flitted between them.

"Yes."

They had worked so well together, without even the need for words.

As she looked at the beast's body below, it was a sobering reminder of the darkness that seemed to be growing within her beloved Tir-na-Alathea.

More would come, Lief was certain, and they could not wait for the Queen's help to arrive.

THIRTY FIVE

Marielle's mother thanked them profusely, clinging to Aedon and sobbing. He patted her back gingerly, looking uncomfortable, muttering soothing words, until she released him.

"Thank you," said Kat'har fervently with shining, tear-filled eyes, grasping Aedon's hand tightly.

"It's no trouble."

"Anything you need, *anything* at all, just ask and it is yours."

Aedon glanced at Lief beside him and gave her a small smile. Her eyes were glazed over with exhaustion, and he could tell from the slight furrow in her brow – a small tick of hers he was growing to recognise – that she was in pain.

Her wound.

His smile faded. "Honestly, anyone else would have done the same." Aedon turned to Kat'har. "For now, all we desire is sleep."

Kat'har chuckled. "Well, I did say anything, and that is easy to grant. Go. Sleep as much as you need. I shall make sure you are undisturbed and there is food waiting for you to break fast."

"Thank you. Set a guard. Just in case."

Kat'har grimaced. "Yes. Now we know that they can climb…"

He barked out orders, and two of his nephews rushed forwards. They babbled in their native tongue before darting off.

"They have the keenest eyes and the sharpest aim. We shall know if anything more comes tonight."

Aedon nodded, then hovered his hand over Lief's lower back and steered her away.

"You were incredible." His grin widened, but her own answering smile was thin. "Queen of archers…" Aedon winked.

Lief chuckled mirthlessly. "You weren't too shabby yourself. I thought you were dead when you ran right towards that thing."

Aedon's spirits lifted at the appraising glance she shot him. It had been a long time since he had felt such camaraderie, and he had missed it more than he realised.

"I still have some tricks up my sleeve," Aedon said airily.

He stood aside to allow her to climb the ladder. She ascended slowly, favouring her injured arm. By the time they both reached the top, her face had paled, looking stark in the moon's light.

"Are you all right?" he murmured.

"Fine," she strained out with a grimace.

"It's hurting, isn't it?"

Lief did not answer.

"Are we near where the *aleilah* grows?"

"Yes."

"It'll be okay." Aedon was not sure whether he reassured her or himself. "Do you want me to take a look at it?"

Lief shook her head. "Let's sleep."

He rubbed his eyes. "That sounds good to me." The rush of adrenaline had faded, and he longed for nothing more than to shut his eyes. He kicked off his boots, stripped off his blood-stained tunic, then clambered into the hammock.

Lief eyed his bare chest, pausing for a moment, before she climbed in beside him, fully clothed, her back pressed to his front.

"Good night," she said.

"Sleep tight. Don't let the beasties bite." He laughed, then grunted when she elbowed him in the ribs. "Honestly, you wood elves have no sense of humour."

She wriggled around to glare at him, eyes narrowed. This close, her eyes were deep, dark pools, unfathomable and alluring. Aedon shut off the thought and grinned devilishly. She huffed in annoyance and turned away.

Aedon could not suppress the genuine warmth blooming inside him at the mischievous spark that had started to develop between them. Her body was warm, albeit stiff, as though she purposefully did not allow herself to relax. It was strangely intimate and vulnerable, and he was unsure how to feel about it.

Nothing more than convenience, I suppose.

Yet it had awoken his desire for more – to celebrate life again, and all that it entailed. He gently draped his arm over her and buried his head into the soft fabric of the hammock, his heavy eyes drifting shut as he breathed a deep sigh of contentment.

She stiffened momentarily before relaxing slightly. He was grateful to her, he realised. For as much as she infuriated him, as much as she had been insufferable, as much as he was under no illusion that they were anything more than companions of convenience, she had also reminded him of laughter, friendship, and the joy of life.

He turned away from thoughts of her slowly relaxing against him. How natural it felt to hold her close. She was attractive – in both looks and fiery, determined, self-assured nature – but it could never work between them. To her, he was no more than a thief and an inconvenience, and he could sense her walls were built thick and high to keep everyone out.

Don't ruin this, Aedon. You work well together. Nothing more.

THIRTY SIX

Long-lost faces swirled through a dark storm, taunting him. Valyria's craggy, scaled visage hovered above them all, a constant, brooding, reproachful presence, as though, from somewhere beyond the grave, she bore him ill, blamed him for her death.

He sank even deeper, and Valyria shifted, now under him, in a memory he hated but could not escape. The heaviest of the ghosts that weighed upon him. They soared over rugged mountains, grey and pallid in the seething late afternoon light under skulking clouds, dark and heavy with the promise of rain.

Shrieks echoed through the sharp valleys, and Aedon crouched lower over Valyria, urging her faster still, as the scarlet cloak of the Winged Kingsguard billowed behind him, the pin of the general's rank, a golden dragon head, keeping it clasped firmly at his neck. He knew what happened next now, but his past self did not as he flew, inexorably forwards, closer to their doom.

Below, dark shapes scurried across the barren landscape, keeping pace with Valyria. Dark blood rained down from the deep gashes in her wings, spattering the stone. He could hear her laboured breathing as she fought to keep them airborne, feel it shuddering through his legs, and Aedon, exhausted though he was, continued forcing the small, dribbling dregs of his own magic to her, trying to repair the damage the goblins had caused, though he knew it was a lost cause.

He had been arrogant to think he could face the horde alone. He should have waited for reinforcements, for the full might of Pelenor's legendary Winged Kingsguard to descend upon the goblin scourge and rain down fire and death. Fury had overshadowed his judgment. Instead, he faced them alone. The beginnings of despair stirred within him, knowing they may not make it out of the mountains alive.

"Keep going, Valyria. We can do this," he urged.

Her only reply was a laboured groan.

Slowly, their altitude dropped, and they soon flew below the peaks. The scourge kept pace, racing up sheer, vertical cliffs, across steep ledges, and over deadly drops, shrieking with glee. Aedon raised a fist and snarled, sending blasts of magic at their pursuers. Most went wide, but a few struck with satisfying yelps. He wished he could burn them all for what they had done to the villagers, for the pain they had inflicted upon Valyria.

Aedon eyed the peaks rising ahead, the narrow valleys they would have to wind through to reach the plains beyond. They were so close.

"I cannot…continue…," Valyria gasped, shuddering. Her wings stilled and she glided, slowly descending. She had done so well, but they had been cornered, Valyria bearing the brunt of their attack to protect him. Her wings were torn, bloody masses, and he did not have the strength to repair them.

Bitter fury rose within Aedon. This was not how it was supposed to end. He was General of the Winged Kingsguard, atop his mighty, feared, revered dragon, Valyria. The goblins were nothing more than malevolent beasts, only worthy of extermination. He could not give up. They could not give up.

Yet the moment came, as it inevitably did every time Aedon relived the nightmare, when Valyria's wings gave one last, laboured flap, then she shuddered. And failed. They plunged from the air and crashed into the ground, Valyria's bulk and momentum ploughing a long trough into the rocky earth.

Aedon leapt from her back, his hands blazing with magic, but even that sputtered, his remaining strength spent trying to heal her. His blade would be little use against the claws and teeth of the scourge. Even knowing it was hopeless, he gritted his teeth and sank into a fighting crouch as the shrieking, clamouring horde charged them, baying for blood.

Valyria dragged herself to her feet. Her neck drooped. Her sides heaved. Her tail lay limp.

"I'm sorry," Aedon said, his glance flicking to her. "I failed you."

"We are together in this, as we have always been. We failed each other." Valyria's giant, golden eyes blinked slowly, then she swung her head back to the advancing rabble and growled.

"But I will make sure my death is not in vain, Aedon Lindhir Riel. Either we both die, or you live. I choose you every time, my soulmate of heart and wing. I will not meet my end in the manner of their choosing. Carry my fire with you always."

She began to croon, and her fire brewed brightly in her neck. Suddenly, she slowly rose up, her neck arching, tail lifting, wings extending with renewed strength.

"No!" Aedon shouted in horror as the fire building in her throat

became white hot. He had only ever heard of this in the old records of ancient wars. That a dragon might sacrifice itself as a weapon, burn up their inner fire in one giant blaze of glory.

Aedon woke with a start, panting, staring into the darkness, as reality came back into focus. Lief's smooth, dark hair catching the faint moonlight. The warmth of her body moulding to his. The deep rise and fall of her chest under his arm. The soft fabric of the hammock pressing against his cheek. His own thumping heart, drowning out any of the sounds of the night-time forest.

The nightmare always stopped there, but when he awoke, he always remembered what came next.

How he had woken in a giant crater blackened and singed, but miraculously unhurt, thanks to the protection she had bestowed upon him with the last of her strength. How she had been reduced to a pile of embers and ashes, even her bones eviscerated into nothing, her Dragonheart gone. How there had been nothing left of the goblins but their burnt remains.

The air had tasted of death and smoke that day, and he would never forget the feeling as he retched upon the ground until there was nothing left. When the shock had worn off, grief and pain set in. They had been his constant companion in the years ahead.

He remembered feeling that tiny, flickering ember deep inside him, the beating core of what had once been her vast power, the only remnant left of Valyria. He would carry her always. The gift of her dragonfire. Her legacy. The weight of her death. Valyria had not been the first he had failed, or the last, but she was the one who had cut most deeply, and Aedon would never forgive himself for it.

He lay awake for the rest of the night, his long vigil haunted by the ghosts of all those he had failed throughout his life. Lief, warm and sleeping, was the only talisman he had against the darkness of his bleak thoughts. She would never know what her presence meant to him – her warmth, the reassurance of her quiet breathing, her sweet smell that grounded him against the darkness in his mind.

She had awakened painful desires within him. Desires he had suppressed long ago. His heart longed to be permitted to open, be loved, accepted, wanted…yet it was too excruciating. Opening up always meant loss, and he could not bear the thought of that.

Aedon closed his eyes to block out the very sight of her. He could not care for anyone else, not even one hair, in case he lost them, too. Lief had already wormed her way in, with her fiery nature, determination, and vitality. It already hurt to think they would part, go their separate ways. That he would soon lose the closest thing he had to any kind of companion in a quarter of a century.

Don't deceive yourself, Aedon, the dark voice within him callously chided. *It is a companionship of convenience, nothing more. Either she will leave or you will fail her, just as it has ever been.*

He shied away from the thought, even though he knew it was right. *Don't delude yourself, Aedon*, he told himself. *Don't be fooled into letting down your guard. Shut her out. It's for the best.*

Lief groaned and stretched as she leisurely unfolded from sleep, blissfully comfortable. The warm body behind her shifted at her movement. She turned into it, expecting Finarvon, before her consciousness woke enough to remember. Never again would it be Finarvon. She was no longer in Lune. Her shoulder throbbed in an angry reminder, her numb arm tingling.

She blinked the sleep out of her eyes and met Aedon's gaze, momentarily unbothered by their close proximity, which she would have ordinarily shied away from. Perhaps she was softening. Her grudge against Finarvon could not extend to everyone forever.

"Good morning," she said with a yawn and a half-smile. "Sleep well?" She expected a chuckle, a smile, something after the events of the previous night. But Aedon's eyes were hard and cold, his lips set and thin.

"A… Are you all right?" she asked.

"Fine."

Without another word, he extricated himself from the hammock and turned away, his bare shoulders and scarred back closing him off from her. Grabbing some food that had been left, he climbed down the ladder onto the bough below and out of sight.

Lief tried to suppress the hurt his coldness caused, the rejection of her first moment of true openness with him. *Was I mistaken?* Their tentative connection… She had been so convinced it was genuine. So certain she had begun to know the real him, see snatches of the worthy elf he had been.

Lief sat in the gently swinging hammock for a moment, not comforted by the whispering, warm breeze and rustling leaves. With a sigh, she climbed out and washed from the ewer the wood elves had left, then broke fast on the delicate pastries laced with honey and berries – which tasted like ash in her mouth.

With every bite, she berated herself for being such a fool. *He's a thief and a liar. He's probably been taking me for a fool all along. Working to get me to let down my guard so he can strike when I'm vulnerable. I'm a fool to think anything kind of him. To think I need him. I'm better off alone. As I've always been.*

The two of them hardly spoke as they readied to leave, with the warm blessings and thanks of Kat'har and his family, as well as provisions he had insisted they take.

"A day, a night, and another day will see you far into the mountains and to the Wellspring. Please, be safe," Kat'har said as he escorted them to the road.

The two new packs were made of wood, twine, and

handwoven fabric, filled with waterskins, cheeses, meats, breads, and honeyed pastries. Finer fare than they had had since meeting. And for Lief, a dagger crafted of dark metal and rich wood, imbued with light magics.

They were farther off-track than she had realised, and Lief was thankful they had stumbled upon Kat'har, or she might not have reached the Wellspring in time. The tingling numbness had begun to creep across her chest and back. The black veins spidered down her tainted arm past the elbow, and her fingers and hand felt weak and clumsy.

Lief wished Kat'har could stay with them somehow, to breach the painful, awkward silence between her and Aedon. How had it even happened? She dreaded the thought of spending so much time alone with him when he was so inexplicably standoffish. All too soon, Kat'har embraced them, inclined his head, and retreated back to his family in the trees.

Lief watched him go for a moment, before she turned back to Aedon…who was already gone, striding down the road, past Kat'har's son's barrow blooming with small, white flowers that pulsed open and closed. Lief gritted her teeth and followed.

They barely spoke a word all day, the only sounds that of the forest around them, the crunch of their feet upon the path, and the cacophony of her own frustrated thoughts. She had given up asking him what was wrong. He refused to answer, refused to speak, refused to say anything.

Damn him.

With the silence, her resentment only grew. She had started to feel like they were a team, yet he had become a stranger once more in an instant.

I don't deserve to be treated like this! she raged to herself. *Forget about him. This is a job. Nothing more. If he wants to be miserable, leave him to it. Stubborn mule.*

They walked until her feet throbbed in unison with her shoulder, and the sun was setting, before they moved off the road to camp in a quiet nook nearby.

Lief caught Aedon watching her, his face closed and inscrutable. She clenched her jaw to stop herself from asking him what was wrong and turned away. Without a word, she lay down between the roots of a giant, gnarled tree, covering herself with the umber cloak Kat'har's grateful daughter had given her, and closed her eyes, pretending to be asleep.

She cracked open an eye as his quiet rustling settled into silence, too. Aedon sat beneath the tree next to her, legs crossed, staring into the night. At least he had taken first watch. Yet he did not break the silence, even though he looked down and caught her looking before he glanced away again. She forced down her bitter disappointment at the way things had soured between them.

Even the forest echoed their silence, not a living thing to be heard.

THIRTY SEVEN

Every second seemed to yawn into eternity as Vasili strained his senses for any sign of either the dragon he had heard or Icarus's return. He fretted until the moment his dragon swooped into the cave and landed with a thump. It was only then that he released the pent-up breath inside him.

"Thank the skies you're all right."

Icarus allowed Vasili to lean into his muzzle for a long moment. "I sensed nothing."

"I am not mistaken."

"I know." Even Icarus sounded troubled. Vasili had shared the memory in as much detail as he could whilst Icarus rushed back, though he had precious little else but the sound to go on. "It… I would be astounded if it were not a dragon. I took precautions to avoid detection, and I could have sworn I was alone."

They would have to retrace their steps back to the outpost by midday the following day in order to have hope of reaching the garrison at the same time as their fellow riders. If they were tardy,

Tristan would be the first to ask what had happened to delay them when they should have remained within the vicinity of the Dragon's Nest for their patrol.

"We ought to venture farther up the valley before we return." Vasili was curious to see if the valley beyond the waterfall held any clues to the appearance of the strange dragon that had come so close to discovering them.

Icarus paced to the back of the cave but did not lay down. "I agree, but I do not want to wait for dawn. If there is something out there, we would do well to protect ourselves under the cloak of darkness."

Vasili threw a troubled glance outside the cave. It was still dark, but at least the snow had ceased. It went against his training, but he was inclined to agree. The light of day would reveal plenty enough to them – and give away their position. It was the last thing they needed if they had, against all probability, stumbled on the remnants of the Order of Valxiron.

In the dark, they would be handicapped, as well, but with Icarus's night vision and Vasili's magical prowess allowing them to sense far into the darkness, he hoped that flying blind would not be the last mistake he made.

Vasili saddled Icarus, glad for the light saddlebags that would not weigh his nimble friend down. He debated leaving them in the cave for now, but they would be hard-pressed to recall which of the hundreds of caves they had stayed in to retrieve them.

Vasili knew he could sever the straps and cut away the bags to lighten Icarus's load if he needed to. He hoped it would not come to that, because then Tristan would *definitely* ask questions he did not want to answer. No rider would do that without urgent need. Somehow, that seemed worse than facing whatever awaited them in the darkness.

After checking all the straps were secured, he mounted and extinguished the faelight. Darkness engulfed them. For a moment, his heart rate soared before he pushed down the bubbling panic, forcing himself to slow his breathing. His senses melded with Icarus's.

Using his dragon's eyes, Vasili could see in the dark, though far differently than he was used to. The contrast was higher, the world around them shades of grey overlaid with a dark blue-green hue. When he'd first become a rider, it had taken Vasili some time to acclimate himself to Icarus's night vision, but now, well used to it, he knew how to scour the landscape for signs of movement, life, danger.

Icarus crouched and launched himself into the void on silent wings, gliding high above the valley – sensing for any danger – before bringing his wings down in a powerful thrust that blasted them up into the heavens. To the head of the valley he raced, Vasili hunched low over his neck and casting out his magical senses as wide as he could. Vasili could sense no life in the barren valley, save for nocturnal creatures in the forest below that were of no consequence to them.

That all changed when Icarus reached the cleft at the end of the valley.

He tipped to one side, his outstretched wings just brushing the cliffs on either side. Below them, the frozen river was silent, and ahead, a vast, flat expanse of snow-covered ice heralded a lake hemmed in by another rise of mountains.

Vasili felt foreign magic wash over him in a great cascade.

Icarus shuddered beneath him at its touch.

Then the empty valley ahead teemed with life, where there had been none a moment before.

Vasili and Icarus could no longer see barren, rocky outcrops pockmarked with abandoned caves. Light blazed so brightly that Vasili retreated from Icarus's sensitive night vision to his own sight once more.

All around the valley, fires burned in every opening he could see. He could not count them, so numerous were they, and the frozen lake was covered in tracks and temporary structures. People still moved, even this late at night. Black dots moving on a canvas of white.

At the head of the valley, Vasili could see a grander structure than all the rest. Tall columns. Wide, high, arched windows. A grand portal fortified with a portcullis. It was a façade, the true depths hidden in the mountain behind it. If he did not know better, he would think it was the subterranean equivalent of a castle.

As Icarus banked again to circle the valley, hiding in the shadows below the cliffs and rising on a few, sparing wingbeats above the level of the dwellings bored into the rocks, Vasili could only come to one conclusion.

This was a city.

And it was not on the maps.

That meant it could belong to none other than the Order of Valxiron. Who else would go to such trouble to conceal themselves in such great numbers?

Now, Vasili felt somewhat foolish to have ever presumed they could single-handedly discover the Order of Valxiron and bring them to task. Above the sea of lights, he felt as inconsequential as an insect.

Across the valley, movement flickered. Vasili's attention snapped to it automatically, and his heart stuttered. A giant dragon arose, launching into the sky.

Dread struck Vasili to his core, and he felt Icarus's fear bleed into him at the sight.

It had not sensed them – yet. For, over the wind whistling through the peaks, Vasili and Icarus could hear another sound. One that masked their presence. One that had taken him too long to comprehend, for he had never heard its like before.

The keening of dragons in pain echoed around the valley. He could also make out several voices in the wails, all originating in the depths of the mountains. Vasili cast out all of his senses as Icarus did the same, until they traced the source to one side of the valley.

Careful to avoid the notice of the giant dragon at the opposite side of the basin, which wheeled up and away from them, Icarus swooped around the lake, using a sparse forest on one edge for cover for a few precious moments.

"There," Vasili breathed with horror.

Before them, gouged into the very mountain itself with the savageness only tooth and claw could make and covered with spiked, iron grills were three giant pits. As Icarus flew over, using the shadow of a passing cloud for cover, scant though it was, they caught a brief glimpse within.

Dragons.

Broken dragons.

Blood, open wounds, bone.

Proud creatures slumped in defeat.

Small, pitiful, unmoving figures huddled with them.

Open to the elements, Vasili did not envy them one bit. The snowstorm that had just passed them, whilst Vasili had remained safe and warm in his cave, had dumped snow into the pits, forcing the dragons and their riders to cower against the walls to escape what they could of the cold.

Vasili suppressed the urge to vomit as the acrid stench of waste and decay rose to meet them. Icarus growled softly. Vasili could feel his surging anger, boiling the dragon's very blood. It seemed they had discovered far worse than anyone had expected. Not only had they found a settlement that could only belong to the Order of Valxiron, but the missing patrol, as well. In no fit state to travel, by the looks of it.

"We must help them," growled Icarus into Vasili's mind. Rage laced every word.

"We cannot." Though Vasili wished it were not so. Despair cowed him. It was a fool's mission. Yes, he was arrogant, but he was not an idiot. "We have to get help – Tristan, Elyvia, the Wings – and we have to get them *now*."

They had been there for precious minutes. Which meant it had been minutes since they had broken through the protective enchantments shrouding the valley. Neither of them knew whether that meant whoever dwelled in this valley was now alerted to their presence. Vasili had never felt an enchantment as powerful. He suspected whoever had cast it would never have allowed such an obvious omission in their wards.

"I will not leave them." Icarus was the most stubborn being he knew, and he could not be forced into anything. Vasili gritted his teeth. This was above both of their arrogance.

"If someone took the trouble to hide what is in this valley, that means they will be sure to know if and when someone stumbles upon it. Someone like *us*. And I have no desire to discover who they are without the Wings behind us. We're leaving, Icarus. Now." He filled his voice with as much authority as he could, even though Vasili was under no impression he had any semblance of control, yet he could not help the edge of fear that slipped through. Upon Icarus's back and strapped in, he was, ultimately, at the dragon's mercy.

Behind and below them, the keening of the dragons intensified, then silenced as shouting arose and the crack of whips snapped through the crisp air. Shrieks of new pain rang out.

Vasili could feel Icarus's body stiffen as he attempted to silence the roar he so longed to unleash. With every wild call of agony, the dragon trembled…until he could contain himself no longer.

Icarus erupted, and dove into the valley.

They shot towards the frigid ground, the wind stinging Vasili's eyes as it sliced past him. Flames illuminated the night, and he was half-scalded and half-frozen as Icarus's fire blasted, mingling with the icy air.

"What are you doing?!" Vasili screamed, but he could feel the walls of Icarus's mind slam shut against any attempts by him to penetrate. "Stop!"

They would certainly be discovered now. As Icarus slowed his descent and the dazzling brightness of the fire ebbed, Vasili's vision cleared… and his heart plummeted. Shouting figures quickly converged on them from across the frozen lake and around the pits. Icarus landed with an almighty crash that jarred Vasili, sending shooting pain through him, but it had the added benefit of sending those running toward them sprawling to the ground from the force of the impact.

Icarus ran. Vasili clung on for dear life, hunching low over the dragon's neck. With one hand, he hung onto the pommel for dear life, his knuckles whitening, whilst he blindly reached backwards with his other to draw his sword from one of the bags, where it lay wedged amongst his bedroll. The dagger at his waist felt altogether worthless.

Another blast of fire lit up the night as Icarus blazed a great swathe around them, thundering towards the pits.

A vast shadow fell over them.

The blow that smashed into them with the force of a mountain falling crushed Vasili.

THIRTY EIGHT

It was the stillness that jolted her awake. The forest was too quiet. Instinctively, she knew something was amiss. Lief opened her eyes and slowed her breathing, taking care to be still, shrouded from view by the cloak.

Clicking.

The canopy shuddered.

Lief was alert immediately, awareness coursing through her veins, the sluggish remnants of her magic trying to force its way to her aid.

Aedon still sat as he had when she had fallen asleep, his back to the tree, but now his head rested back against the rough bark, his mouth gaping open, and his eyes closed.

"*Aedon!*" she shouted into his mind, but he did not respond. "*Wake up!*"

Nothing.

Unease stirred in her belly as she moved her eyes, taking a careful look around the forest and seeing small beasts and insects lying motionless…in plain sight. The clicking emanated again, and the shuddering canopy rustled closer this time. It sounded like something heavy approached. Something dangerous, too, if the forest creatures that ought to have fled lay prone with her travelling companion.

Why am I unaffected? Lief wondered, having no answer.

Fear curled in her. She had hardly any magic remaining, and the wound physically slowed her, as well. Regardless of their sundered relationship, she needed Aedon's help for them both to survive whatever came.

I cannot do this without him, she admitted to herself, though she would not have said it aloud.

"*Aedon*!" she shouted into his mind again.

Nothing.

Lief hissed a silent curse.

She was alone.

She could run, but she would not get far alone, nor could she, in good conscience, leave Aedon to certain doom at the hands of whatever dark creature had taken hold of their corner of the forest.

Lief forced her breathing to slow, forced herself to calm. *Think. What are my options?*

She glanced around. Her bow lay within easy reach. The new dagger was tucked under the cloak, close to her head. She'd need to move quickly to use either.

Aedon would have to be the distraction, the bait, to give them a fighting chance against whatever creature was dark and devious enough to send the forest into slumber.

Lief rose silently, keeping the cloak around her, its brown colour and rough texture helping her blend into the shadows. She grasped the dagger, then her bow and four arrows from her quiver, wincing as they rattled ever so slightly. Fortunately, the sound was masked by the shivering canopy above and the clicking, which had increased in volume and frequency, as though whatever creature it emanated from grew excited – or impatient – to see the fruits of its labour.

Lief slipped around the tree trunk and tucked herself into a hollow. The scent of earth and rotting vegetation, damp and pungent, filled her nose. Just as she folded herself away, a shadow engulfed the area, blotting out the pale moonlight. It slowly advanced upon their clearing, its bulk causing the branches to creak and groan, and Lief's heart stuttered in her chest as she beheld the beast.

A thing of legend.

A terror of nightmares.

Eight thick, hairy legs. Giant, bulbous body. Enormous, slick pincers.

A gigantic *arakea,* twice her height, descended on silent webbing towards Aedon.

Lief screamed silently, the only expression of her terror she could make without drawing its attention, and gritted her teeth, desperately trying to slow her thundering heart, calm her ragged breathing. Her bow, a small dagger, and a dribble of magic suddenly seemed infinitesimally inadequate in the face of such an enormous beast.

Her hand tightened around the arrows. *Lief, hold it together*, she told herself sternly. She had taken down big prey before. Nothing quite like this, but still.

It's just you and the prey, she said, as though this were like any other hunting expedition. As though the beast had not already landed on hairy feet and clicked with excitement.

Its giant pincers snapped open and closed as it lowered its head, with all of its bulbous eyes, and advanced towards Aedon…

Lief silently drew her arrow, gritting her teeth against the pain of her injured shoulder. Aedon needed her. There was no time for fear. No time for doubt. Only time to act, or he would die

She stepped from the hollow for a clear shot, and brought her foot down heavily, deliberately, upon a twig, both relishing and fearing the crunch. The sound echoed through the clearing. Time slowed. The *arakea* spun around, focusing all eight eyes on her.

It hissed, its pincers clicking.

Lief loosed.

The arrow flew true, striking the creature in one of its eyes. It burst, and black liquid gushed forth. The *arakea's* screech cut through her, blinding her with momentary pain as the noise cleaved her head in two.

Yet despite the clamour, Aedon and the creatures around the clearing continued to slumber.

The creature lowered its head, its legs writhing, rubbing, trying to relieve itself of the pain. A hairy leg snapped the arrow shaft in two, but the point remained lodged deeply within. It keened again and raised its head, shuddering. Now it focused on her, Aedon lying forgotten.

Lief drew and loosed again. The arrow clattered off its hard pincers and flew into the undergrowth. She bit back a curse, nocked, drew, and loosed again, just as the creature charged her.

Another arrow buried in an eye, another shriek of pain, but the creature did not stop. Lief realised she was trapped, her back against the tree, its terrible pincers stretched wide and ready to tear her to shreds.

Time slowed with every thunderous beat of her heart. Hot, moist air stinking of death and decay roiled over her. Its remaining eyes were fixed upon her, black, oily, and malevolent. This close, she could see the wiry hair covering its body, the sharp pincers glittering with poison.

Fumbling for a heart-wrenching moment, Lief nocked her last arrow and loosed, having no time to aim.

As it lunged, the arrow drove straight into its open maw.

With a screech, the *arakea* reared up, writhing. Its legs flailed as it tried to wrench the arrow from its mouth, to no avail.

Gurgling, bubbles frothed from its mouth, and as it contorted in pain, black, boiling globules of blood flew, hissing as they landed and burning whatever they touched.

Lief could see the tough, thick hide of its underbelly, scarred and scratched – and covered in pale, glittering powder that flaked off with every movement…

The powder!

Lief glanced around. It had settled upon the clearing, sending everything it touched to sleep…except her. *The cloak!* Unwittingly, the elf-girl's cloak had protected her. Yet the great beast was still too close, and too alive, to think about anything else right now.

Lief dropped her bow, her arrows spent, and drew the dagger, wishing she had a longer blade. She would have to venture dangerously close to deliver a killing blow. The *arakea's* pincers were longer than the dagger she held.

She did not quite dare to leave the paltry protection of the hollow tree just yet, watching the creature writhe upon the ground. Black blood and pus leaked from the wounds. It still tried desperately to force the arrow from its mouth, but could not, its bloody legs sliding off the smooth shaft.

Taking a deep breath, Lief edged around the clearing to Aedon. No matter what, she had to protect him since he could not protect himself. In the chaos, he had slipped sideways and now lay in a crumpled heap upon the ground.

Without taking her eyes off the keening beast, Lief crouched and touched his neck, feeling for a pulse. Weak and faint, but there. Relief washed over her.

He's alive, thank the stars.

The creature clicked and hissed in pain and fury, one of its legs lashing out towards her. Lief swiped at the hairy, black mass, almost stumbling backwards. The *arakea* shrieked as the blade connected, half severing its leg, and drew back, before coming at her again.

The air became a whirl of black, hairy limbs, flashing steel, and a hail of black blood as Lief forced her tired body to meet every attack, until at last, a leg swiped at her and knocked her off her feet. Winded, she lay there gasping, her dagger arm trapped under her, as the creature dragged itself closer.

It loomed above her, mouth open, soiling her with frothing, stinging, black blood and green pus.

Lief had but a moment to think before the creature struck. She rolled to the side as the pincers drove into the moist ground, just missing her. Her dagger arm free, she rolled back just as it pulled itself free.

A slash across three more of its eyes, and blood cascaded down upon her, coating her in sticky, stinking, stinging liquid.

When it came at her again, she thrust up, holding her shaking arm as steady as possible. As it struck, she rammed the point of the dagger home. Deep into its maw.

The *arakea* wrenched itself away with a scream, dagger still embedded within it, and fell backwards, writhing upon the ground in its death throes.

Lief had no energy left, and no weapons. If the creature attacked again, she would be done for. Slowly, painfully, she rolled over, dug her fingers into the wet earth, and hauled herself forwards, one painstaking inch at a time, to where Aedon lay in a heap, her eyes fixed upon the dagger at his hip.

Behind her, the keening of the creature crescendoed, then slowed. Lief's dirtied, slick fingers slid upon the hilt of the dagger until she finally drew it, holding it with a shaking hand as she turned and propped herself up on an arm, expecting to feel the sharpness of death slice into her.

But the *arakea* subsided, folding in upon itself, its great legs curling across its belly as terrible shudders wracked its body. For a moment, she felt sorry for it. No wood elf killed for sport or without good reason. Then she remembered the maw coming at her, the stench roiling her stomach, the malevolence in its eyes.

Lief shuddered. *It was kill or be killed.* And, if she had not intervened, Aedon would be dead.

With its last death throes, the *arakea* finally stilled. Its keening faded, and its shuddering jerks ceased. Yet Lief did not let down her guard for even a second. She waited, stiff and poised, ready to fight or flee, though she knew she had the strength for neither.

Lief waited in the silent forest, until she was cold, frozen against the ground, still propped up on an elbow and clutching the dagger. Behind her, Aedon gently snored. Still, she did not dare move. Did not dare believe it was over. Every part of her remained tense and taut, ready and waiting.

In the distance, she could hear the faint sound of life returning to the forest. It approached slowly, a rippling wave of life as birds, insects, and small creatures rustled through the undergrowth and canopy once more.

Only when she could hear things moving nearby did she move. The forest itself told her it was safe once more. No creature would have emerged otherwise. Lief suppressed a groan as she rose to her feet, her stiff, cold, exhausted limbs aching. Dagger held out and trembling, she circled the giant creature. Even in death, curled up, it was the same height as her. The powder glistened on its belly and legs. Pincers open in a silent, eternal scream. Remaining eyes glazed and dull, unseeing.

Appalled by its bulk, shock and fear now rolled through her, as well as relief that she had survived a creature so lethal without an ounce of magic. A shuddering sob took hold of her. Gagging at the stench of it, she slowly retreated to Aedon's side.

Lief dropped to her knees, the moist earth quickly soaking through the fabric of her trousers, and dragged him to sit upright once more, shaking his shoulders with increasing ferocity. "Wake up, Aedon! Damn it. Wake up!"

He was as pale as death, but still breathing faintly. When she felt his neck, his pulse was still lazy and sluggish.

Lief glanced around desperately. How long would he remain asleep? "Aedon!" she called again urgently. He did not move. As she held his cool, clammy face in her hands, looking into his slack face, so peaceful and carefree in slumber, she realised if something happened to him, she did not know what she would do with herself.

THIRTY NINE

Despite his infuriatingly elusive and aloof nature, Lief did not want him to die. As much as she did not want to admit it, she needed him. Could not do this without him.

Not knowing what else to do, she grabbed the waterskin, took a long gulp of it to soothe her parched throat, then tipped the rest over his head, washing away the remnants of the powder glittering upon his cheeks.

She waited so long for him wake it felt like she had petrified. Lief forced herself to her feet, stumbling on her deadened legs. She paced around the clearing to tease some life back into herself, glancing at the creature every so often. At the shimmering in the *arakea*'s mouth, she paused. And swallowed.

My dagger…

There was nothing else for it. Though her body recoiled from placing herself within reach of the terrible maw, Lief gulped in a breath and darted forwards, reaching for the dagger. With a sickly, sucking sound, she yanked it free.

It stank. She quickly retreated to Aedon once more, never taking her eyes off the beast, and began to clean the blade of dark gore on the grass, waiting for Aedon to wake.

He finally stirred, to her soaring relief, and moaned. "What is it with you and rude awakenings? I was having the loveliest dream of a feast–"

Lief wanted to be furious at him, but she was so relieved they were both alive that she let out a muffled sob as she pulled him into a tight embrace.

"Oh…" Aedon stiffened, then patted her back gently as he looked over her shoulder…and spotted the giant, dead beast. He sucked in a breath. "Wh-what did I miss?"

She choked out a laugh at his sheepish tone. "You slept through a crisis, Aedon Lindhir Riel. You very nearly were the main course at the feast you dreamt about. What kind of companion are you?" *I needed you.* But after his unexplained coldness the previous day, she could not bear to admit it.

Aedon groaned and rubbed his eyes. "Clearly a poor one. I feel like I've been trampled by a horse. Or maybe a dragon…"

"Try an *arakea,*" Lief said, leaning to one side so he could fully see the beast.

Aedon's eyes widened as he looked at it. "It's dead? You're sure?"

"Yes."

He swallowed, and a small faelight bloomed. He shuddered as it fell on the hideous creature. "I've never seen one in real life, and I can't say I'm that enamoured."

"I wasn't that thrilled to have to fight it singlehandedly, either – without magic." She glared at him. He had the good grace to duck his head.

"Sorry. I don't know what happened." He did sound sincere.

"I do."

She briefly explained what had transpired, right down to the paralysing powder, which explained Aedon's unbreakable slumber and the ache in his body, as the toxic magic worked to paralyse and subdue its prey.

"I think Mirielle's cloak protected me. I guess the powder has to touch your skin to work?" She shrugged.

Struck by inspiration, she glanced around and found the empty husk of a giant seed. With an apprehensive swallow and a glance at the beast again, she darted forwards and scraped some of the shimmering powder into the makeshift vessel, before scrambling backwards and closing her hand around the husk to seal it around the precious powder inside.

She held it up. "Might come in handy."

"Well... Thank you, Lief," said Aedon, a hint of awkwardness in his voice as he met her gaze, then swiftly looked away. "I appreciate you not leaving me to become dinner..."

"Goodness... That's a change!"

Aedon furrowed his brows. “Hmm?”

“When we first met, you wanted nothing more than to be left to your own punishment.”

“I suppose… But since meeting you, I’ve… I’ve realised I no longer want that fate anymore. Whether I deserve it or not, I’m done rotting in this forest. When we reach your Queen, I’ll be taking my freedom back…one way or another.”

Lief was impressed by his fire, though she could not help but think his cocksure attitude both risky and foolish. She did not remark about it, though.

“Well,” she said lightly, “I suppose we had better get there soon then, so you can be done with this realm.”

He gave her a strange look, saying nothing.

“Come on. I don’t fancy sleeping here anymore.” Lief stood, brushing herself down. Dirt and debris from her skirmish littered the forest floor.

“I agree. The ambience is sadly lacking,” Aedon murmured, rising. “Can we find somewhere without giant, elf-eating spiders?”

“Certainly, sir. Right this way.” Lief mockingly bowed and gestured for him to walk ahead of her. And as suddenly and inexplicably as it had arrived, the coldness between them dissipated. At least they were on speaking terms again, could joke with each other, even if it were nothing more than that.

FORTY

Venya retreated slowly, not taking her eyes off the beast, heart hammering, limbs shaking as she called forth her magic. Her back bumped against the rough metal bars of a cage. A snarl erupted behind her. She scrambled away, turning to see what was within, whilst keeping an eye on the beast approaching. The grimoire inside, which was almost as tall as her with teeth as long as her fingers, retreated to the corner of its cage. She shuddered.

Turning away, careful not to get too close to the cage, she faced the beast once more, Nyx by her side, and Sylvio lurking behind her, tethered to her wrist. The beast gave her a vicious smile, its tail lashing eagerly. Venya nodded slightly at Nyx, then they launched into motion, charging the beast. A ragged cry burst from her throat, a scream of fear and anger, and magic blazed at her fingertips.

The beast lowered itself onto four legs and became a blur as it launched itself at them. It barrelled into Venya, sending her flying and crashing into a bookshelf with a grunt. Grimoires tumbled from its heights, screeching and roaring in protest.

She crumpled to the floor, winded, the taste of blood in her mouth. Sylvio had landed hard upon her thighs, and Venya could already feel the bruise starting to form from his sharp corners.

She turned to see the beast readying to leap upon her. It sprang into the air. She threw up her hands, knowing she could not truly defend herself from it…then a familiar tug yanked at her.

Dizzying darkness… Then Venya found herself falling onto the floor, confused for a moment. She looked around, relief washing over her.

Sylvio!

The grimoire had transported them feet away, yet far enough, even though they were now trapped between the creature and the cage again. She did not have a chance to dwell on the budding idea within her at Sylvio's actions, as the beast rounded on them with an angry snarl.

With a screech, the beast lowered its head, its toothy grin widening. Its foul breath washed over her, carrion and decay, as it huffed and stalked closer, step by careful step, watching and waiting for her to try to escape again.

"Vee?"

They all froze at Beatrix's shaky voice. Venya glanced beyond the beast. At the end of the aisle, wearing her nightclothes and dressing gown, stood Beatrix, with a familiar, compass-shaped charm in her open palm.

"W-what's going on?" Beatrix's attention slid to the beast, and she blinked, eyes widening, as if only just realising what she saw.

A strangled cry escaped as she took in the horror before her…and realised she was powerless. Beatrix had no belt, no weapons, no protections upon her. She was little better than naked, for all the good her clothes would do her.

Time froze.

Before she could react, the beast lunged.

It was quickly on Beatrix, who went down with a gargling cry of pain and terror. Venya charged, her legs and lungs burning. By her side, Nyx morphed, growing into something huge and terrible – a great bear, Venya realised – and leapt upon the beast, tearing it off Beatrix.

Nyx and the beast tumbled down the aisle, locked together, teeth and claws flashing, shelves shaking and grimoires flying. Venya skidded to a halt beside Beatrix and crashed to the floor, ignoring the painful jolt of her knees upon the stone, desperately dragging Beatrix's head onto her lap.

To Venya's relief, she was breathing, though unconscious, a nasty gash across her chest blooming red and soaking her nightclothes, her face bruised and pale.

Venya smoothed her tangled hair back from her forehead, cursing the fact Beatrix had come, that she had been foolish enough to follow her, even though Venya could hardly blame Beatrix for her own folly. Of course, Beatrix would have wanted to make sure she was all right, had not come to harm…and she had paid the price. Venya berated herself; anguish, guilt, and shame threatening to engulf her.

Down the aisle, the beast and Nyx caused carnage. Taking advantage of the brief respite in the maelstrom, Venya stood and pulled Sylvio close on his chain, telling him her idea.

"Can you do it?" she hissed, glaring at him.

"Well, I must say, that sounds like rather a lot of fun. I shall give it my best shot." Sylvio's wolfish grin was audible in his voice as he considered the devastation of it.

Nyx's screech of pain cut through her. Yelping, he backed off, and Venya saw him gingerly put his weight on a hind leg, limping. The beast circled, almost lazy in its movements, sensing it had the upper hand. Its mouth and claws dripped with blood, and its furless skin was smeared with the darkness of it.

Venya could sense her chance slipping away – Beatrix prone upon the stone, Nyx injured, and only her and Sylvio left to withstand the beast…if the unreliable grimoire could be counted upon. All seemed to be lost, and only desperation remained. The defiance not to die just yet.

"Oi!" Venya shouted at the top of her voice, then charged.

With one hand, Venya reached for a pouch at her hip, wrenching it free. With her other, she called forth the binding magic. As one, she threw and thrust out her hand. The pouch shot through the air, the net of golden, binding magic with it.

The beast turned, but too slowly. It twisted free of the net, only to land in the path of the pouch, which exploded, casting shimmering, mauve powder all over it. It shrieked. Nyx rushed back in, now in the form of a wolf – still slightly limping – and sank his teeth into the beast's leg. It howled in agony, but Nyx held fast. Venya skidded to a halt and used both hands to cast a bigger, stronger binding spell. Once more, a net of fine, golden threads burst from her palms.

This time, held fast by Nyx and slowed by the potent magic inside the pouch, the beast could not move as the net wrapped around it. The more the beast writhed, the firmer the net stuck. Nyx released his hold and twisted away before it could ensnare him, too. His head hung, and he panted heavily.

Venya moved, Sylvio still bound to her wrist. "Now, Sylvio!"

She leapt into the air.

She reached behind her, one hand grasping the chain on her belt, the other a padlock. Behind her, Sylvio flung open, this time to a dark portal full of stars and obsidian, surrounded by shards of crystal. Larger and larger the portal grew.

The beast raised its head, its teeth bared in a snarl, a hint of pain on its wretched face as it struggled against the net, its movements sluggish and clumsy, thanks to the infusion of Venya's immobilising pouch. Venya flung the chain out before her like a whip and landed upon the beast. The chain coiled around it.

She gagged on the fetid stench, recoiling from its moist, clammy skin. The beast, net and all, wrapped its long, spindly arms around her, its jaws stretching wide…

Sylvio landed upon them both, and his portal engulfed them. For a moment, the beast's foul smell vanished into a cool, calm breeze, before they materialised back in the living world once more…crammed inside one of the empty cages. Sylvio squawked in protest at the close confines, unable to do more than flutter his pages and shriek in dismay as the beast's claws tore at him, reaching for Venya.

Claws pierced Venya's arms as the beast latched onto her, pulling her closer. Despite every instinct screaming at her to fight, to free herself, she let it. The closer it dragged her into its deadly embrace, the more she fumbled for the other end of the chain to draw around it. Tighter and tighter, it squeezed the breath from her. Finally, she grasped the two ends of the chain in her hands.

And slipped the padlock through them.

Crack.

She could not be sure whether it was the padlock closing or her ribs snapping, but she felt it click shut, the magical power of the chain and padlock amplified by their joining. The beast threw its arms wide, trying to shrug off the chain that slowly tightened around the creature's spindly limbs.

Venya threw herself backwards from its looming jaws,

retching on the stench. Sweat dripped into her eyes. She tried to blink it away, ignoring the sting of her wounds and the warm blood trickling down her rent skin, soaking into her torn clothes.

"Now!" she screamed.

Sylvio sprang into action once more, folding over her. She grasped onto the void willingly, as though her life depended on it…which it did. The beast's claws latched onto her ankle as Sylvio whisked her away, and for a heartbeat, Venya panicked as it began to tug her back. She shot her other foot out, hearing a satisfying crunch and a cry of pain as her boot connected with the creature. Its claws slipped from her bloodied leg, and Venya wrenched it away.

Into the abyss.

FORTY ONE

They followed the road in comfortable silence until the fork Kat'har had detailed to them, taking the right up into the mountains.

Aedon had been extra vigilant on the way, mostly shamed about his failure to help Lief face the giant *arakea.* He had never seen anything like the beast before, and it was bad enough dead. He did not want to imagine what it might be like to face one alive. He suppressed a shudder. She was a braver elf than he.

Lief's warning hiss distracted him from his thoughts. She motioned for him to come forwards, and he stepped up alongside her, halting at her outstretched arm.

Without a word, she pointed at the trail ahead. Aedon frowned. What was that? A small, black, twisted thing the size of a large rodent… A husk of something that had once been alive.

Beyond it, smaller creatures littered the way. A gruesome trail of death.

"The blight is here," Lief said in a low voice, glancing at

Aedon, her amber eyes dark under drawn brows.

"What does that mean for the Wellspring?" Aedon asked, looking up the path.

Lief swallowed. "I don't know."

They continued walking, slowly, shoulder to shoulder, arms bumping with each cautious stride, silently scanning before, around, and behind them.

The mountain valley closed in, steep sides funnelling them forwards upon the trail that would lead them to the Wellspring…and whatever else lurked there.

Saying nothing, Aedon paused, placing a hand on Lief's arm to halt her, deepening the wards upon them. Wards so eyes would turn from them. A cloak of silence, so none would hear their passage. A charm of evasion, so those who perceived them would quickly forget and turn away.

Lief smiled thinly as the warmth of magic washed over them, then he gestured for her to continue.

Aedon examined her for a second before he followed. She was paler than he had seen her, her once tan, vibrant skin looking gaunt and pallid. Her arm was a mess, pale and hanging limp, spidering veins almost down to her hands.

The farther they walked, the more the stench of death and decay grew. Soon, even the plants, which should have possessed extra vitality and vibrancy from the Wellspring, looked like they were withering and dying.

Aedon drew his dagger. Lief did the same. Ahead, the steep cliffs converged into one jagged ravine, a light beyond.

They stole forwards, Lief leading with Aedon in the rear, casting his senses and magic out as far as he could. So intent on their surroundings, he bumped into Lief when she stopped abruptly, gasping.

Before them, the cliffs parted to reveal a small, concealed valley, a guardian to the wide, open cave on the far side in the precipices that ringed the area with an impenetrable wall.

Aedon could tell it once had been lush and verdant, brimming with life and vitality, but now, it was a forest of nightmares. Dead, decaying trees, oozing blood-red sap, looked like jagged, broken teeth jutting from the earth.

Yet this was not what caught his eye. Horrifying, lumbering creatures wandered through the forest, flickers of movement within the darkened canopy that remained. He could sense the dark magic roiling off them and swayed at the potent power of it. Every manner of beast had the same, stumbling gait, missing fur, missing limbs, gashes oozing dark blood…

Aedon did not need to draw any closer to know that these beings were dead, yet animated in the same way the elves of Lune had been.

Lief and Aedon shared a dread-filled look. It would be impossible to sneak past so many of the dark beasts to enter the cave beyond, where the Wellspring, and the *aleilah*, awaited.

FORTY TWO

Heavily warded, they made a hasty, tense retreat back the way they had come. Aedon breathed easier with each vibrant, leafy tree they passed, but the small, dead creatures scattered upon the path was a stark reminder of the proximity of the threat lurking in the valley above. The threat that, Aedon assumed, would come down from the valley with the night to feast anew.

If they became trapped, it would be impossible to escape or defeat such a great number of the dark beasts. But he knew Lief was fading. She did not say as much, but he could see it in the way her shoulders hunched, hear it in her ragged breathing, not to mention the way her eyes seemed to have lost some of their spark and lustre. Every time he glanced at her, his heart dropped, dreading the moment he might see that they had become black and dead, too.

"We have to find somewhere safe to spend the night," he murmured, his sweaty fingers clenching around the handle of the dagger, if for no other reason than to reassure himself it was still there, that he had a means to defend them, though he had no doubt it would be a futile gesture.

"In a tree," Lief muttered, looking up, a frown knitting her brows.

"Are you all right?" Aedon asked, reaching out, then stopped himself. He knew she would hate him trying to support her. Would see it as a sign of weakness.

Lief momentarily scrunched her brows together, then shook her head. "No. We need to find somewhere soon."

Aedon swallowed and looked around. They had deviated from the path, picking their way up the steep slope. Beyond, the rocky cliff soared into the sky, impenetrable. Ahead, Aedon spotted a large tree that had split in two, its mighty trunk contorting around a small nook off the ground…a cradle for them to spend the night. There would be no fire, no noise, nothing that would draw attention when the dark beasts came down to feast.

Aedon bent and cupped his palms for Lief to climb into the tree.

"Thank you," she murmured, grunting with the exertion as she hauled herself up, her limbs trembling.

Aedon wondered how much longer she could endure. He clambered up the tree behind her, not daring to voice his concerns.

They settled in the bough of the tree, its leafy branches concealing them. Lief sighed and wrapped the cloak around her shoulders. It was warm in the forest of eternal summer, yet she shivered, her pale lips trembling. It made Aedon's heart sink further. They were quickly running out of time.

"Lief, I know you're not one to stand idly by, but you must conserve your strength. I'll go alone tonight. Hopefully I can sneak–"

"Absolutely not. Out of the question. You'll never make it."

"I understand–"

Lief leaned towards him. "No, Aedon. It's too dangerous."

In the shadows, her skin looked even paler, her eyes even darker, and for a second, it made Aedon's stomach drop. A glimmer of the setting sun lanced through the rustling leaves, and her eyes were golden once more for a split second, but it was enough to still the ferocious thundering of his heart.

"Lief…," he began, then stopped. What could he say? He had no right to tell her what to do. And she had no obligation to heed him, no matter that he spoke out of concern for her wellbeing.

"I can help somehow," Lief uttered, filling his silence, as though she understood what he had not said. "You cannot face that alone."

"It's too dangerous," Aedon said simply. "The *aleilah*… The first time I stole it was not luck, I shall not do you the dishonour of suggesting it was, but this time will be far more dangerous. At least I have my magic and strength. You are–"

"Don't you *dare* say weak," Lief warned, her eyes flashing

with ire.

"I would never think that about you, but it would be foolish to believe you could take on the challenge of what lies ahead."

"I would warn you similarly," Lief replied coolly. "If you go in alone, you cannot expect to walk out alive."

"I would rather do that than risk your life." He dropped his gaze to the branch. A jewel-coloured insect trundled along. He held out his hand and guided it onto the back, its tiny feet tickling his skin. He could crush it without a second thought. He felt similarly small against the creatures they faced.

"You don't get to decide that for me."

"And if you are not fit enough to decide that for yourself?"

"How *dare* you," Lief said softly, her tone so scathing he flinched at it. He had not meant to offend her, to take control, but if it came down to it, Aedon knew he would, just to make sure she did not die in vain or come to harm. "I will do as I damn well please, and no Pelenori elf shall stop me."

Aedon stared at her levelly, meeting her furious gaze, and pushed down the flip in his stomach. "We have come so far for you to obtain this cure so we might have a chance of reaching your Queen to warn Her of what taints your realm. If you want to jeopardise that by taking needless risks, you are a fool, Lief na Arboreali."

"Then a *fool* I am, Aedon Lindhir Riel." With that, Lief turned away from him, huddled in her cloak, and was still.

Aedon's eyes slipped shut for a moment as he fought to push down the surge of frustration within him. Lief seemed to instinctively know how best to rile him.

Damn her pride! he cursed silently.

He would have to take matters into his own hands. *I will wait until she sleeps, then go myself without her knowing.* It would be a tall order, but it was the only way to protect Lief from her own foolishness.

FORTY THREE

With a small amount of guilt, Lief watched Aedon sleep. When he had not been looking, she had taken a swig of water, then carefully laced the skin with the *arakea*'s sleeping powder. Unaware, Aedon had taken it from her to have his own fill.

He soon succumbed to a deep sleep, but she had used such a small amount, Lief knew her time was measured by minutes, not hours. Her heart fluttered as she watched him for a moment longer, just to make sure.

His chest rose and fell steadily, his head tipped over awkwardly to one side and mouth hanging open, a quiet snore emerging.

Forgive me, she silently begged. The idea had been born of anger, yet watching him, so vulnerable, she regretted it. Not enough to stop her, though.

Lief dug into the well of her magic, which was nearly empty, pulling on the trickle still within. It came reluctantly and with resistance, but she gritted her teeth and dragged it forth, pouring it into a simple glamour.

No more did she have the magic left to craft an intricate replica, or even a poor one, of herself. This was nothing more than a shapeless lump that she threw the cloak over – a passable imitation of her bundled up and asleep. It would not survive even the closest inspection, but it would buy her the time to do what was needed. Lief hoped.

Most of all, she hoped Aedon would understand and forgive her. This was necessary. He had no reason to endanger himself for her, and she did not want him to risk his own life…especially now she had seen what they faced.

She would retrieve the *aleilah* herself and get them out of this mess. She ignored the small voice in her head that told her it was all her fault. That if she had just listened to Aedon in the first place and not headed back to Lune, she never would have gotten into such a mess, and they could have been in Emuir already, safe.

With a last look at Aedon, Lief pushed down her guilt, suppressed the rising coil of fear, and clambered down the tree.

Aedon woke with a groan. His head throbbed, and his neck was stiff. Why had he fallen asleep sitting up? The thought nagged at him as he tried to wet his dry, foul-tasting tongue. Water. He needed water. He stirred with another groan at the lance of pain through his neck and reached for the waterskin lying between them.

Across from him, Lief was nothing more than a lump huddled under her cloak. He regretted that they had ended the day with an argument, but he was not about to wake her to apologise.

He did not even recall falling asleep, but he must have been on watch. Hopefully she would never realise he had fallen asleep on duty. Aedon winced.

He ought to wake her, for the moon was near the zenith of its ascent, but as Aedon reached out, something made him pause.

Perhaps this was the best opportunity he would receive.

With her sleeping, perhaps there was no better time to take matters into his own hands. Aedon rolled onto his knees and rose, stretching out his neck. With meticulous silence, he strapped Lief's dagger around his waist, wishing he had a better weapon with which to defend himself. With such a short reach, it would put him perilously close to anything he had to fight. He shuddered at the thought of those rotting, sharp teeth sinking into him, cursing him with the same painful blight affecting Lief.

Aedon turned towards her sleeping form. *I had better check on her*, he thought, guilt twisting his stomach. She was so still. He had not even heard her breathe. *She's so weak now. The blight has taken such hold…*

Aedon would hate himself forever if he let her down. *It will be just a few hours*, he convinced himself. *A few hours, and I'll be back with the aleilah. She will never even know. By morning, she will have started healing and we'll be on our way to Emuir.*

Aedon nodded sharply. This was for the best. He should leave without waking her. She could be mad at him later. He would not care as long as he procured the *aleilah*, the only hope for her.

Even so, he felt strangely protective of this wood elf who had literally crashed into his life, fiery temper and all. Sending a silent apology her way, he rested a gentle hand upon the tangled cloak shielding her.

At his touch, the cloak collapsed, pooling upon the branch. It took a long moment for Aedon to comprehend that Lief was gone.

He swore viciously. Anger blazed through him, all-consuming, that he had been duped, even though by his own hypocrisy, he had been planning to do the same.

For a moment, he considered leaving, too…but in the opposite direction. *I never wanted any part in this in this first place. It's none of my business, and if she thinks so little of me, I ought to leave her to it.*

Yet as his eyes dropped to her bow hanging on a branch, his feet twitching to leave, Aedon sighed, closed his eyes, and hung his head. He could not do it. His honour would not let him. As intolerable as Lief was, he could not bear to see her hurt, or worse, knowing he could have prevented it.

"Damned honour, and damned wood elves," he grumbled to himself as he descended from the tree. Back on the path, he glanced once down the way to freedom, then sighed and turned up the hill.

A blood-curdling howl rang out before him, another one behind, making Aedon jump. He quickly checked his wards. They would hold for now, but he was too obvious on the path. He scrambled off it, shrinking into the shadows of an overhanging tree as a large, furry mound, mouth open and teeth dripping, bounded down the trail, treading a large paw print into where he had stood but mere seconds before.

Heart thundering in his chest, Aedon forced his breathing to slow, trying to tamp down the fear that rose in him at the utter stupidity of what he and Lief were attempting.

FORTY FOUR

The beast's angry shrieks were the first thing to greet Venya, its grating keening stabbing into her head as Sylvio threw her out and sent her sprawling onto the stone flags. Venya flailed, instinctively covering her head, before she realised they were out of the cage.

Several feet away, the beast stood in the small cage, its limbs folded up, the cage too small to stand in now it had constricted to fit its subject. She felt a momentary pang of regret, of pity, before it turned its murderous, venomous gaze upon her once more and let out a blood-curdling howl of fury.

"Time to go," Nyx said sharply.

She looked up at him, once more in his bear form, standing upon his hind legs and holding Beatrix's limp form carefully in his giant paws as he cradled her to his chest. Venya scrambled to her feet.

Sylvio did not wait. Seconds later, they were in the cool, still silence of his vault. They stood for a moment. The din of her pounding blood and the echo of the beast's screech still jarred through Venya's ringing ears, and she glanced around, convinced that they could not possibly be safe. That she could not have just managed to bind the beast. Yet as the ringing in her ears faded, true silence fell, broken only by Nyx's snuffly breathing and Sylvio's angry muttering about his slashed cover.

Venya closed her eyes on a sigh, relishing being alive, and leaned into Nyx's large, warm form, appreciating the much more welcome scent of his natural musk than the beast's foul, acrid tang.

"I'll get you repaired, Sylvio. I promise."

"I want a new binding," he growled. "Else I'm telling the first librarian all about this *little adventure.*"

"You wouldn't dare," yawned Venya, suddenly overcome with exhaustion. "Else *I'll* tell them how you escaped all those times. If you keep my secret, I'll keep yours."

At her glare, Sylvio subsided, muttering grimly to himself.

"For now, back to your shelf you go."

Before he could object, she cast a net across him, slipped the chain off her wrist, and used the second of the padlocks to bind him, to his muffled protest.

"Thank you," she whispered to him as she slipped him back onto the shelf, her arms screaming from the weight of him after the night's exertion. "I won't forget this, Sylvio."

Then, with a tired sigh, she beckoned to Nyx. "We have to get Bea to the infirmary."

Never mind that she was bleeding, too. Never mind it would raise questions she did not wish to answer. Never mind that she was so exhausted she could not even fathom making it even halfway there.

She plodded up the stairs, Nyx faithfully keeping pace with her. Now that the rush of the fight had faded, her wounds, bruises, and bloodied slashes stung, until she dropped to her hands and knees and crawled up the stairs, overcome with weakness. Beside her, Nyx faltered as he tried to help her and carry Beatrix at the same time.

Her eyes slipped shut as she lurched forward, her cheek striking the cold stone of the stairs. Ahead, the faint light of dawn trickled down the stairs, mingled with the glow of the Athenaeum's halls. She had nearly made it.

"Just a little rest…," she mumbled, darkness roiling over her.

FORTY FIVE

Having no other option, Aedon ran through the narrow, cliff-lined entrance to the valley, hoping he did not encounter any beasts. The fates must have favoured him, for he charged out of the other side and dove into cover just as more creatures rushed past, snarling and snapping at each other. The scent of death wafted through the air. Aedon gagged.

The cave across the valley now clearly visible in the night, a yawning void against the grey stone, he pulled on his magic and tried to find a tendril of her essence, or the wards he had set upon her.

There…

Lief was already almost across the valley, circling above the tangle of trees that still contained a little life. He followed the same path, hoping his wards would hold and he would not be detected as he was forced to dart between rocky outcrops and across slopes of dangerous scree that skittered underfoot.

She moved slowly, so Aedon quickly closed the distance. He

needed to reach her before she entered the cave. His lungs felt close to bursting as he dashed the last bit of distance, leaping to grab her arm and yank her back before she stepped into the open.

He swiftly clapped a hand over her mouth as she opened it to scream – and suppressed his own grunt of pain as she bit down savagely, her pointed canines sinking into his flesh. She twisted in his arms, and her eyes widened in surprise. The fight drained out of her instantly as she blew out a breath and wrenched out of his hold.

She dragged him behind a rocky shelf. "What are you doing here?" she hissed.

"I could ask you the same thing," he whisper-shouted.

That stopped her for a moment, and she blinked in surprise. "Well, it… It doesn't concern you," she huffed.

"I beg to differ. I can't get out of these forsaken woods without your help, and I wasn't going to wait around whilst you got yourself killed on this ridiculous mission."

Lief snorted. "You're an arrogant prick, thief."

"And you're a fool, but I couldn't care less about that if it means we get out of here alive."

"You could have gone, you know. You'd have eventually found a way to leave the forest and be free." She cocked her head. "Why didn't you?"

Aedon stirred. "I wasn't going to leave you at the mercy of…" He gestured around them, "*this*. I'd never forgive myself."

"I can take care of myself," Lief insisted, but her tone was less hostile.

Aedon gave a lopsided grin. "As well I know. Even so, isn't it better to have somebody with you? A friend to watch your back?" The word slipped out before he realised.

They blinked at each other. Was that what they were? Or just companions built of necessity? They could scarcely go half a day without bickering.

"I suppose," she admitted softly. "Thank you. And I'm sorry about your hand."

Aedon grimaced and looked at his stinging, throbbing hand. Blood oozed from the wounds. "I don't mind a little biting," he said with a wicked smile and a twinkle in his eye, "but softer next time, please."

He warmed as she rolled her eyes and huffed in disgust. "Now I remember why I left. Your arrogance makes me want to vomit."

"You adore it and would be lost without me," Aedon teased.

Suddenly, a growl sounded nearby, then the crunch of gravel and a horrible, drawn-out snuffling.

"Time's up," Aedon muttered, grabbing Lief's hand and tugging her into the yawning darkness of the cave. "There's only one way we both go from here, and I'd rather it not be in that beast's belly."

FORTY SIX

Lief guided Aedon forwards, her fingertips grazing the wall with a small *sshhh.* Her heart beat fast and hard, and her numb hand tingled as it dragged over the rough stone.

As her eyes adjusted to the darkness, she froze, Aedon bumping into her.

Around them, the stone, streaked with veins of crystal, emitted a faint glow, pulsing in time with the deep throb of magic she could feel far below them. The Wellspring. But that was not why she had stopped. There was something ahead, something…*wrong*, yet the feeling itself was foreign to her.

A great beast came out of the darkness and prowled towards them, stumbling. As it drew closer, she realised it was a bear…or had been at one time. Lief pressed her back against the wall, Aedon following suit. It passed them – none the wiser to their presence, thanks to Aedon's wards – its rumbling and growling covering the sound of their movement. The scent of rotting flesh was unbearable, and Lief swallowed hard as dizziness and the urge to vomit threatened to overwhelm her.

The strange sense prickled again, and the hairs on the back of her neck stood on end. She knew instinctively there would be more creatures ahead. Lief's eyes slipped shut. What if the Wellspring itself had been tainted? She had never heard of such a thing, but then again, she had never heard of the blight before, either. Dark magic was at play, and she did not know its rules.

"*There are more ahead,*" she spoke into Aedon's mind. "*I can somehow sense them.*" She did not voice her suspicion that it had something to do with her own affliction. That it somehow bound her to them as a kindred spirit… Lief shuddered and pushed the thought away.

"We must be quick then," he whispered out loud. "Where is the *aleilah*?"

Lief paused as a wave of dizziness assaulted her. "Farther," she ground out.

She could feel the power of the Wellspring, but it seemed to both attract and repel her, as though it sensed her two halves – the wood elf and the blighted. If she could but drink from the Wellspring, it might give her strength, but it would not cure her. They needed the *aleilah*. However, as Lief looked around in the darkness, she could see no trace of the small plant.

"Does it not need light to grow?" Aedon asked.

"No. The plants within these caves are fed by the magic of the Wellspring. It is a light, of sorts, just on another plane that we cannot see."

"Incredible."

She did not reply, creeping forwards, glad for his reassuring presence at her back. The cave was dark and echoed with the scratches, clicks, snuffling, and snarls of creatures she could not see but sense. She guided them carefully past the creatures, thankful for Aedon's wards that kept them unseen and unheard.

A screech rang out above them. With a gust of air, a great, winged creature appeared from the gloom, heading right towards Lief's face. She flinched and threw up her hands, one holding the dagger outstretched. Aedon's magic flaring, the creature fell, shrieking.

"Run!" cried Lief, reaching for Aedon's hand and tugging him along, for she now sensed all the creatures in the cave alert and searching…for them.

Aedon moved in front of her, guided by the push of her hands as he veered to the left, right, right again, left again, through the darkness, trusting their footing to fate. With ruthless efficiency, Aedon dispatched any creatures that rushed at them, using his dagger to slice though tendons and muscles to incapacitate them, then a flare of fiery magic to end them.

Each time, the light within his magic flashed, illuminating a grisly scene before them – horrific creatures prowling through the cave as they soaked up the nourishing magic of the Wellspring. Lief and Aedon kept running, knowing if they stopped, fear would paralyse them.

Finally, not sensing any creatures in front of them, Lief allowed herself to stumble to a stop. Her head hung with exhaustion, her shoulders slumped. Everything hurt, but they were so close.

"Light," she whispered hoarsely. "There are…no creatures here. We need…light."

Warm light bloomed, and she drank it in hungrily, blowing out a breath.

"The plant will be here somewhere, probably in a nook. Start searching."

A few tense, silent minutes later, Aedon whisper-shouted, "Here."

She rushed to him and breathed a sigh of relief.

Behind a jutting, sharp edge of rock, nestled in the crevice, lay a tangle of *aleilah*. Delicate, pale green vines clung to the rock, heart-shaped leaves the size of her fingernail growing from them. Nestled in clumps was the precious bloom itself – tiny, white, star-shaped flowers that curled outward and framed delicate, golden anthers dusted with the precious, shimmering pollen that gave the plant its potent healing powers.

"This is more than I've ever seen in my life," Aedon breathed with wonder, tipping his head back to regard the flower that climbed up the crevice and scattered over the ceiling of the cave in a giant constellation of living stars.

Reverently, he leaned forwards to cradle a bunch of *aleilah* in his hand, then carefully snipped it off with his dagger.

"I'll take it." Lief held out her hand, and he passed it to her. She tucked it into the breast of her tunic, feeling the velvety scratch of the smooth leaves and vines against her skin, desperately hoping the plant could offer her salvation from the blight.

"Now to get out…" Aedon turned. The cave had several tunnels. "Which way is it?"

Lief swallowed, looking around. "Um…"

"Oh no," Aedon groaned.

Lief could feel no movement, see no light, sense nothing that would lead them out of the blighted caves to freedom beyond. She could sense dark creatures moving at the edge of her periphery, as well as the tug of the Wellspring, which was close. She said as much to Aedon.

"Perhaps the opposite direction of the Wellspring will lead us from here," she mused.

"Or perhaps not." Aedon grimaced. "I don't know about you, but I'm exhausted. Maybe we should make for the Wellspring, replenish our strength, then we might be ready."

She heard what he did not say. *Ready to find our way out of this hellhole. Fight our way through those fiends.*

Lief leaned against the rock, her vision spinning. Maybe Aedon's idea was sound. She did not have the strength to face anything else right now.

She nodded. "All right."

They both looked around the cave one more time, quickly deciding on a direction. Aedon in the lead, they slipped through a narrow, tall fissure in the rock, following the invisible tug of the Wellspring.

The ground gently sloped downward, then more abruptly, until they staggered down it, hands braced against the walls for support. They opened to wider than an arm span, and Lief and Aedon had little choice but to struggle ahead in the pitch black, nothing but the faint, ambient glow of the crystal in the rock around them for illumination.

Suddenly, loose stones shifted under Lief. She twisted and fell as a cascade of stones loosened and skittered down the steep path. The sound was jarringly loud in the silence as she slid down the steep slope, landing in a heap at the bottom. Her head struck the rock, and darkness closed in.

"Lief!" Aedon yelled.

Without a care for his own safety, he dashed down the precipitous slope after her, stumbling and slipping. He slid to a halt beside her and dropped to his knees, a tiny faelight blooming in front of him. She was so pale and still, Aedon feared the worst. He reached down and gingerly scooped her up, standing just as noise erupted around him.

Hissing, screeching, chittering, snarling…

Movement flickered just beyond the range of his faelight.

They knew he was there. It would do him little good to hide. Aedon cast out the widest faelight he could.

For a moment, he wished he had not.

Creatures swarmed the cave, which had widened into a large, high space. They emerged from various fissures, cracks, and holes in the stone, clinging to the walls, the ceiling, advancing across the ground, their sharp claws clicking on the stone with every step.

They were trapped.

A blow struck him in the middle of his back. He stumbled to his knees, and Lief spilled from his arms, rolling several feet away and lying utterly still upon her belly, an arm trapped beneath her. Aedon scrambled to his feet, ignoring the burning pain. He noticed every beasts' attention on him.

Never mind that she was far more vulnerable and within easy reach, the creatures did not give Lief a second glance. Foreboding rose within Aedon, before a glimmer of hope broke through.

Lief is like them. They do not attack her because they sense the same darkness within her. Maybe that will help me save her. For now, I am the prey. Fresh meat.

He could not bear to acknowledge the hopeless notion that perhaps it was too late for Lief. He could not afford to crumble. Not now. It would mean both their deaths.

Aedon drew his dagger and slowly turned, watching the

creatures that hissed and snarled around him spread out in a giant arc, just within the dome of his light. Beyond them, he could hear the rush of falling water at the far end of the cave. *The Wellspring!* The power rumbling from it was unmistakable, though this one was more powerful than any he had previously encountered.

The faelight was so bright, it made his eyes water, but he brightened it further and watched with satisfaction as the creatures recoiled.

They are blinded by light. It seemed he still had some small weapon in his fading arsenal of power.

But he had only one chance to make it work.

FORTY SEVEN

Snow and sky tumbled over one another as Icarus fell under the force of the impact. Bones crunched – Vasili was not sure whose – and he could not breathe. Icarus's weight pressed upon him, crushing his leg and sword arm. Stars danced in his vision, and white-hot pain lanced through him.

Icarus's weight shifted as the dragon was lifted from the ground by something far larger. Horrified, Vasili let go of the pommel, grabbed his dagger, and quickly sliced through the leg straps. He plummeted to the ground several feet below, crunching onto the rocks. His chest burned, unable to draw breath. But glancing up, he realised he had acted in the nick of time.

A great dragon that seemed to take up his entire field of vision, far bigger than any he had seen before, clutched Icarus in its brutal, gore-covered claws that were as long as Vasili's leg. With the barest effort, the beast flung Icarus.

Icarus sailed through the air and smashed to the ground, but he immediately pushed to his feet, roaring, even as Vasili felt his dragon's mental walls tremble with fear at the foe he had so foolishly engaged in his moment of fury and the absence of common sense. He looked so small in comparison.

The dragon roared its challenge to Icarus.

Blackness laced Vasili's vision as he continued to gasp for breath, not able to draw in even the smallest gulp.

Then hands grasped him. Dark silhouettes against the night. Wrenching his dagger free from his grip. Fingers digging into his arms. Turning him. Pushing his face into the earth. Jagged rocks cutting into his cheek. Binding his hands so tightly that the rope cut into his wrists. Then binding his legs. The world righted itself as they hauled him up.

Icarus froze, a moment of indecision shining in his emerald eyes.

The dragon before him was undefeatable. And Vasili was impossibly outnumbered.

Figures still surged towards them, like a pack of wolves coming in for the kill.

At last, the pressure on Vasili's chest eased just a little as his muscles loosened once more. He gulped in a breath so great it seared his lungs. "Flee!" he screamed at the dragon.

Icarus roared at his command, his plea, and Vasili could feel his friend's raw pain as Icarus realised what he had done to them both. The only option either of them had was for Icarus to reach the outpost alive. To tell the tale. To get help. Before it was too late for them all.

Icarus bolted, thundering down the slope as quickly as he could. Those who got in his way were trampled as he took a running leap into the sky from the rocks jutting over the edge of the lake, battering them all with gusts of wind as he ascended.

The black dragon took chase, roaring in glee at the pursuit. Icarus was one of the fastest dragons in the outpost, but against the bulk and might of the beast hunting him… Vasili did not know whether his friend stood any chance. He moaned in pain – both physical and the mental anguish of knowing he could do nothing but watch helplessly as his companion fled.

Fly fast, fly true, and do not falter.

Vasili prayed to the skies that Icarus would reach Tristan and raise the alert of what they had stumbled upon.

But he did not see whether Icarus achieved his freedom. Something large struck the back of his head, and Vasili knew no more.

FORTY EIGHT

Aedon gathered the remainder of his power, clutching his dagger close. He swiped at a long-limbed creature with claws as long as his hands that drew too close. His dagger clashed, sliding against those slick claws, and caught so viciously in the serrations that it nearly wrenched from his grip. The beast screeched and fell back, but circled still, its bloodlust only fed by his defiance.

His faelight wavered. The creatures surged forwards, almost trampling Lief before he shored it up again and they fell back, hissing and snarling. Even with their aversion to light, he knew he could not hold them back forever. And it seemed they also knew that, for they circled with all the predatory intent they had held in life.

Lief lay prone upon the ground. He could see a sticky, dark mass of hair on the back of her head. *She's bleeding. Think, Aedon. Think!*

There was no way he had the strength to carry her and fight

his way out, yet he could not bear to admit that he might have met his match.

He blinked. This was so similar to just before Valyria's death, it was uncanny. Was he doomed to die in such a cruelly similar fate?

Then, he had been with Valyria, not Lief, though still under a mountain and surrounded by a horde of goblins. Valyria had bought him time with…

Fire.

Aedon stilled at the simple brilliance of the notion. The light kept the creatures at bay, but perhaps fire would destroy them, just like it had the scourge of goblins that had been Valyria's demise. She had left him her gift of fire. But it was currently a dying ember, sparking deep inside.

Aedon needed magic, and quickly. He had to reach the Wellspring. He could feel its throbbing power.

So close, yet so far.

Unfortunately, he could not take Lief with him. He had to trust that the wards he had placed would protect her. That, and the blight spreading through her that made her similar to these beasts and invisible to their predatory intent.

Despite the futility of their predicament, he could not bear to give up. Could not bear to willingly walk into those teeth and claws. Despite the insurmountable odds, he had to try until his last breath.

And so, he gathered up every dreg of his remaining strength

and blasted out a ball of light so pure and bright it even blinded him. Then he ran.

In the white light, creatures appeared in his path, keening and screeching as his light cut right through them. The dark beasts fell back, clawing at themselves, their distraction affording Aedon the chance he needed.

He sprinted through the cave, though he was so exhausted each step felt like it was to be his last. He hacked, slashed, pushed, and barged his way through the horde. They split before him like sheaths of grass in a summer's meadow, until there were no more, the dark, smooth pool of the Wellspring before him.

He dove into its depths.

Here, the water was a gentle ripple, not the pounding rumble of the waterfall tumbling into the pool from high above at the far end. Aedon quickly surfaced, staggering to his feet in the waist-deep, icy water, relishing in the glory of the raw power coursing through him.

Then he sucked it in.

More…and more…and more.

It called to him, filling the deep, void-like well within him. It hummed and vibrated, resonating with the very fibre of his being. All trace of pain and weariness vanished as energy tingled through his body, the magic healing his wounds, banishing his exhaustion, and momentarily soothing his fear and despair.

He was a conduit of magic, a doorway between its own plane

and the living one, a tool to shape it. And shape it he did.

Just like Valyria had, long ago, Aedon opened up to his inner fire, her last gift, and incinerated everything.

The inferno consumed all around him. With it, Aedon launched himself forwards with fresh vigour and a roar of challenge. His blazing dagger held before him, he sliced through any that came close, the creatures paying him no heed in the face of their obliteration. Their shrieks and ragged cries were silenced with the insatiable crackle and roar of the flame's own voice.

The power of the Wellspring charged through him with the strength of a dragon unleashed as Aedon rushed back through the cave and the disintegrating beasts, their darkness cleansed from the world.

Before him lay a small, huddled lump, flames all around… *Lief*. His wards had marked her as his own. The flames had not touched her, despite the blight. He raced to her side and scooped her up into his arms.

"Lief?"

When she did not respond, Aedon cursed, gritted his teeth, and rushed up the steep incline, leaving nought but fire, death, and devastation behind.

Filled to the brim once more with energy and power, Aedon blasted aside any creatures that stood in his way, obliterating them. Out of the caves he charged, instinct leading him through the honeycomb, away from the raging power of the Wellspring and into the valley.

He raced straight through the valley and into the heart of the dark wood that clogged its bottom. The fire dashed with him, like a line of blazing horses charging to battle. Hungrily, the flames followed him, consuming all they found in the cursed valley. Fire was forbidden in the realm of Tir-na-Alathea, but as Aedon raced through the rotting forest, where all smelled of death and decay, and he saw no sign of the living, he did not regret his choice to remove that blight from the face of the world.

It was still dark, but before them, beyond the narrow, cliff-lined path into the valley, the purple of dawn was just beginning to bleed into the sky. Aedon sprinted down it, his endless strength beginning to wane as the adrenaline faded and the power of the Wellspring burnt out with the inferno behind him.

Daylight was welcome. Daylight felt safe. The soft, muted purples turned to pinks as he ran, then jogged, then strode into the forest with Lief in his burning, shaking arms, until the canopy above them hid the sky and he was once more surrounded by life.

Aedon stopped and took a deep breath. Never had he been so glad to hear the simple rustle of insects and animals, the swish of the canopy dancing in the breeze, and…*Skies above*…birdsong.

He paused for a moment and tipped his face skyward, appreciating the light, the warmth, before he continued, scouring the forest before him for the sign of their previous passage. When he saw the scuff of footsteps and the broken fauna, Aedon veered off the path towards where they had sheltered, though he could not carry Lief up the tree. Instead, he placed her gently in the mossy loam at its base, cradled between two roots, and clambered up the tree to retrieve their packs.

Once back on the ground, he raised her head and sat behind her, cradling it in his lap and dribbling a tiny amount of water between her blackened lips, but she did not move. Aedon swallowed, taking in every detail of her pale, dirty face. Her auburn hair was a tangled mess, pulling free of its braid with flyaway hairs framing her face.

He smoothed it back, and his lips thinned as he felt how hot her forehead was. Under the dirt, her lips were bleached of their usual warm colour, and for all intents, Lief looked more dead than sleeping – yet she had a pulse. Faint, but steady. He swallowed.

He would have to work quickly. He was certain he had obliterated the worst of the creatures in the valley, but he did not want to discover if he was wrong once night fell again. They would not linger there if he could help it.

Aedon tended to the wound on her head first. Her hair was matted with blood, so he cleaned it as best he could, then used magic to knit together the sundered flesh of her scalp. To his relief, it was only a surface wound and there was no damage to her skull.

Filled with apprehension, he took a deep breath, then gingerly lifted the neckline of Lief's tunic, the once soft, fine fabric now crusted with blood, sweat, and dirt. His heart stuttered with relief when he beheld the *aleilah* still tucked there, though it was battered and crushed, pressed against her delicate collarbone.

He extracted it, being careful not to touch her bare skin, for it felt like too much of a violation, never mind the circumstances, and set to grinding it into a paste using a rock as a pestle and a small recess in the tree as a mortar. Adding a dash of water from their dwindling supply, he continued until the sage-green paste was smooth, flecked with small pieces of white petals and golden dots so tiny he could barely perceive them – the precious pollen that gave the flower its healing properties, second only to the nectar.

Then, silently begging Lief's forgiveness, Aedon pulled aside the top of her tunic, exposing her wound. Had it not been for the dark blight that tainted it, he would have lingered on the beautiful way her slender neck arched into an elegant shoulder. But with the festering bite, it was an eyesore. Stinking pus leaked from the black-rimmed, open wound, the black veins spreading from it thickly.

Aedon's heart sank, and pity washed over him. He could not imagine how incredibly painful it must have been for her to travel with it, spreading so virulently through her body, yet she had borne it without complaint. He felt no small measure of respect for that.

He ground the paste one last time for good measure, then separated a small measure of it. Tearing off the cleanest part of his tunic, he doused it with water and dabbed at the open wound. Even in her unconscious state, a moan escaped through her parted lips as she shifted restlessly. He fed his magic into the wound, separating dirt, pus, and rotted flesh from the clean flesh below. All the while, Lief moaned and squirmed, her brows knitting together, but did not wake.

Grabbing a leaf, he scooped up the larger of the two measures of *aleilah* paste and pressed it into the wound, packing it in as gently as he could. He ripped off a long strip from the bottom of Lief's cloak and bound it around her shoulder to keep the *aleilah* compacted in the wound. He inspected it. It was crude, but secure.

Aedon gulped down all but a mouthful of their remaining water, soothing his parched mouth and throat, then mixed the last of it with the small measure of paste left and dribbled it between Lief's lips.

True healing *aleilah*, distilled into a clear, precious liquid, was so potent that a single drop could heal most ailments. This would do nothing so miraculous, but he hoped the freshness and vitality of the plant's natural properties would be enough. If it did not work, he was out of options.

He pushed aside that thought. All would be lost if he gave himself over to despair.

She had ceased moaning, but as the *aleilah* liquid trickled down her throat, Lief shuddered upon his lap.

Her eyes suddenly opened and focused on him. Aedon's heart plummeted. Her once beautiful, amber eyes were deep voids of black. Terror engulfed him as he rushed to call forth his magic, expecting an attack. But her eyes flickered closed.

"Aedon…," she whispered, then drifted into slumber again.

Scrambling to his knees, her head resting upon his thighs, Aedon watched and waited, heart hammering, magic still ready to call forth, worry and fear surging through him – partly for himself, but mostly for her.

He had not allowed himself to care for someone in many, many years, but Lief na Arboreali had found a way inside his defences, and he knew he would be devastated if harm befell her.

Part of him fleetingly wished he could erase it all, return to the quiet solitude of his prison before he had met Lief. It had hurt too much to care for Valyria and all the others since, then losing them one by one through death or other partings.

And now… How had it happened that he had begun to care for this fiery, stubborn, determined, passionate wood elf?

She appeared in slumber once more and no threat, though he had not yet entirely dismissed the notion. And, if he was not mistaken, the tiniest hint of colour had returned to her freckled cheeks. He tucked a stray strand of copper hair behind her slender, pointed ears, wishing he could do more.

He sat there for hours, feeding healing, strengthening magic into her, until his body was stiff with it and the noon sun was high overhead. Aedon was certain her lips had gained some of their plump pinkness, her cheeks their rosiness, and her breathing seemed deeper and fuller. Then, with a small smile, he noticed the black, spidering veins were slowly retreating up her arms. Aedon did not dare to hope too fully that the *aleilah* might have worked.

Needing to move, he shifted himself from under her sleeping form, wrapped her carefully in her cloak, and walked around the area, placing protective wards around them. Then, after asking the forest's forgiveness and permission, he built a fire to both warm them and keep predators away – whatever predators might be prowling. For once, he hoped only *living* ones might chance upon them.

He sat once more, returning her head to his lap. As he watched her sleep, the peaks behind them became silhouettes of jagged teeth with the setting sun. Became silent sentinels. He hoped the forest would watch over them, if only for Lief's sake.

She slept as he kept an exhausted vigil all night, until his eyes were gritty and sore, his head drooping, sustained only by the slight lingering magic of the Wellspring. Aedon did not dare fall asleep, wards or not. Yet he must have drifted off, for it was the shift of movement in his lap that jerked him awake, his eyes snapping open.

In his lap, Lief's head turned from side to side as she stretched, pulling off the cloak. Slowly, so slowly, her eyes opened.

Her beautiful, amber eyes.

FORTY NINE

Comforting warmth, and the delicate scent of lavender and lemon, greeted Venya. Her dry mouth tasted sour, and she hurt all over. A groan escaped as she cracked open her eyes to find herself in the softly lit infirmary, upon a comfortable bed with cosy blankets piled high, her head propped up by plump pillows.

The infirmary… That meant… *We made it.*

"She's awake, Nieve," a voice called from somewhere above her.

Venya turned her head, moaning. Even that hurt. She glanced down at a strange sensation. Her fingertips grazed the woollen coverlet, but her arms… Her arms were wrapped in clean, white bandages, and the sting of the wounds had vanished because of whatever healing balms and magic the matron had used.

She wore a simple nightgown under the duvet, and on the wooden floor beside the bed lay a tangled heap of her bloodied, soiled, tattered robes, her belt coiled upon the top. A sudden thought struck her.

Nyx! Where is he?

Her breathing hitched as she wondered fearfully if he had been found, before she saw a small, mousy nose pop up from within the tangle of her clothes. His bright eyes watched her, and deliberately, slowly, he turned his head and winked.

Venya sighed with relief, but it was short-lived as Nieve appeared in her periphery, striding into the small room and sinking onto the bed beside Venya.

"You look dreadful..." Nieve's brows were creased with uncharacteristic worry. "What happened?"

"How... How did I get here?" Venya croaked, rubbing the back of a hand across her bleary eyes.

"You and Beatrix were found on the stairs, both of you in such a terrible state that we feared the worst. You were brought here at once. The injuries you both bear–"

Venya quickly sat up, ignoring the pain. "Is Bea all right?"

"She will be. Her injuries are minor – concussion, some flesh wounds. Nothing too difficult to patch up."

"Here's some water, dear." The matron, an aged, expert healer, strode in, bobbing her head apologetically for interrupting and waiting as Venya took long, soothing draughts of the sweet, cold water.

"What happened?" Nieve asked again, her stare boring into Venya, who squirmed under her scrutiny. The matron took the cup and left. Venya cast her eyes to the coverlet.

"Venya..." Nieve's voice was both softness and steel.

Reluctantly, she dragged her gaze up to meet Nieve's. Part of her was desperate to lie. To shirk any responsibility. To avoid losing everything she had worked so hard for. Yet she could not. Not when three of them had been so badly hurt, though she considered her own injuries deserved.

So Venya swallowed and told her the truth.

Nieve listened in grave silence as Venya described how the beast had attacked her and she had fled, not thinking anything of it until she had noticed the wards fraying...but had been too scared to mention it.

Yet, and she did not quite know why, she omitted any mention of Nyx, *The Book of Beasts.*

"And so, when Beorn was hurt..." Venya swallowed past the lump in her throat, "I knew it could wait no longer. I took matters into my own hands."

When Venya ended with her final memory of falling unconscious upon the stairs, Nieve shook her head. "You were very foolish, Venya."

Her tone held no anger, just disappointment. Venya thought that was worse. She hung her head.

"I can understand why you acted the way you did, and I respect your convictions for doing the right thing, but you should have immediately told someone."

"Will I be struck off?" Venya whispered, not looking up, barely daring to ask. But she needed to know if all hope had been lost. If her career, the one thing she had nurtured for herself, would be over.

Nieve regarded her, and the moment seemed to stretch into eternity as she considered her answer. "No," she said at last. Venya's head shot up. "I thank you for righting the situation. You have ensured no other librarians are placed in harm's way. When the vault is put back to order–" Venya winced at the state she had left the archive in, "–the creature will be rebound into its grimoire form and placed under stronger wards to ensure this does not happen again. It is not a grimoire that should ever be freed, as you know.

"However…"

Fear and nausea coiled in Venya's stomach.

"You *will* be punished. You did not do your duty to the fullest of your obligations. You ought to have reported the grimoire at once, and you most definitely should not have attempted to re-ward the door on your own or bind the beast yourself, putting your own, Beatrix's, and your fellow librarians' lives in danger, not to mention jeopardising the containment of any number of grimoires caught in the crossfire."

"I'm sorry," said Venya glumly, her shoulders slumping.

I really have been stupid. This would have been so much easier to fix had I simply swallowed my pride and asked for help. I deserve to be punished.

She only hoped it would not be too severe – and dreaded her parents discovering her misdemeanour.

"I accept your apology. Do not let it ever happen again."

The warning in Nieve's voice was enough to tell Venya what the consequences would be if it did.

"As for your punishment... You will be relegated to filing and retrievals only for the next month, and all your grimoire work shall be supervised."

Venya nodded. "Thank you," she whispered. It would be dull, monotonous work, but it was fair. Perhaps fairer than she deserved.

"Then I shall expect you back to your full duties, and to catch up on any additional work or training you have missed on your own time." Nieve's tone was unyielding. She had the highest expectations.

Venya sat up as straight as her injured body would allow, raised her chin, and nodded. "I will. I promise."

"Good." Nieve stood and turned to leave. "Rest now. You had quite the ordeal."

"May I see Beatrix?" Venya blurted, then froze, worrying she had overstepped.

Nieve inclined her head. "You may. Good day."

And with that, she left.

Venya shuffled down the corridor, forcing one burning leg in front of the other, feeling ridiculous swathed in bandages over what seemed like her whole body. The matron watched her but did not intervene, save to open Beatrix's door. Venya entered, and the door gently shut behind her.

"Vee, I'm so glad to see you."

Beatrix's voice was weak. She was pale and looked exhausted, but otherwise well, with only a couple of bandages on her arms, and some bruising to her cheek.

She propped herself up with a groan. "Are you all right?"

Venya rushed forwards and collapsed onto the bed. Beatrix wrapped her arms around her, pulling her close "I'm so sorry, Bea. This was all my fault," she cried, her voice muffled.

It all spilled out, every part of it – even Nyx – and she could not stop until she had told Beatrix everything.

Beatrix lay in stunned silence as Venya trailed off after her daring escape with Sylvio, Nyx, and an unconscious Beatrix.

"I understand if you hate me," said Venya, swallowing past the lump in her throat. "I'm so sorry."

"Why would I hate you?" Beatrix loosened her hold, and Venya glanced up to meet Beatrix's frown. "You were incredible! I can hardly believe that *you,* of all people, broke so many rules and threw yourself into danger like that! Things make sense now. You have been acting awfully strange these past few weeks."

Venya shushed Beatrix, lest the matron hear, but she did

crack a rueful grin.

"I don't hate you, Vee. I was just so scared that something terrible had happened to you and I wasn't there to help." Beatrix laughed, then winced and held her head with a groan. "I suppose it was the other way around in the end. I was the damsel in distress who needed rescuing."

"You wouldn't have been there if it wasn't for me." Venya's eyes dropped to the coverlet, still guilt-ridden. Faced with Beatrix's injuries, she wanted the floor to swallow her up to hide her shame.

"Don't be so hard on yourself." Her voice softened, and she grasped Venya's hands. "You did the best you could in a tough situation – and you saved more from being hurt if the creature had remained free. No one can ask any more of you than that. Nieve has punished you already, so don't punish yourself, all right?" At her silence, Beatrix squeezed her hands. "Hey. Promise me."

Venya met her eyes. Beatrix gave her a reassuring smile.

"Venya, there's a dragon somewhere inside you. You ought to have more faith in yourself."

"Hmm…," Venya replied noncommittally. She was in no rush to repeat the experience. "I'm just glad you're all right."

Beatrix winked. "No lasting damage." Her smile faded. "It doesn't make you want to quit, does it?"

She frowned. "*What?* No! Of course not." Already, she itched to return to the vaults. The Athenaeum was her home, the grimoires her companions. Besides, she owed Sylvio a repair…

No doubt I'll never hear the end of that from him.

"Good. Umm… Venya?"

Venya looked at her, brows furrowed at the humour in her tone.

"Can I meet Nyx?"

She blinked. "You want to meet him?"

"Yes! I always wanted a dog growing up. I mean, I realise he's not *actually* a dog, but still. A talking dog that can transform into anything he likes sounds more interesting anyway. Plus, I need to thank him. After all, he saved my life." A shadow crossed her face before her customary roguish smile returned.

"All right. You can meet him."

"Excellent! It's a date. As soon as we get out of here anyway."

"I guess so."

Venya's shoulders relaxed as a smile unfurled on her face, unable to be stifled. She had survived the beast, kept her position, gained a new, albeit animalistic grimoire companion…and finally procured a romantic date with Beatrix.

Perhaps everything will be just fine after all.

FIFTY

"Oh, thank the stars," Aedon exclaimed as Lief, disorientated, bolted up, taking stock of their surroundings. He suppressed the urge to embrace her as she turned to him, her mouth open, a question in her eyes.

Relief bathed him in a dizzying glow as he looked her over. Her skin had regained some of its warmth, her eyes were amber again, and the spidering black veins that had crept up her neck and onto one cheek had all but disappeared.

"What happened?"

"We made it." A laugh escaped him at the outrageousness of it. He still could not figure out how they had survived.

Lief gaped at him. "How?"

As he replayed the events, her mouth only widened in amazement.

"That really happened?"

"You doubt me? I am wounded…" Aedon smirked through

his mock indignation, ruining the effect. Then his smile faded. "It did. We would not be here otherwise. How do you feel?"

Lief noticed his gaze drop to her arm, and her own followed. It took a moment to realise the numbness had faded, along with the stabbing, aching pains that had plagued her. Most importantly, her skin was clear and unblemished by the black veins that had ensnared it only hours before.

Her eyes widened. "How?"

Her heart fluttered. It was too much to hope that the nightmare might be over. That this was not just a cruel dream. She raised her head and took a deep breath, feeling the warmth of the breeze upon her skin, the freshness of the air, untainted by death, the light of day.

"The *aleilah*, of course, and the magic of the Wellspring." Aedon smiled at her with a hint of shyness that she had not expected to see.

"And you… You made this possible, Aedon. Thank you," she said, meeting his gaze fleetingly before she looked away, picking at a moss-covered stone nearby.

"You're welcome, wood elf. I'm always available to help damsels in distress."

She whipped her attention to him with a fierce glare, but his grin only widened. It seemed the cockiness she was beginning to both like and loathe had already returned.

"I was managing just *fine*, thank you."

"Hmm...," Aedon hummed. "You don't have to do it all alone, you know." His voice softened. "When I realised you were gone... It scared me, Lief."

I scared him? It touched her that he would even care, but it muddied the water between them further.

What is this? For no longer were they captor and prisoner. Desperate individuals trying to survive. Companions by convenience and necessity.

Yet... Were they friends? She had been through more with him than half of the elves in her garrison. A part of her already rebelled against the fact there could never be anything between them. Soon, they would be in Emuir. Soon, the Queen would have Her report from Lief. Soon, Aedon would once again be Her prisoner.

They could never be anything more than what they were, even though she hated to admit it. For now, though, the tentative alliance between them bloomed, hatred replaced by wary mutual respect. Lief turned away from the dangerous thought that she might actually *like* his company.

She swallowed. "Well, *you* don't have to lie down and accept your fate, either, Mr. Tortured Past."

Aedon rolled his eyes with a smirk. "All right. I'll agree to stand up and accept my fate if you'll agree to not run away in the middle of the damned night like a fool."

Lief narrowed her eyes, but Aedon only laughed.

"I can tell you're feeling better already, Lief na Arboreali. Your venomous gaze stings me."

She punched him softly in the arm, but Aedon's smile did not fade.

"Where to now then? Since you are much improved, we should not tarry. The *aleilah* will suffice for now, but I cannot guarantee you are healed. You should be checked over." Aedon's attention strayed to the peaks behind them that held the secret valley within their protection.

"No indeed." They now had even more reason to hasten to Queen Solanaceae. The darkness was more prevalent than she had realised. "At least your healing isn't as shoddy as I thought." Lief smirked at him as she buried her worries beneath her hard exterior once more.

"Hey! I was working with very limited constraints!"

"Only a poor workman blames his tools," Lief replied airily.

"Or his patient," Aedon said, a wolfish smile spreading across his face under twinkling, mischievous eyes.

"As far as I understand it, Aedon Lindhir Riel, I was unconscious. You'll never find me more agreeable than that."

"O-ho. Is that a challenge or a warning?"

Lief glowered at him. "Come on. We have a long journey to Emuir, and I would rather not tarry here a moment longer than necessary."

Aedon rose and shouldered his pack, holding out a hand to help Lief up.

After a brief hesitation, she took it, her cold, small fingers slipping into his big warm palm. He pulled her to her feet and helped her fasten the cloak around her shoulders. She noticed that he had re-packed all the provisions into one pack, leaving nothing for her to carry. It touched her that he would be so considerate, but she was slowly realising that she ought not be so surprised by that.

Aedon looked at her, his eyebrow cocked in silent question. *Friends?*

It was a stupid notion, one that would not last once they reached Emuir and their roles were returned, but nothing could break what they had endured together. The fact Aedon had *chosen* to put himself in terrible danger to save her.

She could hardly believe it had been mere days ago when he had been nothing but a stranger, a criminal, worthy only of incarceration with no redeeming qualities. Now, she could hardly imagine travelling without him. She would enjoy it while it lasted.

Lief smiled in return and nodded. They would reach Emuir together.

Friends.

THANKS FOR READING

Thanks for reading *Flight of Sorcery and Shadow*. If you enjoyed it, please leave a review on Amazon, Booksniffer, Bookbub, and Goodreads. These help new readers discover the magical world of Altarea!

Ascent of Darkness and Ruin, the next book in the series, is available to order now. Want to read more from the Altarea World? At the front of the book, you can find all of the sister series currently available.

Happy reading!

Meg

If you want to reach out to me, I love hearing from my readers.

You can find me in the following places:

Follow me on…

- Amazon
- BookSniffer
- Bookbub
- or sign up to my newsletter.

Say hi via…

- Facebook
- Instagram

Join my communities on…

- Facebook
- Patreon

You can find links to all the above on my website at: www.megcowley.com.

ABOUT THE AUTHOR

Meg is a USA Today Bestselling Author and illustrator living in Yorkshire, England with her husband and two cats Jet and Pixie. She loves everything magic and dragons.

Meg thanks her parents for her vivid imagination, as they fed her early reading and drawing addiction. She spent years in the school library and in bed with a torch, unable to stop devouring books. The first story Meg remembers writing as a child was about a clever fox (it was terrible, and will never see the light of day). At school, if Meg wasn't reading a book under the desk, she was getting told off for drawing in all her classwork books.

Now, she spends most of her days writing or illustrating in her studio, whilst serenaded by snoring cats.

Visit www.megcowley.com to find out more, discover her books, and join her reader's group newsletter.

Printed in Great Britain
by Amazon